BELOW THE BELT

A MIAMI JONES FLORIDA MYSTERY
BOOK 16

A.J. STEWART

JACARANDA Drive

Jacaranda Drive Publishing

Los Angeles, California

www.jacarandadrive.com

Cover artwork by Streetlight Graphics

ISBN-13: 978-1-945741-59-3

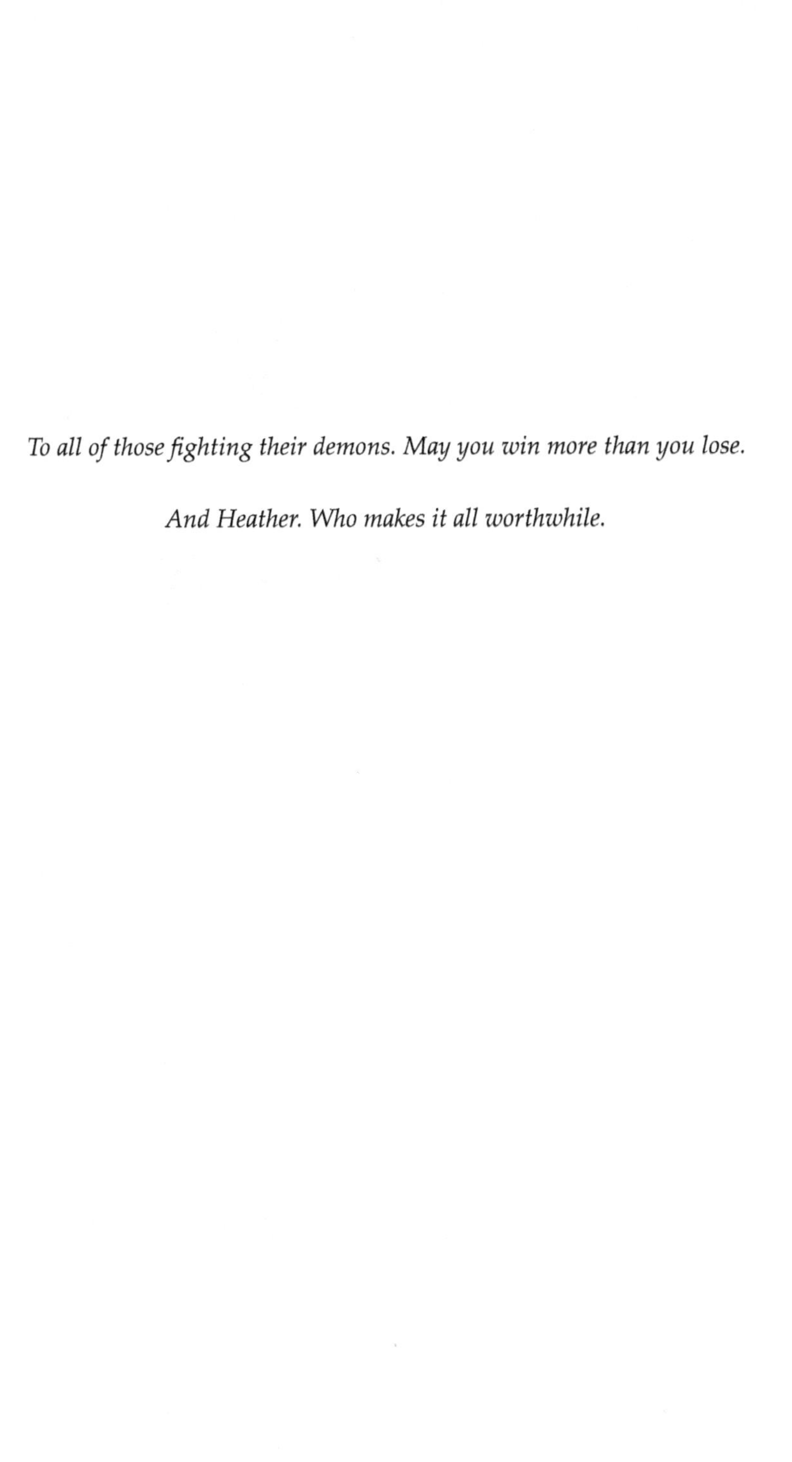

To all of those fighting their demons. May you win more than you lose.

And Heather. Who makes it all worthwhile.

CHAPTER ONE

The snowbirds know. When winter bites and mounds of black snow start piling up along the roadsides of Ann Arbor and Lowell and Quebec City, the snowbirds are gone. They've packed up their RVs and hopped their flights, and they're bunkered down in trailer parks and golfing communities and apartment complexes across Florida, basking in *the season*.

The sun shines, but it's not so hot. The water beckons but only to those who don't live here permanently. And the traffic snarls, so walking becomes a smart man's best form of transport.

The snowbirds flee south to escape their winter, bringing their troubles with them. Paradise is a breath of fresh air, but it isn't the antidote to worry. Not if you carry it in your suitcase or in your mind. I know this because winter is the busiest time of year for a private investigator in South Florida.

People bring their affairs and their deceit and their suspicions. If they were committing fraud in the summer in Cleveland, they are probably thinking about doing it in the winter in Boca Raton. If they were inclined to rhumba behind their spouse's back at home in Ottawa, they've probably got a wandering eye in West Palm.

Which made the fact that Ron and I were sitting in the office with nothing to do the exception rather than the rule. Ron was kicked back on the sofa in my office, reading a book about offshore nautical navigation, and I had my feet up on my desk with a computer in my lap, pretending to work but really poring over the stats that might unlock the secret to how the Patriots could turn their season around.

The door to the outer office was closed because Lizzy was doing a winter clean, reordering her files, and contemplating a new paint scheme. I didn't hear the front office door open or anyone come in, but my office door opened, and Lizzy poked her head around with a quizzical look on her face.

"Um, Miami?"

"What's up?"

"There's someone here to see you."

"A client?"

"Not sure."

"You wanna give me a hint?"

Lizzy pushed the door wide open and stepped aside. The man who entered wore a tank top and shorts along with an expression that matched Lizzy's.

"Mick?" I said.

Ron dropped his book to his chest and looked up. "Mick," he said helpfully.

Mick glanced at both of us. He didn't look surprised that we were both so recumbent at work, but there was clearly something on his mind.

"Is something wrong at Longboard's?" asked Ron. He said it like he was concerned a close friend had gotten bad news from their doctor.

"No," said Mick.

Ron let out an audible sigh. Longboard Kelly's was more than Ron's favorite bar. It was his spiritual center, his home away from home. My wife might have suggested it was the same to me.

I dropped my feet and closed the laptop. "Take a seat, Mick."

Mick came in and Lizzy shrugged behind him then closed the door. As Mick sat down, Ron sat up.

"What's news?" I asked.

"Not much." Glib repartee was not really Mick's thing.

"But nothing's wrong at Longboard's?" Ron asked again.

"Nup."

"So what can we do for you, Mick?" I asked.

He looked like a little schoolboy sitting opposite the principal, except that he had a five o'clock shadow at 10 a.m. and was built like a fire hydrant. Spotting him outside his natural environment—behind the bar at Longboard Kelly's—was rarer than a Sasquatch sighting, and the nervous vibe he was giving off was so unlike him it was giving me the heebie-jeebies.

"Need help."

"You got it, pal. What do you need?"

"Me, nothin'. But I got a friend."

I'd heard the *I'm asking for a friend* line more than most. "Okay. Your friend needs help."

"He's sick."

"Has he gone to the doctor?"

Mick frowned like that was a really dumb question. "That's the problem."

"Okay. Let's cut to the end. Why don't you tell me how I can help your sick friend."

"He's a boxer."

"Right."

"Least he was. Long time ago. Now he's sick, you know, in the head."

"He has a mental health issue? Still not seeing how I fit in here."

"He's in this fund. Insurance thing. Supposed to get money when he gets sick."

"And he can't?"

"Doc says he don't qualify."

I looked at Ron. This was his raison d'être. He worked on all our insurance cases. It was pretty much the standard playbook of the less reputable firms to deny claims in the first instance, and often every other instance.

"Does your friend pay premiums?" asked Ron.

"Nup."

"So how does he pay for this insurance?"

"Fighting."

"He pays in from the purse?"

"Uh-huh."

"Okay," said Ron. "Do you know the name of the insurer?"

"Nup."

"And what about your friend?" I said. "What's his name?"

"Johnny Cabrini."

"Does Johnny know the details of the coverage?" asked Ron.

"Doubt it."

"Does anyone?"

"His wife."

"Johnny's wife? She handles all the paperwork?"

"I'd reckon."

"Do you want us to have a chat with her?" I asked. "Get the lowdown?"

"Yep."

"All right, then. Let's do that." I stood. "Is Longboard's open?"

"Nup."

"Do you need to be there to open up?"

"Nup. Muriel."

I nodded. Muriel was the bartender at Longboard's, and it wasn't an overstatement to say the place couldn't run without her. It had never occurred to me before, but I now had the thought that she was to Mick what Lizzy was to me. Like Muriel, Lizzy had skills, many of which she hid away until required, but Muriel had one skill Lizzy didn't have: she knew how to tap a keg.

"Muriel can open," I said. "Good. You wanna go see this Johnny Cabrini now?"

"Nup."

"You're busy?"

"Nup."

"So why not?"

"Dunno where he is."

I didn't know where to take the conversation, so I looked at Ron.

"What about his wife?" said Ron. "Do you know where she is?"

"At home."

"Do you know where their home is?"

"Yep."

"All right," I said. "Now we're getting somewhere. Let's go see Mrs. Cabrini."

CHAPTER TWO

We piled into my Jeep, Mick and I in the front and Ron in the back. Mick directed me down I-95 toward Lake Worth, which at some point had been renamed Lake Worth Beach, even though there was only about two hundred yards of beach in the whole city. There really wasn't a lake either, given Lake Worth Lagoon was technically just part of the Intracoastal Waterway, but that was the way names rolled in Florida. Hyperbole stretched to the point of snapping.

I got off the freeway at Forest Hill Boulevard. Mick pointed me west, then down South Military Trail and around the city of Palm Springs, until he directed me to the side streets just past 10th Avenue.

The area was single-family residential, no sidewalks, parched streets, and front yards that were as much sand as grass. Most of the houses dated back to the middle of the previous century and were fiberboard over asbestos, except for the handful here and there that had been razed and rebuilt using hurricane-proof cinder block.

The house we stopped in front of had not been painted in fifty years and hadn't been washed in twenty. It might have been white once upon a time, but now its hue defied the color wheel. The lawn had a length and color that suggested it was recovering from a hangover.

We walked up a cracked concrete driveway that led toward a one-car garage. Mick stepped across the grass to a front door with no porch and knocked. We waited in the pleasant breeze.

A grim woman in jeans and a black T-shirt opened the door as if smiling was just too damn hard. She nodded at Mick.

"Teens," said Mick. "This is the guy."

The woman first looked at Ron and then at me, then she returned to Mick. I got that. It happened a lot. Ron wore a polo and trousers; his silver-gray mane gave him an air of dependability. I wore a palm tree-print shirt with board shorts, and my blond mop looked like I had just rolled out of bed.

"Come in," she said.

I followed Mick and Ron inside. The living room was small but neat, family pictures on the wallpapered walls, an old sofa and two vinyl chairs. I spotted a kitchen off the living room and a short hallway leading to three doors: I figured two bedrooms and a bathroom. I got the impression that any disrepair was the fault of the landlord more than the tenants.

I offered my hand to the woman as I stepped by her: "Miami Jones."

She glanced at Ron again, then nodded. "Tina Cabrini."

I looked at the photos on the wall. "Your kids?"

"Yeah."

"How many?"

"Three. Sofia is twenty-four and she lives with her boyfriend up in Palm Beach Gardens. Our two youngest are Anna and Josephine. Fourteen and sixteen."

"High school? Tough years."

"They're good girls."

"I'm sure they are."

Tina offered us seats, which we took, and water, which we did not.

"So, Mrs. Cabrini, Mick says you're having some issues with an insurance claim."

"It's Tina, and yeah, it's something like that."

"Is your husband home, Tina?"

"No."

"Okay. Well, we might need to talk with him too, since I understand the policy is with him."

"If you say so."

"This is my colleague, Ron. He's our insurance expert. Perhaps if you tell him a little about what's happening . . ."

Tina blinked slowly, suggesting she had told the story one too many times. "It's not insurance, not exactly."

"What is it?" asked Ron.

"They call it a fund, an athlete's fund. The way I understand it is, it's supposed to take care of boxers after they call it quits. My husband was a boxer—you knew that, right?"

"Yes, ma'am," said Ron. "Mick mentioned it. What can you tell me about this fund? How did you pay into it?"

"Part of the money he earned from each fight went into it."

"Do you know how much?"

"Twenty percent."

"And has he ever made a claim from this fund before?"

"No."

"Not when he was boxing?"

"No, he couldn't then. This was only for after the end of his career, if you want to call it that."

"Tina, do you have any paperwork from this fund? Contracts, letters, that sort of thing?"

"Yeah." Tina pushed herself up out of her chair with long, slim arms and wandered away down the hall.

"How long did Johnny box for?" I asked Mick.

"Pro, twenty years. Five or six amateur."

"When did he retire?"

"When they stopped calling."

"Which was . . . ?"

"Maybe ten years ago."

Tina returned with a shoebox in her hands, then sat and opened the box. She started pulling out papers and handing them to Ron.

"This is one of the GBC fight contracts. The fund split is on the last page."

"GBC?" asked Ron.

"Global Boxing Council."

"Yeah, okay."

"This is the letter we got from the fund denying payment."

Ron looked at the letter. "Post office box in Palm Beach. No street address."

"Is that a problem?" said Tina.

"Not really. Do you have a notice of what the coverage is?"

"We never got anything like that. The girl at the doctor's said it was on the GBC website, but I don't have a computer."

"No problem, I'll check it out," said Ron. "It says your husband was denied because he didn't meet medical criteria. Do you know who made that determination?"

"*Their* doctor."

"I see," said Ron.

"Their doctor?" I said.

"That's right."

"As opposed to *your* doctor?"

"Yes."

"So you had a second opinion?"

"What do you mean?"

"Johnny saw two doctors."

"Yes."

"Who was their doctor?"

"Dr. Wrexham."

"And he said Johnny didn't qualify?"

"That's right."

"And your doctor? Who was he?"

"Dr. Abe." She pronounced it like Lincoln's first name.

"And did he agree?"

"No, he said Johnny needed treatment."

"And you need the fund payout to cover the treatment?"

"I need the fund payout to cover the rent."

"How did you find your doctor?"

"He's with the university. He's doing some kind of study on old fighters. The doctor's visits and some of the medications are free, so Johnny did it."

"Do you have contact details for those doctors?" I asked.

Tina walked into the kitchen, and I heard the click of magnets on the fridge. She returned with two business cards.

"I'll need them back."

"That's okay." I took a photo of each card with my phone and then gave them back to her. "I should get your number too."

She put her hand out, so I gave her my phone. After punching in her details, she tapped out something else, and I heard a whoosh on my phone followed by a ping on hers.

"Now I've got your number as well."

"Good."

Ron held up the shoebox. "Do you mind if I take these for a day? I'll copy them and return them to you."

"That's fine, I guess. So what do you think you can do?"

"We'll need to look into what the specific terms are for the fund and see if Johnny really does qualify. Sometimes a denial of payment is just a tactic. They hope you'll take it on the chin and leave it alone. But often if we make a bit of noise with the right people, we can change their view on it."

"What people?"

"I'll find that out," said Ron.

I stood, and Ron and Mick followed my lead. "Tina, why did you see this other doctor, Wrexham, if you already had seen Dr. Abe?"

"They said we had to."

"The fund?"

"Uh-huh. One of those letters there. They said we have to go through their doctor."

I looked at Ron. He nodded.

"All right. Thanks for your time."

We walked out to the car as Mick said goodbye to Tina. We

scrambled into the Jeep, sitting as we did before, and I drove back toward the freeway.

"Well?" asked Mick.

"We'll check it out," I said. "What do you think, Ron?"

"I'll need to confirm the terms of the fund. Under workers' compensation rules in Florida, your employer can designate which doctor you have to see, so that might not be so strange, but the variation in diagnosis is interesting."

"Tina mentioned having to make rent," I said to Mick. "Are things that close to the bone?"

"I guess."

"Does she work?"

"Cashier at a drug store."

"And Johnny?"

"This and that." He looked at me. "Don't worry, I'll pay your bill."

"I don't care about the bill. I just don't want to see anyone out on the street. Listen, Mick, in your opinion, how bad is Johnny's condition?"

"Good days but a lotta bad days. Can't keep a job."

I nodded and kept my eyes on the road. I figured Mick had given up all the information he was going to, and it was of limited value anyway.

Time to start digging elsewhere.

CHAPTER THREE

I parked in the lot beside my office building on Banyan Boulevard, and Mick headed for his car. Ron and I took the stairs up. It wasn't exactly running a marathon, but those little spurts of energy helped offset the beers at Longboard's—a trade well worth making.

Lizzy was standing in the outer office with her hand to her chin like an art critic, staring at color swatches on the wall. There were a lot of pastels.

"Anything but coral," I said.

"Coral is very soothing."

"Not to me."

"I'm more concerned with your clients. They don't usually come here unless they're under some kind of stress."

"They'll be under more stress if I have to look at coral."

"What's wrong with coral?" asked Ron, not acting like a proper wingman. I planned to have a word with him about that.

"Flashbacks to childhood. Enough said."

"How did you do?" asked Lizzy.

I outlined the dearth of information from Mick and Tina, and Ron divided up the work. He would take the fund and insurance angle, and Lizzy would look into anything else that popped up, which didn't leave a lot for me to do. Ron went into his office—he preferred to keep it more as a storage room—and Lizzy worked at her desk. I contemplated a nap on the sofa but felt guilty about not pulling my weight, so I wasted time on my laptop looking up Johnny Cabrini.

There wasn't a lot. He had never played Vegas—I wasn't sure that was the right turn of phrase, but I was running with it—and had only made it onto pay-per-view a couple times, and never as the main event. Many of the articles on him used the word *journeyman*. I wondered about the reference. To me, a journeyman was a football or baseball player who was good but not quite good enough to make it stick, so he regularly got traded. I knew guys who had played for a different minor-league team every year of their careers, moving from town to town and state to state, looking for the elusive big break. They would fill holes when a team needed cover for an injured player or a guy who had been picked up by the majors. But there seemed to be a limit to how many teams a guy could box for.

My research told me that Johnny "Slumber" Cabrini spent most of his twenty-year career getting beat. I noted that his record was still active. I didn't know if that meant he hadn't officially held a press conference to announce his retirement or if he had and no one had bothered to turn up. But as it stood, his record was 13-81-3. I took that to read thirteen wins, eighty-one losses, and three draws. Outside of Jacksonville I couldn't figure out how that was a viable sports career.

After a couple hours Ron and Lizzy debriefed me in my office.

"So, according to the online documents, the fund is referred to as the fighters' fund," said Ron. "It's there to provide support for medical issues faced by former boxers who have retired from the game. It's not insurance per se; it's a pool of money to help guys who can't afford to pay their medical bills. The only caveat is that the health issues have to be related to having been a boxer. So if you blew a knee in a bout and later in life needed a knee replacement, you should get assistance. But if you twisted your knee in the bathtub, then you wouldn't qualify."

"So how are they saying Johnny Cabrini doesn't qualify?"

"I don't know. If his issues are mental, then I would think a case could be made that it is related to boxing. Getting hit in the head doesn't seem healthy to me."

"And this guy got hit in the head plenty, if his record is anything to go by. So why the denial?"

"As I told Tina, some less reputable firms deny every claim initially. So we need to push back. Nine times out of ten that gets a result, especially if the claimant has gotten outside help."

"Like us," I said.

"Or a lawyer," said Ron. "But the letter isn't specific about the grounds for denial. It says he doesn't qualify but not why. That broad terminology is probably deliberate, to give the claimant nothing to argue against."

"So how do we make it specific?"

"We'd have to get the records from the doctor—copies of test results, that sort of thing."

"Can we?"

"Not easily. There are HIPAA rules in place, to protect patient privacy, but they also make it easier for these kinds of people to hide what they're doing. We can have Johnny request the results in writing, but in my experience, we'll get a lot of meaningless numbers and no explanation of how they made their determination."

"So who knows how it was determined?"

"The doctor."

"So we talk to the doctor."

"He won't tell you anything," said Ron. "Again, HIPAA rules."

"I'm not loving these rules."

"You would if someone was trying to get your medical records. It's a double-edged sword."

I looked at Lizzy. "What do we know about the doctor?"

"Doctors," she said. "There's a Dr. Wrexham. He's the one from the fund. He has a clinic in Mangonia Park. Appears to be a general practitioner. I couldn't find anything on his website about neurology or mental illness."

"Okay. And the other guy?"

"Dr. Abe." Lizzy pronounced it *Ah-bay*.

"Is that how you say his name?" I asked.

"Yes, I watched him in a video about sports-related head trauma."

"Sports-related head trauma? He sounds a little more on point."

"He's a neurologist and neurosurgeon, and head of a research team affiliated with Florida Atlantic University, looking into brain trauma from contact and combat sports, like football and boxing."

"Tina said they were providing their assessment for free?"

"Yes," she said, holding up a document. "Johnny Cabrini signed on to be part of a study that Dr. Abe is doing. It included all medical checkups, physiological and psychological screening and support, and some medications."

"Okay, I think I need to go see these doctors."

"I'll try to arrange appointments," said Lizzy.

"Thanks. Anything else?"

"I'm still digging into who is actually behind the fund," said Ron. "The contracts that Johnny signed for his fights—and there aren't many in this shoebox, so I assume most are handshake agreements—are typically drawn up by the promoters of the fight, but that's not always the same organization."

"The GBC website mentions the fighters' fund but not how someone gets into it or initiates a claim from it," said Lizzy.

"Right," said Ron. "And the GBC is the sanctioning body for every fight I can find paperwork for."

"So what do we know about this Global Boxing Council? What is a sanctioning body exactly?"

"It rubber-stamps the fights. Think of it a little bit like the NFL. It doesn't own football, it just authorizes and promotes games between specific teams under its banner. But these days there's also the USFL and the XFL, arena football, and so on."

"But the NFL is the biggest of them all."

"Sure, and in boxing it's the same. There are bigger, more well-established sanctioning bodies, like the WBO and the IBF, and there are less well-known ones. The GBC is one of those."

"So like a minor-league boxing thing."

"Sort of. Boxers tend to stay in their own sanctioning body until they become a champion, at which point they might fight a champion from another sanctioning body. Sometimes one person holds all the titles for the main bodies and will become the undisputed champion."

"Okay, so the GBC runs this fund for its boxers."

"Maybe," said Lizzy. "There's mention of it on their website, but, Ron, you said the address you have is in Palm Beach."

"A PO box. That's all."

"Well, the GBC isn't based in the United States."

"Where's it based?" I asked.

"British Virgin Islands."

I nodded. "British Virgin Islands, hey?"

"No," said Lizzy.

"It's not in the British Virgin Islands?"

"Yes, it is, but, no, you are not going there."

"I might need to, you don't know."

"I do know. I also know that not long ago you told me to remind you not to take a case north of Fort Pierce or south of Fort Lauderdale."

"I did say that."

"You did. Besides, the GBC might be based in BVI, but I think we'll find that's a tax dodge thing. They hold most of their fights in the US and Mexico."

"So they must have a US presence of some sort. They obviously recruit boxers here. We need to know more about them."

"I can keep trawling the internet," said Lizzy.

"Do," I said.

"What will you do?" she asked.

"I'm going to the source."

CHAPTER FOUR

THE CENTER OF MY UNIVERSE WAS A PERSON, NOT A PLACE, BUT IF IT were a place, it would be Longboard Kelly's. The umbrellas in the courtyard were open, and the soft glow of winter sun was throwing shadows across the surfboard with the bite out of it that hung on the far wall. Our barstools were under the shade of the palapa over the outside bar. Muriel stood behind the bar with hands on hips, watching us as we walked in.

"Lunch, gents?"

"Actually we're looking for Mick," I said.

Muriel crossed her arms. "Is he okay?"

"Mick? Yeah. There's a thing going on with a friend of his, that's all."

"He's not sick?"

"No. Honestly, this isn't about him."

"Hmm, all right. Let me get him."

She disappeared into the darkness of the bar's interior. We each slipped onto a barstool and waited.

Mick came out alone. "All right?"

"We wanted to get some background on this GBC—the Global Boxing Council, is it? Is there much you can tell us?"

"Bit. Know more at the gym."

"Gym? What gym?"

"Stone's."

"Is that where Johnny trains?"

"Johnny don't train no more."

"Does he hang out there?"

"Doubt it. Maybe."

"Perhaps we'll take a look after lunch. Can you give me the address?"

"Hang on." Mick walked back into the depths of the bar.

We waited for either of them to return so we could put in a lunch order. Ron was eyeing the condensation on the beer taps like he'd spent the week in the Sahara Desert.

Mick came back out through the patrons' side of the indoor bar and stepped out into the sunshine behind Ron.

"Come on," said Mick, and he headed for the courtyard exit. Ron looked at me, mouth agape.

"Don't worry," I said. "We'll find you a hot dog or something."

Mick stood next to my Jeep, and again we climbed in. Mick directed me back to the freeway.

"You didn't need to come for this," I said.

"Not much for strangers," he said.

"Who?"

"Gym."

Mick turned to the window, so I dropped it. I headed back toward Lake Worth again and the same exit, Forest Hill Boulevard. Shortly before North Military Trail, Mick pointed to a low-slung strip mall. I pulled in and cruised by a tobacco shop and an Indian restaurant. I parked at the end of the building, across from a double storefront that had all the windows blacked out with paint to keep the heat and light at bay.

I got out and looked above the windows. On peeling stucco were letters that looked like they'd light up at night. The sign read *Samson's Gym*, but under the word *Samson's* was the dirty outline of older signage that had once read *Stone's*.

"Stone's?" I asked Mick.

"Uh-huh."

"But it says Samson's now."

"Yeah."

Mick led us across the lot and in through a creaky old glass door covered in posters for fight nights and PPV events. I glanced along the storefronts and noticed an ugly kid—his elongated face and nose made him look like a rat—leaning against the stucco between the blacked-out windows and the next place. Wearing a leather jacket that was unnecessary given the weather, he cocked his head to look at me as he chewed on a match. He was working hard to look like he was doing nothing at all, but I knew when a person was loitering with intent.

The smell hit me as soon as I stepped inside the dark and musty gym. Not unpleasant, really, but definitely earthy—a mix of sweat and leather and talc, with overtones of Tiger Balm and Pine-Sol. Fluorescent tubes gave the guy who was lifting weights at the front a sickly glow. Two women on Assault bikes pumped away, and several men stretched in a large area covered with mats. Along one wall was a collection of speed balls next to where a woman and a man independently took their frustrations out on heavy bags. As I followed Mick deeper into the space, I saw a boxing ring at the rear. A lone guy inside the saggy ropes was gracefully dodging and weaving, his feet against the canvas making deep thuds like a bass drum.

Mick led us to a man with slicked-back hair who was looking up at the ring. He could have been from Mick's family; they had a common build, short and thick through the chest, although this guy had a little less beef and stood a tad taller.

Mick walked up next to him and watched the boxer in the ring dancing around nobody. Up close I saw it was a kid, maybe eighteen, sweating like a sumo wrestler, throwing punches at his imaginary opponent so quickly that his gloves were a blur.

In an instant, the kid stopped in place and turned toward the corner of the ring. A white-haired, older man I hadn't noticed jumped up some wooden steps and spoke to him. The Brylcreem model finally nodded to Mick, who returned the gesture.

"Seen Johnny?" asked Mick.

"Nah, man. Not in a week. He don't come 'round here much no more."

"Don't come or not welcome?"

"Is there a difference right now?" The guy turned to Mick and caught sight of Ron and me. "Help you?" he snapped.

"They're with me," said Mick.

"Yeah?"

"Johnny's due some dough from that fighters' fund. We're trying to get it for Tina."

"Good. But like I say, I ain't seen Johnny. We can't have that going on down here, you know that, Mick."

"Have what going on?" I asked.

The guy looked at me but didn't speak. He was a good four inches shorter, but everything about him felt bigger. His neck, his biceps, his thighs. He was way too old to be a boxer, but he wasn't standing in an old-fashioned gym for nothing.

"Miami Jones, Ron," said Mick. "Allan Samson."

Samson raised his chin in lieu of a handshake. Ron and I reciprocated. He jangled a large keyring in his hand that held thirty or more keys as he looked at Ron for a long moment, enough to sum up that Ron was a lover, not a fighter.

He turned his attention to me. "Miami? You born there?"

"No, college."

"They call you after your college."

"They do."

He looked me up and down. "You box?"

"Nope. Too slow in the feet, I'd reckon."

"It's good for a man to know his limitations."

"Plus I value my brain too much. So what is it you can't have going on down here?"

"Fighting."

I frowned. "Isn't that what you do here?"

"No. What we do here is box. Fighting is what morons do on the street. And I'm afraid Johnny was tending that way."

"Being a moron?"

"Losing his cool. Meltdowns."

"Not his fault," said Mick.

"We all know why, Mick. I'm not saying there ain't a reason. But we have to have discipline. Gotta keep it in the ring. You know that."

Unsurprisingly Mick said nothing.

"It's a nice place you got here," I said.

"Yeah?" He eyed me like he was searching for sarcasm, which was fair enough. It wasn't the most sincere comment.

"Not that busy though."

"Most guys come after work."

"You do group classes?"

"This ain't LA Fitness, pal. Listen, Mick, I got stuff to do. I'll see you 'round."

Samson spun the ring of keys around his fingers like a gunslinger and strode away toward an open doorway, presumably the locker room. As I watched him go, Mick spoke.

"Apple don't fall far," he said.

"Meaning?"

"Stone always carried them keys. Flicked 'em just like that."

Samson disappeared through the door, so I turned back to Mick.

"Meet Harv," he said. "Don't piss him off."

The boxer in the ring eased through the ropes and jumped down, then he too headed toward the locker room. The older man, whose dark, deep-set eyes seemed decades younger than the rest of him, stepped down from the corner and gave Mick a tight smile. His skin looked like he stole it from a lizard.

"Micky," he said.

They bumped fists, and Mick turned to the two of us: "Miami Jones, Ron, this is Harv."

Harv offered his hand, so we each shook it, the skin tough as canvas.

"Boys," he said.

"You seen Johnny?" asked Mick.

"Nah. Sorry, bud. Slumber lost his cool, and Steamtrain gave him the boot. Haven't seen him in a few days, maybe a week."

"You a trainer, Harv?" I asked.

"Yep. Fifty years."

"Seen a lot."

"More than most, bud."

"Seen a few fighters go downhill like Johnny Cabrini?"

Harv took a small towel off his shoulder and tossed it into a metal bucket. "Some guys take a lot of punishment in their careers and don't wear it well later."

"Punch-drunk."

"You could say."

"I'm helping to get Johnny's wife some money she's due from the GBC."

"Good boy. Tina needs all the help she can get."

"So, Harv, do you know anything about this fighters' fund?"

"A little. It's meant to help guys who suffer from long-term injuries get medical help after their careers are done."

"What about during their careers?"

"There's always insurance if they get hurt in a fight. The athletic commission requires that. But for anything else, like getting hurt in training or whatever, or getting sick, that's health insurance and it's the responsibility of the individual."

"How many boxers have health insurance?"

"Unless they're covered by their parents' plans or their wives get something through their work, well, I don't rightly know of any."

"Do they have to put money into the fund?"

"Yeah, if they want to box under the GBC they do. But honestly, most guys around here don't think about it." Harv gave me the once-over. "You did something; you were an athlete."

"I played football at Miami and minor-league baseball. Six years."

"Right. And what did you think back then, about your body, your health?"

"I thought I was unbreakable, even when I was injured."

"Yeah. That's what young minds are supposed to think. Otherwise, they'd be too damn scared to do anything great. It's for the old minds to think about the future, what might happen later. To make them pay into insurance and funds and boring stuff so they have something down the line."

"But Johnny keeps being denied coverage by this fund. You know anyone around here that has gotten money from it?"

"Not around here, but like I told you, it's mostly young guys in the gym. The ones still with stars in their eyes. But I gotta be honest, now you mention it, I can't think of anyone who's gotten a payout from that fund. But if anyone did, they'd be old-timers."

Harv picked up a spray bottle and rag. "You wanna talk to old-timers, you best try the Pugilists' Club."

"Pugilists' Club?" I looked at Mick and he nodded.

"Yeah," said Harv. "You go see Maxine. She'll know about that."

As we made for the door, I asked Harv if he had any thoughts on where we might find Johnny, if not at the gym.

"You try the car wash?"

"Which car wash?"

"The dinosaur, down near the Walmart. He works there sometimes for cash money."

"The dinosaur. Thanks, Harv."

He walked us out into the sunshine. The rat-faced guy, still loitering against the wall, spotted Harv and spat on the concrete then walked away.

"You know that guy?" I asked.

"Ricky the Fudge."

"Ricky the Fudge? What kind of name is that?"

"I know. He used to work out a little here, but he's banned now."

"Banned? Why?"

"He's a dealer. A minor-league thug with just enough brains to be dangerous. To himself mostly."

"He deals in the gym?"

"He tries. It's not like the old days. Old Stone woulda busted his face for dealing anything, but guys like Steamtrain will put up with the minor stuff like steroids and painkillers and whatnot, but he draws the line at the hard stuff. And that's where Ricky the Fudge went wrong. A gym owner doesn't need that kind of attention."

Harv twirled his spray bottle around his finger as Samson had done with his keys. "Anyway, boys. I've got work to do. Best of luck to you with all you're doing for Tina."

"Appreciate your help, Harv."

He waved the bottle as he walked inside, and I looked at Mick. "Who is Old Stone?"

"Previous gym owner. Stone Mitchell."

"And what does 'guys like Steamtrain' mean?" asked Ron.

"Steamtrain, that's Samson."

"The current gym owner?" I said.

"Uh-huh."

"Is that like a nickname?"

"Fightin' name."

We got in the Jeep, and I asked Mick if he had to be back at Longboard's immediately.

"Nup. Before customers."

"What customers?"

"You, knucklehead."

I smiled and pulled out onto Forest Hill Boulevard, looking for a dinosaur.

CHAPTER FIVE

It didn't take more than three minutes to find the car wash with a dinosaur on the sign. It was one of those places where you could go through the automatic wash and have your car dried by hand or you could up the ante and get the full-service job: hand wash, interior vacuum, and even a wax if you had more vanity than sense.

I pulled into a full-service bay under a sunshade.

"You want the full wash?" asked the guy.

"Is Johnny around?"

"No."

"Johnny did my car last time. I'd like him again."

"He's not here. This is my bay. You wanna wash or what?"

"So where would Johnny's bay be? In theory."

He shrugged like it was above his pay grade, then held out a hand. I'm a PI, not a priest, so I'm not above using cash to facilitate the transfer of information. But I also know when I'm being had. There weren't that many bays in the place, and there were many more sources of information, so the supply-and-demand equation didn't fall his way, but mostly I just didn't like that he was playing me. I understood that guys washing European sports cars didn't earn the kind of dough that saw them rolling around town in one, but attitude counted for something. Someone was going to benefit from my largesse today, but I'd be damned if it was going to be this joker.

"See if you can spot Johnny, will ya?" I asked Mick. He got out and walked away.

The car wash guy put a hand on his hip. "You don't want a wash, you gotta move."

"And I will, just as soon as I know where I'm moving to."

"I need this bay. I got more customers."

"Then perhaps next time you'll be a little more friendly."

"MJ, down here," called Mick from across the lot. I winked at my man, backed out, and followed Mick down to the end of the concourse. Mick pointed me into a slot at the end that didn't look like it was seeing much action, and Ron and I got out.

Mick led us over to the end of the automatic car wash, where a man in overalls stood waiting for a soap-covered car to get rinsed off and roll out of the wash. He was yet another variation on a theme: a good three or four inches shorter than my six two but powerfully built.

Mick called to him, and the man looked up without breaking into a smile. They bumped fists.

Mick turned to me. "Johnny, Miami. He's getting your fund money."

Johnny had a small head and large neck, which seemed like a good combo for a boxer. He held a chamois in his hand, so I didn't offer to shake it. Instead, I just took him in. He didn't look good. Besides his thick belly, his papery face seemed as if it had been torn and mended a thousand times, with broken blood vessels visible on his flat nose, the hallmark of a man who hit the bottle a little too hard a little too often.

"Thanks, man," he said in a voice that sounded like he had spent the previous night screaming at a football game.

"Sure, no problem. Listen, have you got time to chat?"

"Let me finish this one." He moved toward an Acura that was coming out of the car wash. He chamoised the windshield first, then worked his way down the hood and around the car with quick feet. He finished the job at the driver's side window and the occupant handed him a dollar like he was passing over a fifty. Johnny thanked the driver as they pulled away, then waved to an old guy who was sitting in a plastic chair at the exit. The man nodded without enthusiasm.

Johnny led us over to a wooden bench that might have been where customers waited for their cars back in the days before every place became a coffee shop. We sat, four of us in a row, like a backgammon group looking for a table. Mick asked Johnny to tell me about what was going on. Johnny spoke in a soft, raspy voice.

"So you know I'm a boxer, right?"

"Yeah," I said. "Tell me about that."

"Done it all my life, you know? Started training when I was a kid." He looked at Mick. "We all did, right? It kept us off the streets and taught us a thing or two. Some guys did their fighting on the street, and some did it in the squared circle. Those first guys mostly ended up in the pen. Training kept us from going off the rails, didn't it?"

Mick nodded and Johnny continued.

"It's all I've known. I've always been a boxer. And was okay at it."

"Better than okay," said Mick.

"Yeah, I had my chances. I was crafty, quick on my feet, I suppose. Good, but not good enough. I had a decent amateur record, and then I went pro and got ranked and got my shot. After that, the shots dried up."

"But your record says you had a lot of fights."

"Yeah, I did."

"Were you paid to lose?"

"No, no, don't get the wrong idea. I was a journeyman, the away guy. And crowds don't pay to see the away guy win. I never threw no matches, but when the judges made their decisions, they usually favored the other guy. The guy selling tickets."

"And you did this for twenty years?"

"As a pro, yeah. I ain't retired though. I could get fit for a fight in a month if something came along. You never know."

"So what happened to the money?"

"What money?" Johnny shook his head. "The opponent doesn't get what the home guy gets, and most of my career was undercard, you know. The big bucks are in the main event, and if you can get onto TV or pay-per-view, whoa boy, that's when you make some green. I was on HBO once. That was a good payday. And TV a few times, but mostly not. So after the manager took his thirty percent and the promotor took his twenty-five and the trainer got his ten, there's not a lot left over. Some nights I fought for gas money."

"So why do it?"

"Because it's what I do."

"I get that. When was your last fight, Johnny?"

He frowned at Mick and shrugged.

"Ten years ago," said Mick.

"Not that long," said Johnny.

"A while."

"So tell me about the fund," I said. "You paid into it after every fight?"

"Yeah, that's right. I've been in the GBC my whole career, so I paid in every time."

"How much. Do you know?"

"Over the years? No idea. It was twenty percent off my cut."

"A good chunk."

"After taxes, I probably put as much into that damn fund as I ever earned."

"And now they won't give any of it back," I said.

Johnny clenched his jaw. "Yeah. Their doctor says I don't have nothing wrong with me. No busted bones or bad knees or whatever. And the stuff up here"—he pointed at his head—"he says there's nothing proven. You know he actually told me it was all in my head. All in my head! I said, 'No kidding, Doc.' But nothing from him."

"What about the other doctor?"

"Abe?" He pronounced it like the president, and I didn't correct him.

"Yeah."

"He said it was my brain. He said I took too many hits. I didn't need no doctor to tell me that. He said every time I got punched, my brain bounced around inside my skull and it got damaged. Over time the damage got worse. He said the right uppercut was the worst. Dunno why."

"How do you feel?"

"Today? Okay. I mean I hurt. I'm a boxer, so I'm used to that, you know. Aches and pains are part of the game. The body I can handle. But the head? That's something else. Some days my head's like a splitting watermelon, like the whole thing's gonna crack open."

Johnny shook his head and stared at his feet for a moment. "And there's the moods, you know. Sometimes I get so angry and I don't even know why, and I can't do nothing to stop it. Like if a guy cuts you off on the highway, you got a reason to lose it, right? But I can be sitting at home, watching a movie with my girls, and then bam! Suddenly I'm so angry I want to punch something. It just comes from nowhere, and I can't stop it."

I could see the veins tensing in his neck. He took a deep breath. "The doc gave me some pills, you know. They help a bit, but they turn everything into a funk. It's hard to work, hard to do anything. And I need to work, right. I gotta have money for Tina and the girls."

Johnny rubbed his face with his gossamer hands. "I'm no good to 'em now. No use around the house. I can see they're always walking on eggshells around me, trying not to set me off, but I can't explain that it ain't about them. The fuse gets lit inside my head. So I need this money, Miami. They need it. 'Cause I just ain't no use to them otherwise."

"Hey, you working today, Cabrini, or what!" I looked up to see a man in a shirt covered in vintage cars holding his hands out near the automatic wash. The old guy had resumed his position in the plastic chair.

"My boss," said Johnny. "I gotta go."

I stood and walked over to the boss man. "Just getting the deep clean."

"He don't do cleaning, he does drying."

I stuffed a twenty in the guy's shirt pocket. "Five minutes."

"I ought to fire his—"

"I have a question: how much you pay these guys?"

"What?"

"How much do you pay them? Minimum wage, right?"

"They're drying cars."

"Yeah, I'm sure for minimum wage, not just for tips. That would be illegal."

"Who are you?"

"I'm the patron saint of car washers, and if I hear of anything bad happening to Johnny, like losing his job or getting his hours cut, well then I might have to come back with my team of attorneys and have the state go through your books. Make sure everyone's getting what they're due by law. You get me?"

He didn't look happy about it. "Five minutes."

"Not even. And by the way, having the grumpiest guy in your crew as the first face your customers see probably isn't doing you any favors."

"It's my brother-in-law," he said, defeated.

"Well, forget that, then."

I turned back and found the others walking toward me.

"I should get back to work," said Johnny.

"Yeah. Listen, Johnny, we'll do our best, okay? We know how this system operates. We'll work these guys over and get something for Tina."

"I appreciate it."

Johnny walked back to the car wash as a sun-faded pickup came out. He flicked out his chamois and got to work.

"You sounded like a gangster just then," said Ron as we turned toward the Jeep. "'*We'll work these guys over.*'"

"You think?"

"Like Joe Pesci."

"What do you think, Mick?"

"Dreamin'."

CHAPTER SIX

THE NEXT MORNING I MADE POACHED EGGS AND LOX WITH SOURDOUGH toast while Danielle sat at the breakfast bar and watched. Our old kitchen had been destroyed in a fire, and although the rebuilt version lacked the seventies kitsch that I loved so much, it gained in functionality. The cooktop now burned hot, and the fridge produced ice cubes by the pound.

"How are you settling in?" I asked. Danielle had recently transferred from the Miami office of the Florida Department of Law Enforcement to the West Palm Beach branch. It wasn't exactly a career move. In her business, careers got made in Miami or Tallahassee, not the Palm Beaches, but she had decided to trade up in terms of lifestyle.

"It's a good crew. I like it."

"You miss Miami?"

"The city?"

"Yes. I haven't taken to referring to myself in the third person."

"No, I don't miss it. Do you?"

"Nice place to visit. Glad I live here."

"It was never you," she said, scooping up some egg.

"And too much confusion with my name."

"You could use your real name."

"That is my real name."

"I mean the one on your birth certificate."

"Nah, I'm like an actor with a stage name now. Like Reggie Dwight. If I change it, no one will know who the hell they're talking about." I bit some toast and pointed the remainder at her. "Do you think I should change it?"

"Hell no. So what's on your plate today?"

"Going to see the doctor."

She stopped chewing and frowned.

"Not my doctor. Johnny Cabrini's doctor."

"Why does Johnny have a doctor and you don't?"

"He's sick."

"And how do you know what your status is?"

"I listen for a cough."

Danielle shook her head and resumed eating. She didn't wear a uniform anymore, but she leaned over the plate to make sure her blouse didn't get egg bombed.

"You think you can get some money for him?"

"I think so. Ron just needs to track down the right person to speak with."

"And you?"

"I gather up the ammo so that when we do, they'll think twice about playing games again."

We polished off breakfast, and I put the dishes into the dishwasher while Danielle finished getting ready. She always looked like a million dollars to me, but I supposed there was *professional* million dollars and *lying around at home making me think about how I got so lucky* million dollars. When she came out of the bathroom, she was both.

I stopped at the sliding doors and looked across the back lawn toward the Intracoastal. It was cool for Florida and still early, so I didn't see any boats, but the water sparkled and filled up my energy reserves like a video game character.

I kissed Danielle goodbye and followed her off Singer Island, then along Blue Heron until we got to the freeway, where she headed south to Boynton Beach and I cut north to Jupiter.

I found the South Florida Neurology and Spinal Institute in a building of medical suites not far from the Jupiter campus of Florida Atlantic University. I parked in the large lot as far from the building as I could get and walked over. Then I followed the suite number signage that seemed to be some kind of bastard child of the Dewey decimal system and hieroglyphics, before resorting to asking a security guard where I was supposed to go.

Dr. Cameron Abe was listed at the top of the principals of the institute, so I figured Johnny was in the right hands. The reception was larger than most emergency rooms but held only two other people, so I checked in with the receptionist and took a seat.

I waited an hour and a half, which would have been longer than necessary had I been an insurance case, but Lizzy had made it clear to the doctor's assistant that I was not a patient likely to make him any money, nor a test subject likely to garner him any fame, so she was told I would be seen *as and when*. I was almost to the end of a *Sports Illustrated* article about a fourteen-year-old Japanese boy with a ninety-mile-an-hour fastball when I was called in.

Perhaps it was years of conditioning, but I had expected to meet a doctor in an exam room, so I was surprised to be ushered into a large office with a view of a man-made lagoon.

"Dr. Abe," said the medical assistant. She pronounced it *Ah-bay*, so that case was definitely closed. "Mr. Jones."

Dr. Abe looked like a doctor on television. I didn't own a TV, and when I happened to be seated near one it was usually tuned to some kind of sport rather than any kind of hospital drama, but I figured he had the right look. He was about six foot and wore a white coat over a blue shirt, no tie. He had dark hair and intelligent eyes—a good-looking guy. I was sure Danielle would have agreed.

He stepped around his desk and offered his hand. "Dr. Abe."

"Miami Jones," I replied, although I was tempted to go with *Mr. Jones*.

Abe directed me to a couple plush chairs by a round coffee table near the window. "Water?"

"Sure, thanks."

He retrieved a filtered pitcher from a small refrigerator, poured out two glasses, then returned it.

"So, I understand you are working on behalf of Mr. Cabrini."

"That's right."

Dr. Abe put the water on the table and sat. "I should begin by saying that I can't discuss the particulars of his case with you."

"HIPAA."

"Exactly. Plus, some of what we are studying with Mr. Cabrini is proprietary."

"Proprietary? Like work secrets?"

"Research intelligence."

"So you're a brain doctor, is that right?"

"In layman's terms, I suppose. I'm a board-certified neurosurgeon and research fellow at the Max Planck Institute."

"That's at FAU?"

"Yes. On the Jupiter campus."

"So you're not treating Mr. Cabrini."

"Oh, yes, we are. See, I am leading a research project into the long-term effects of contact and combat sports on the human brain. All the participants in the study receive cutting-edge treatment for their conditions as part of our study."

"For free?"

"That's correct."

"And what are you hoping to show, that boxing is bad for the brain?"

"No, that's been proven. There's no doubt. Being punched is a potentially concussive event, and repeated trauma over time leads to demonstrated negative outcomes."

"So what are you doing with Johnny?"

"I can't discuss specifics."

"What is it you are studying, in general?"

"We are trying to establish the baseline for chronic traumatic encephalopathy and develop diagnostic tools for it."

"In English?"

"Have you heard of CTE?"

"Sure, repeated concussions leading to brain injury. Lots of NFL players get it."

"More or less. But currently, we can't say definitively what it is, what exactly causes it, or who has it."

"Seriously? I thought it was about repeatedly getting hit in the head."

"It is, but what does that mean for an individual? Did you ever play sports?"

"College football, pro baseball."

"Get injured?"

"Not really. Niggles, sore shoulder, that sort of thing."

"But you knew players who did?"

"Sure. Most."

"Take a knee injury," said the doctor. "Say a cruciate ligament. What happens? You feel something in your knee, give it a rub, maybe a rest. But then it happens again. Is it worse? Is it the same part of the knee? What do you do?"

"Get a scan."

"Right. A diagnostic tool to help determine the nature and severity of the injury, which then determines treatment. But imagine you can't scan, you can't know for sure. Then what do you do? Treat the best way you can. But repeated injury leads to a chronic condition. Years after you retire, your knees have degenerated to the point where you cannot walk. Imagine in this world that your knees are mission critical to your life function like your brain is. Now what? We do knee replacements these days, but we can't do that on a brain."

He took a sip of water before he got going again. "So with head trauma, the challenge is that no two brains are the same. A light knock that does nothing to one person might concuss another. Two people might have a major collision and both suffer concussions, but one recovers that day, and the other might not recover for months."

"But we're talking repeated hits over a long period of time, aren't we?"

"Yes, but how many is the baseline? Is ten too many? A hundred? A boxer might get hit in the head fifty thousand times in a career—most of those in sparring sessions, which is something we are trying to address—and that's sure to be over any safe limit, but then how is it that some boxers don't get CTE?"

"They don't?"

"No."

"I thought the tests they did on those NFL players showed almost a hundred percent get CTE."

"The subjects tested had all exhibited signs of trauma when alive—depression, aggression, headaches. It was like selecting only people who limped and saying a hundred percent of them had bad hips. The fact is we don't know. The numbers are clearly not good, but the data we have are flawed."

"So you can't say what percentage of boxers get brain damage?"

"Oh, I'd wager the answer to that is a hundred percent. But then you have to ask what is the extent of that injury? The brain is complex. It has a remarkable ability to repair itself, or to even reroute processes around damaged areas. But a concussion, by definition, is damage. The question is how bad and how much does it recover? Sometimes fully, sometimes not at all."

"But Johnny Cabrini has obvious symptoms, doesn't he?"

"I can't speak to a specific case."

"Okay, but if a subject had depression, anger issues, headaches, trouble holding down a job, that would be proof, wouldn't it?"

"You could say yes, but it isn't definitive. Can a person who hasn't experienced multiple concussions suffer from depression?"

"Yes."

"Sure they can. Most people who have depression are not boxers or football players. And studies have shown that at any one time up to twenty percent of the population has a headache. Most of them will not have had concussions. And take a boxer who has been punched repeatedly over the years and another who has not. Maybe they each had some success in their heyday, made some money.

Twenty years later, each is living in poverty, his glory days well behind him, maybe estranged from his family. Could that induce depression-like symptoms, substance abuse issues? Nothing more than life circumstance?"

"Yes."

"Sure. So, CTE could be the problem, or not. What we know is that head trauma is bad, and it can lead to devastating outcomes later in life, but not in every case. So we search for a baseline above which we have some certainty of negative outcomes, and for a diagnostic tool to determine if a subject indeed is in the early stages CTE."

"How do you tell if they have it now?"

"A neuropathologist cuts open the brain after death."

"Not so useful."

"Not for the individual."

"So the doctor who examined Johnny was right to deny him fund money?"

"While I can't speak on a specific case, I will say this: when you attempt to diagnose this kind of issue, you don't just look for one marker, you look for a broad spectrum."

"Meaning?"

"If the subject has severe headaches, one marker, that is not enough. But if a subject has multiple markers—headaches, depression, mood swings, anger issues—combined with a history of concussive trauma, like being a boxer, that would more likely lead to a CTE diagnosis. More markers, more likely it is."

"Johnny Cabrini has all that."

Dr. Abe lifted his eyebrow.

"Have you seen the terms of the fighters' fund?" I asked him. "Should a patient with a broad spectrum of markers be covered?"

"It would seem the only reason to have such a thing. It's not designed to cover getting cancer, is it?"

"No. So you think the other doctor was wrong?"

"I can't speak to another neurologist's diagnosis. I don't know what data they've seen or what testing they've done."

"The other doctor isn't a neurologist. He's a primary care physician."

Abe frowned. "Then his first step should have been to make a referral."

"Would you share Johnny's test results with the court if he asked?"

"If that was the subject's wish, then yes, of course."

I took a sip of water. It tasted smooth, whatever that meant. "Dr. Abe, you said subjects in your study were offered cutting-edge treatment. What would someone with symptoms similar to Johnny's get?"

"I'm afraid it sounds more impressive than it is. Mostly we treat the psychiatric issues using medications and some counseling. But we can't treat the damage itself. That's a ways off."

"So for a subject with symptoms like Johnny's, you're saying you can't make them better?"

"No, we cannot. When you treat symptoms and not the disease, all you do is buy time. How much time is anyone's guess."

"So he won't get better, the depression and so on?"

"Mr. Jones, there is no cure for depression, and that's without substantial damage to the brain. It can ebb and flow through a person's life. It can often be managed with medications, counseling, and possibly lifestyle changes, such as fitness and eating behaviors, but it is never cured."

"One last thing. Johnny told me that you had said something about the right uppercut being the biggest problem. Is that correct?"

"In a sense. What I meant was, the skull and the brain are designed to take front-on punishment, like a jab. It seems the worst damage is done when the force causes the head to rotate, to snap. In boxing that would be a cross—like a haymaker—or an uppercut. They cause the head to rotate, often resulting in damage to the brain stem—where the brain connects to the spine. But a good boxer usually sees a cross coming and prepares for it. The uppercut often hits unseen. If you watch enough matches, Mr. Jones, you'll notice that many knockouts have something to do with an uppercut."

"Why the right uppercut?"

"Most boxers stand left foot forward, so the right glove is the power shot. If it was a southpaw, I'd be watching for the left uppercut. Same principle."

"Doc, I've taken up enough of your time." Abe walked me to the door. When we got there I stopped.

"Dr. Abe, what's going to happen to Johnny?"

"Outcomes?"

"Yes. I know you can't get into case specifics, but he has a family."

"I wouldn't put it like this to the family, Mr. Jones, but with you, I will be blunt. Subjects with Mr. Cabrini's markers don't get fairytale endings. The depression will likely get worse, as will the mood swings and the anger issues. Subjects find it increasingly difficult to work or to be around people. We can up the medications, but all that does is dull the pain. These drugs, like all drugs, have side effects that must be managed. Such subjects often descend into alcohol and substance abuse. An alarming number end up dying by suicide."

"That's pretty bleak."

"Yes, Mr. Jones, it is."

"So what can we do?"

"The best we can. This is why we research. This is why Mr. Cabrini comes here. Once upon a time, prostate cancer killed most men who developed it. Now five-year survival rates are in the high nineties, and most of the deaths that do occur are because men of your age don't go to the doctor until it's too late. We may not be able to save Mr. Cabrini, but Mr. Cabrini may be able to save those who come after him."

I shook the doctor's hand and thanked him, then walked back through the halls that felt more like a brokerage firm than a medical clinic. I nodded at the receptionist as I strode by but didn't stop, walked swiftly to my Jeep, and started it before I even closed the door. I laid rubber and got far, far away.

CHAPTER SEVEN

I spent the day at loose ends. Ron was working at home on the island, digging up what he could on this fund and handling a few insurance client cases. Lizzy was doing her thing, whatever that was. I paced for a while, then I sat at my desk and thought about whatever flapped its way into my mind. I ended up daydreaming: I was on the field with my high school baseball coach, Coach Dunbar, except I was only a child, maybe six years old. I threw the ball to him behind home plate, and he tossed it back. This went on and on, and I was only pulled from it by the sound of police cars speeding down Olive Avenue, sirens screaming.

I went for a walk down Clematis Street and perused the lunch places but bought nothing. As I got near the water, I saw E.R. Bradley's Saloon, which made me think of Longboard Kelly's. I tossed around the idea of one of Mick's fish sandwiches, but something kept me from going. It was as if my professional life and my private life had collided at Longboard's. The notion made little sense since clients often came and found me underneath the palapa, and Ron and I habitually talked through cases while sitting at the bar. Those compartments had breached and intermingled a long time ago without causing me any stress, but now I didn't know what I was thinking or where I should be. The axis of my planet was tilting, and it was all I could do to hang on.

So I walked. Down Flagler Drive past the bridge named after the same man, until I got to Providencia Park, where I did a loop and then headed back the other way. I walked straight by Clematis Street and the amphitheater and along the water until I reached the long boardwalk out to South Cove Islands.

The nature area on the biggest of the islands was nothing more than hardy mangroves and sand and rocks, and there was nothing natural about it. It was manmade, an attempt to resurrect the estuary habitat that had existed before Flagler and his trains arrived. It was Florida all over. It looked like how the state had been two hundred years ago—scrub and sand—but it wasn't real. It gave a sense of natural peace within earshot of the traffic on Flagler Drive, and egrets and herons stood with me looking at the skyline of West Palm Beach.

When I got back to the office, Lizzy glanced up but went straight back to work. I grabbed my car keys and told her I was heading out. The traffic had built as the afternoon had beckoned the evening, but the slow pace along Route 1 suited my mood. I wasn't in any hurry. Getting to where I was going later was just as good as sooner.

I crawled down toward Lake Worth until I reached 10th Avenue, then I headed west. I had an address that my phone's GPS found shortly before Congress Avenue, but I had no idea what I was searching for. It looked like any old two-level strip mall: glass storefronts at street level and windows on the second floor that suggested office space—the kind of place you might expect to find a private investigator's office, at least if you were reading a Dashiell Hammett novel.

I saw a barbershop that was closing up, and a payday lender and a dollar store still open, but nothing that looked like a club. Someone behind me sounded their horn, so I scanned for a place to park.

A second horn blared. I moved forward and turned down the side street, where I pulled into a parking lot behind the stores. I eased along the rear of the building, just solid doors on this side, turned left at the cinder block wall, and parked in the rear. I wandered over to the building. It was after five, and the lot was about a third full, but I saw no one around. At the dollar store, a note taped on the steel door said they were open and to come on in for bargains.

I left the bargains behind and walked the sidewalk along the rear of the building. I pulled on the door to the barbershop: locked. There was a five-foot-wide gap in the building, like a missing tooth, and I looked into the dark alcove where a steel door was propped open, revealing the bottom of a set of stairs.

I stepped into the alcove and saw another piece of paper taped on a door. This was on the inside of the door before the stairs, I assumed so it could be seen when the door was held open. There was a coat of arms on the paper with boxing gloves and interlocking capital letters *P* and *C*. Below that it read *Pugilists' Club*.

Having confirmed I was getting warm, I took the stairs up. As I ascended I picked up the sound of soft chatter and the drone of a television. At the top there was a locked door to my right and an open door to my left, which I stepped through.

The Pugilists' Club, looking like a relic from another age, took up the entire floor above the barbershop and the dollar store. The stained, paneled walls were filled with photographs of boxers in the ring and in various set poses. Stackable metal seats surrounded chipped wooden tables, and worn leather chairs clustered by the windows. At the end was a tiled bar not unlike an Italian café, with a large espresso machine and rows of liquor bottles at the back. Beer taps behind the bar offered two kinds: Bud and Bud Light.

Only the flat-screen televisions mounted around the room appeared to be from this century, all tuned in to boxing matches but muted. There were roughly a dozen people in the whole place.

I weaved in between tables toward the bar, where three people were chatting with the bartender. She looked like the original article. Her hair was bottle blond and the lines at the corners of her mouth suggested she had smoked for a long time. She put a beer in front of one patron and followed it with a wink.

I took a leather stool at the end and waited for the bartender to come my way. As she did, I noted her eyes were welcoming but her mouth was not.

"Help you, darlin'?"

"Can I get a beer?"

"Sorry, this is a private club."

"So I heard. Harv suggested I come by."

"Did he now? You don't look like a boxer, darlin'."

"No, ma'am, I'm not. My name is Miami Jones. I'm helping Johnny Cabrini get some money to cover his medical costs."

"That right? How is Johnny?"

"Good days and bad days."

"And his wife?"

"Tina's doing it hard, to be honest."

"It must be tough on those boys of his."

"Not really, given he doesn't have any boys. But Tina's trying to shield their daughters as best as she can."

The woman smiled out of one side of her mouth. "What'll you have?"

"Whatever's cold."

She stepped away to the taps and poured two beers, placed one in front of an old-timer, and brought the other back to me.

"Cheers," I said before taking a sip.

"Back at ya," she said, sucking what looked like ginger ale through a candy-striped straw.

"You Maxine?" I asked, wiping my lips.

"One and only."

"Tell me about the Pugilists' Club."

"You don't fight, do you?"

"How'd you know?"

"You're too pretty."

"I've never been accused of that before."

"You're not marked up, hon, and your nose has been busted but not often."

"Correct on all counts."

She sucked on her straw and then put the glass out of sight. "So I started this place about thirty years ago. Back in the day, they were just starting to show the big fights on HBO, you remember. But the thing is, most fighters don't make a lot of money. They can fight on HBO, but they can't afford to pay for HBO. So my husband and I got the idea to pool our resources with some other fighters and start a club, somewhere they could watch the televised events and later even PPV. Somewhere comfortable and just for them. It sort of grew into a home away from home for a lot of guys."

"I know that feeling. So were you a boxer?"

"Do I look like a boxer?"

"No, ma'am."

"Cut the ma'am stuff, fella. I'm not your grandma."

"Sorry."

"Yeah, well, not me. My husband was a boxer for a while and his father, but my Stone became a trainer. Damned good one. Hang on, darlin'." She stepped away to a guy with eyes so puffy I wondered how he could see. He looked about sixty, and his eyes the result of repeatedly being cut open in the ring. Maxine poured a couple beers and shared a joke with the guy. After checking that no one else had run dry, she ambled back to me.

"Where were we?"

"You were telling me your husband was a trainer. Stone, you said. Anything to do with Stone's Gym?"

She sighed. "Yeah, that was him."

"He sold it though. Is that right?"

"I sold it. He died."

"I'm sorry."

"Not as much as me, darlin'."

"Can I ask why you sold?"

"It was Stone's place, the gym. I couldn't run that place and this one, and this was my thing."

"Did you know Samson before?"

"Oh yeah, I've known Allan since he was a boy."

"He looks like a boxer."

Maxine stared at the tiled bar. "Yeah, he was a boxer. Until he wasn't, like all of them."

"Meaning?"

"You don't know Allan's story?"

"No. Only met him once."

"But you know Johnny's story, obviously."

"I know he was a boxer. I know he still thinks he is."

"How did you wind up working this for him? He wouldn't have asked for help."

"A friend we have in common, Mick."

Maxine smiled. "Young Mick. How is he?"

"You know Mick?"

"Yeah, I know Mick."

"He's well."

"Let me show you something." Maxine lifted the end of the bar, stepped around, and led me to a nearby wall. She nodded at a photograph. It was one of those square photos that I remembered from my own childhood, the washed-out colors and orange tint of seventies photography. This was a picture of three boys, maybe fifteen years old. They were all leaning over the ropes in a boxing ring, shirtless and sweating, gloves on their hands and irresistible smiles on their unblemished faces. I recognized the eyes of one boy.

"Is that Mick?"

"Yep. And that's Johnny, and that's Allan."

"They're so young."

"Aren't they?"

"So they knew each other as kids?"

"They grew up together. Peas in a pod."

"I can't imagine Mick as a kid."

"He was a good boy. Quiet, shy. But he knew his mind."

"That sounds like Mick."

Maxine moved along the wall to another photograph. It was a

picture of a young man straight after a fight, gloves held high in victory, his face puffed and red but high with adrenaline.

"Johnny?"

"Yeah. That was the night he earned his title shot."

"What kind of title?"

"GBC welterweight world title."

"I take it he didn't win."

"No, he didn't win. He got knocked out good and proper. The other guy was better, no doubt about it. But he fought for a title, on television and everything. And that was back before fights were on TV all the time. Now any old dog can get on ESPN. Back then it was something."

"So what happened to Johnny? I've seen his record. It doesn't make for good reading."

"13-81-3," said Maxine.

"You know that by heart?"

"I know the records of all my boys."

"But you see what I mean. It's not exactly a world champion record."

"No. Johnny was a good boxer, and he earned his shot, but there were some things Johnny was not good at. You know much about selling tickets in boxing?"

"Nothing."

"It might not seem like it, but there's usually a home guy and an away guy. The home is expected to win. The away guy might be a chump or he might be a journeyman, but what he isn't is a ticket seller. See, fans go to see their favorites. If you've got a good style and you talk the talk at the weigh-in, then you get fans and you sell tickets for the promoter. If you don't catch people's attention, then you don't sell tickets, and promoters aren't interested in putting you on the card, at least not as the home guy."

"And Johnny wasn't a ticket seller?"

"No. Johnny could be abrasive. Heart of gold but not a people person. He didn't come across well and got stage fright at weigh-ins, so he looked rude and mean when all he was was scared. So after his shot, the promoters around town decided Johnny wasn't a ticket seller, and once that's decided, your title days are done."

"So how did he fight so many fights? It's nearly a hundred. Isn't that a lot?"

"It is a lot. Johnny loved boxing, and he wasn't much good at anything else, so he took on the role of the other guy—the opponent. A journeyman. Even the ticket sellers have to fight someone, and back in those days promoters would set up fights for the ticket sellers as they rose through the rankings. Johnny was a technically strong fighter—decent feet, proper stance, fast hands. So he was a good test for an up-and-comer. But Johnny learned quick that if he wanted to keep fighting, he couldn't be knocking those guys down, even if he was better. Fans don't want to see the opponent win."

"So the matches were fixed?"

"Hell no. Fixing a fight is like when a guy goes down in the fourth round on orders. Johnny never did anything like that. But he'd box in a way that ensured a points decision. He'd fight properly for three rounds, then move around or hold on for three, then he'd box for two. And most often the judges would go with the ticket seller."

"It doesn't sound completely kosher."

"It's not like that at the top. Contenders want to win, champions want to win. But is there any sport where judges or referees or umpires aren't prone to making hometown decisions?"

I shrugged. "So Johnny went from contender to chump?"

"No. Johnny was no chump. He was a boxer, through and through. He wouldn't have become a journeyman if he couldn't box. He learned to fight in a way that preserved him, to not get knocked down too much so he could fight more often."

"Looks like he got hit often enough."

"Yeah, he did. Like you say, almost a hundred fights. Too many."

"That many fights, how did he finish so hard up for money?"

"His last seventy fights were undercard. Not a lot of money in those. Maybe a thousand bucks on a good night, before expenses. On a bad night, a lot less."

"He said some nights he fought for gas money."

"I believe it. But you do the math on that over a twenty-year career. It's not a living wage. He had other jobs, of course. Stone had him cleaning at the gym at one point."

I glanced back at the photo of the three boys. "So how did Samson end up with the gym?"

"His career finished early."

"Why?"

Maxine gestured at the picture of Johnny with his gloves in the air. "What this photo doesn't show is the guy on the mat."

"Samson?"

She nodded.

"I thought they were friends."

"Sure they were. Friends fought each other all the time. In sparring, training, often in amateur fights. But the promoter had two young contenders he couldn't separate, so he set up a fight, one against the other, for the right to challenge the champ. Johnny versus Allan."

"And Johnny won."

"He did."

"And you said Allan got knocked out?"

"Depends who you talk to. Most guys ringside say the judges had Allan in front and Johnny got him with a liver shot."

"What's a liver shot?"

"What it sounds like. A punch to the body, right around the liver. If it hits in the right spot, it sends emergency signals all over the body, like a fire drill, and the body can shut down. I've seen guys get a liver shot and be fine for up to five seconds, then they drop to one knee and you think they'll just get up after the standing count, but they don't. Their bodies won't let them."

"So Samson got this liver shot and went down?"

"Not immediately. This is what guys who were ringside say. We saw it here on the TV. Johnny followed with a cross, and Allan went down. He still claims to this day that he slipped, that the punch didn't hurt him, but like I say, those in the know claim the liver shot was the thing that did him in. He dropped and Johnny got the title chance."

"And then lost."

"It happens."

"Did Allan ever get another opportunity?"

"Allan never fought again. He twisted his knee when he went down and had to do PT to get back. Then he got drunk one night and got in a bar fight, and the other guy karate-kicked him in the knee. After that, it was wrecked. He couldn't move around the ring fast enough."

"What did he do?"

"He became a trainer. He worked for my Stone for years and brought through a few good fighters. When Stone got sick and couldn't do it anymore, Allan just kind of stepped in and kept the place going. Never asked for extra money or nothing. He just took it on. At the end, Stone said he wanted the place to live on after him, and we agreed that Allan had shown he could do that, so after Stone passed I sold it to him."

I glanced one more time at the photograph of the boys. "And what about Mick?"

"Mick loved the game. I think he loved the camaraderie most of all. The brotherhood. He worked hard, but he never had the goods."

"He didn't fight?"

"Amateur, yes, like the rest of them. But he never went pro, because his reach was too short. If you have short arms, you gotta be lightning on your feet, and Mick wasn't."

"So what did he do?"

"He stayed around, you know, training and such. Keeping fit. But he got into the restaurant game, worked in a few kitchens here and there, and kind of drifted away from the others a little because cooks and boxers mostly work nights. Then I think he had an uncle who left him some money—not a lot but enough—and he used it as a down payment with the bank to start Longboard Kelly's."

"I never did ask him where that name came from."

"Me either."

"So I take it he isn't a member of your club."

"Of course he is. He's one of my boys."

"But he's at Longboard's all the time."

"And I'm here all the time. That's how it is, running a small business. But Mick's still welcome anytime he comes."

Maxine turned and walked back behind the bar. She refilled glasses and then loaded some dirty glassware into a dishwasher below the bar, the smell of bleach wafting into my nostrils.

"But you didn't come here just for a history lesson," she said.

"No. Johnny's been denied by the fighters' fund. I think he and Tina are running close to the bone with rent and bills, and the doctor they made him go to claims his ailments aren't boxing related. I spoke to another doctor who disagrees, but I wondered if there were any other guys here who had made claims to the fund."

Maxine stepped to the taps and poured a beer, which she deposited in front of me. "Bring that with you," she said as she flipped the bar open and walked across the room.

CHAPTER EIGHT

MAXINE LED ME TO FOUR OLDER GUYS SEATED AROUND A TABLE, ignoring the boxing match on the television above them. Four sets of eyes were focused on the dominos that snaked out in different directions on the table.

"Gentlemen," said Maxine. "This is Miami. He's helping Slumber and Tina get some dough from that boxing fund. You boys be nice."

"You a boxer?" asked an old man with chin stubble that looked like lint.

"Nope."

"What kind of joint you running here, Max?"

"Can I buy you boys a round?" I asked.

"I like the look of this guy."

"A round for the table, coming up," said Maxine.

"Take a seat, kid," said a guy with ears like potatoes.

I pulled up a folding chair and watched the game for a moment. When I played dominos as a kid, it always seemed a slow and gentle game. But I had seen it played in the Caribbean with a lot of ruckus and laughter. Here the pieces were slapped down with the percussion of Claymore mines, and the trash talk was thick and fast.

"Boom!" said one guy in a flat cap as he drove a piece into the table.

"That's your best?" said Chin Stubble. "No wonder you got knocked down in '85."

"Teddy the Machine?" said Flat Cap. "He was a damn middleweight."

"You're a middleweight."

"I wish."

The old man cackled, and Potato Ears turned to me. "What's your name again, son?"

"Miami. Miami Jones."

"Ooh, that's a good one," said Flat Cap. "You sure you're not a fighter?"

"Only when provoked."

"I'm Roy," said Potato Ears. "This is Zeke, Fozzie, and Lew."

"Gentlemen."

Maxine arrived with two beers and two whiskeys, and we toasted to our good health.

"So you're helping out young Johnny," said Roy.

"That's right. He's not in a great way."

"That boy took a lot of punishment," said Zeke.

"I heard he was decent at not getting hit too much."

"Sure, in any one fight, but over the years? You don't lose that many and not wear a few."

"Right. So he kind of needs whatever help this fighters' fund can give him, but they don't want to play ball."

"What a shock," said Lew.

"Why? Any of you guys got ailments?"

"Son, that's the elephant in the room," said Roy. "Every ex-fighter has ailments. If it's not your head, it's your hands, or your knees, or your eyes—"

"Or the headaches or the memory on the fritz," continued Fozzie.

"So you guys get help from the fund?"

There was a ripple of laughter around the table, but not like they were at a George Carlin show. This was more like someone had told a bawdy story about the deceased at their wake.

"So you didn't get money or you didn't try?"

"We all tried, son," said Roy. "But I'll tell you, I don't know a single man who got money out of that thing. Take Lew here: he don't hear too good."

"What?"

"Funny guy. But he wore a haymaker in the ear back in '87—"

"'86."

"I stand corrected, '86. He was literally deaf for what, a week?"

"As good as. Hurt like hell too."

"It came back, sort of, but over the years it just got worse and worse until now—you're deaf without that Terminator thing in your ear, right?"

"What?"

"Yeah, see? The fund's doc tells him it's just old age. In one ear. The same ear that got smacked all them years ago. We all got stories like that, kid."

"Who was the doctor you saw?" I asked Lew.

"What was his name?" said Lew.

"Wrecking Ball," said Fozzie.

"Yeah, that's right," said Lew. "Wrexham. Doc Wrexham."

"You all saw this Dr. Wrexham?"

"He's their guy. You don't see him, you don't see no one."

"Same guy who saw Johnny, huh?" said Roy.

"Yeah."

I glanced across the room, thinking about Dr. Wrexham, when I spotted a familiar face with murine features: Ricky the Fudge was in conversation with two guys at a nearby table.

"You boys know that guy?" I said.

"Ricky the Fudge," said Roy, like he had just found a raccoon living in his basement. He turned, waved to Maxine, then pointed in the direction of the dealer.

"Hey, I've told you, this is a private club!"

Ricky the Fudge's shoulder went slack as Maxine strode out

from behind the bar with a full head of steam. "Get your keister out of my club."

Ricky put his palms up and took two steps backward. "Chill, nana."

A big guy with shoulders like a freeway overpass stood from a chair by the window and stepped toward Ricky. The kid nearly tripped over himself getting out of the room, his sneakers audibly hitting the steps on the way down. The big guy stood at the top of the stairs watching Ricky, then returned to his seat without so much as a nod to Maxine. She groaned and turned on her heel back to the bar. I got the distinct impression this wasn't a club that needed a bouncer at the door.

"He here much?" I asked.

"He's like a kicked dog," said Roy. "Comes around looking for scraps, gets the boot, and runs away for a while but always comes skulking back."

"This place doesn't look like a hot market."

"Don't kid yourself. Every man in here is hurting in one way or another. And if the whiskey ain't doing its job, maybe a guy goes for a little something extra."

"Like what? Opioids?"

"Yeah, them and weed."

"You can't get all that from a doctor?"

"*If* they wanna give it to ya, or sometimes you just might need more."

The dominos game resumed, and I watched for a while, then I wished the men good evening and walked over to the bar.

"You get what you wanted?" asked Maxine.

"You know what they say: you can't always get what you want."

"But you get what you need?"

"Something like that. Say, that guy, Ricky—"

"Scum of the earth."

"Yeah, I saw him loitering around the gym."

"Doesn't surprise me. Stone would have torn him a new one."

"I heard Samson banned him. You done that?"

"Don't need to. He was never a member. I could put a guy on the door to keep him out, but look around. This ain't a rowdy crowd, and if it gets that way, even the old guys still handle themselves pretty well."

"He come around much?"

"He tries his hand every now and then. Last time was maybe two weeks ago. Johnny was here actually. He tossed him out for me."

"He did?"

"Yeah, like you just saw Big Den do. Only Johnny might have gotten a bit more hands-on."

"Did Johnny ever buy from him?"

"Not that I know of, and for sure not here. That isn't how Johnny dulls his pain."

"How does he do that?"

Maxine held up a whiskey bottle.

"How often do you see Johnny here?"

"Less and less. It's a getaway for a lot of boys, but I can't have him here when he's on one of his downswings. The fights have to stay in the ring. That was Stone's golden rule, and it's mine too."

"So he doesn't drink much here?"

"No, I don't let him drink alcohol anymore."

"That hurt business?"

"It's about more than business, Miami. These are my people, and so are their partners who don't come in very often but have to deal with what happens on the other end."

"Tina said sometimes he drinks. If he doesn't do it here, do you know where?"

"Maybe at home?"

"Not sure Tina would allow that."

"There's no shortage of bars or park benches near liquor stores."

True enough. I handed over some cash for my drink and the round for the domino boys and thanked Maxine for her time.

"I hope you can get some money for Tina and the girls."

"I'll do my best."

"Drop by anytime."

I smiled. "I'm not a member."

"I can make an exception. It's good to be queen."

I gently slapped the bar and nodded goodbye, waved at the domino men as I crossed the room, and descended the stairs into the darkness below. I stood in the alcove for a moment, letting my eyes adjust.

As I reached my car, I caught motion in my peripheral vision. In the shadows of the trees behind the lot, I saw the thin silhouette of Ricky the Fudge moving like a marionette, shoulders before elbows before wrists as if operated by strings. He wasn't alone. It was impossible to say who, but they came together briefly, one inky mass, before the person broke away, strode to a car, and drove off. A customer. When I looked back toward the dealer, he was gone, consumed by the darkness.

CHAPTER NINE

THE NEXT MORNING, DANIELLE HEADED OUT FOR WORK AS I CHOPPED some melon and apple and tossed a few berries into my blender with some ice. Enjoying my smoothie on the back patio, I noticed a pelican flying on the other side of the Intracoastal. He then banked and headed straight for me. For a moment I thought he might land on my lawn, but at the last second, he shot upward and over the top of me, his massive beak leading the way.

I ventured into the office at an easy pace, knowing that my real work wasn't going to happen until the afternoon. Lizzy had attempted to get me an appointment with the guy issuing all the denials for the fighter's fund, Dr. Wrexham. He hadn't been quite as accommodating as Dr. Abe. I didn't take this as any sign of wrong-doing—he might have just had a full slate—but it didn't engender any positive vibes either. Lizzy said that the appointment scheduler had asked for my Florida boxing license number or GBC fighter number. When she was unable to provide either, she was informed that one was required to make an appointment.

"I tried to get you a *late* afternoon appointment like you asked," said Lizzy, "but she said the doctor didn't see patients after two on Wednesdays."

"Of course not."

"I told her you were my brother visiting from Georgia and asked if you could see a doctor there when you got back, and she said no, all fund appointments have to be with this Dr. Wrexham but that he did video consultations."

"How do you diagnose a brain disorder over a video call?"

"How do you do it in person?"

"No idea."

I kept myself busy until it was time to leave, then I drove across the Flagler Memorial Bridge and onto the island. I turned off Royal Poinciana Way and onto Cocoanut Row, and found the address I was looking for. It was a building of medical suites—physicians, dentists, a radiology center—the kind of place that was really just an office building but had been repainted and pitched at the medical community because they were used to paying too much for things like rent and latex gloves, and because they rarely went out of business. Sickness, decline, and eventual death was a growth business in Florida.

A boom gate operated by a credit card stopped me from cruising into the parking lot. Not wanting to leave a trail, I continued along and found a spot in a nearby mall.

I walked back and around the boom gate and found the parking had two sections: the open-air lot, where the cars would bake in the summer, and another strip of slots in a shaded area underneath the raised building. The rear entrance to the building was through a glass door at the back of the covered spaces. This was where I needed to be.

I knew two things about doctors. First, they liked for people to know they were doctors. There was still prestige in spending a decade of your life training for your profession. Second, they liked to have the closest parking spaces to the entrance, although to be fair, most people did. Each space in the area protected from the sun had a metal plate attached to the wall with the name of a doctor. What I didn't see there was any handicapped parking—that was out in the open. Do no harm didn't mean you always had to help.

When I found the metal plate with Dr. Wrexham's name on it, I was unfazed by his black Porsche. I looked around the lot, checked my watch, and sat down on its sloping hood. I rested my feet on the bumper and lay back like a model until I heard my watch beep two o'clock, at which point I sat up and waited. I figured it would be less than five minutes.

It was four.

I knew one other thing about doctors: if they were academics and surgeons, like Dr. Abe, they probably had separate hours for consulting and for researching, but if they were general practitioners, like Dr. Wrexham, not seeing patients after two o'clock was code for having a midafternoon tee time. It was a universal truth that doctors hated to miss their tee times.

"What are you doing?" said a redheaded man in a green polo shirt. I had to assume the guy had never seen a color wheel.

"Sitting," I said.

"Get off my car."

"No."

Dr. Wrexham blinked hard. When you are on top of the food chain of professions, you don't often hear the word *no*, so he didn't seem to know what to do next.

"I am a doctor. I have an important appointment."

"Important?"

"Emergency."

"You playing the ocean course?"

"What?"

"Where's your tee time?"

"Do you know who I am?"

I smiled. It was one of my favorite lines.

"Why are you denying patients access to the fighters' fund when university tests prove they have debilitating injuries?"

"I can't discuss patients."

"I didn't ask you to. I'm asking why you routinely deny coverage to people who show clear signs of trauma from boxing."

"Are you a doctor?"

"No, are you?"

"Yes."

"For now."

"Listen, I don't need to explain myself to you."

"You do if you want to make your tee time."

"You have no standing to debate my diagnosis."

"That's why I'm sitting."

Wrexham took his cell phone from his pocket. "I'm calling the police."

"Don't use 911. That's for emergencies."

"This is an emergency."

"Do you think when I tell the *Palm Beach Post* that you used 911 to make sure you made your golf game that the people of Palm Beach will agree?"

He hesitated.

"I have the non-emergency number for the Palm Beach police if you want it."

Wrexham knitted his brows. I could see the cogs spinning as I gave him the number.

"Yes, this is Dr. Wrexham at Wrexham Medical Associates. I have a delinquent sitting on my car." He listened for a moment. "Yes, sitting on my car. It's a Porsche. No, he refused to move. I don't know his name."

"Miami Jones," I said.

Wrexham frowned deeper. If he kept it up, his eyes were going to merge into one. "He says his name is Miami Jones. Yes, okay. Thank you."

Wrexham ended the call and pouted at me. "They're sending a car."

"They're good like that."

"Look, I don't have time to waste."

"You can't get back a missed tee time, huh. It's tougher than rescheduling a doctor's appointment."

"Listen, my diagnoses are accurate. I don't know what you've heard, but that's the truth."

"No it's not. I've spoken with a large and growing number of former boxers who have obvious medical conditions associated with their fighting careers. Not a single one has been approved by you to access money from a fund that they paid into, many of them for decades."

"Your data set is too small. I've approved many patients."

"Name one."

"I cannot discuss individual patients."

"I'm not asking you to discuss them, I'm asking for a single approval. Just one."

Wrexham said nothing.

"Can't huh? Well, let me tell you something: my data set may be small, but it's big enough for a class-action lawsuit."

Wrexham's jaw dropped, but he regained his composure quickly. Lawsuits were a doctor's worst nightmare, but they were also often a hollow threat.

"Look, do whatever you think you have to. You'll get nowhere. I don't administer the funds. I just do the tests."

"Who handles the funds?"

"That's not for me to say."

"Okay. So I won't go after them. I'll just go after you."

"I hope you have deep pockets."

"I do. I work for an insurance company."

Once again Wrexham's face dropped.

"Mister, I just do the medical tests, I'm telling you. If you want to talk to someone, talk to Priestly."

"Priestly."

"Yes. He runs everything at the GBC. I'm not involved in the decision making at the fund."

I heard the bleep of a police siren in the distance. I slid off the hood of the Porsche and walked away from the good doctor without a word. I ambled out into the sunshine and was walking up the middle of the lot when I heard the Porsche roar to life. The unmarked police car sat on the other side of the boom gate, and as I got closer I saw my old friend and part-time nemesis Detective Ronzoni behind the wheel.

Dr. Wrexham sounded his horn behind me, but I kept on walking up the middle so he couldn't get by. When I got to the boom, I stepped around and approached the police car. Ronzoni lowered his window.

"Fancy meeting you here," I said.

"You're a card, Jones. You think a call comes in with your name attached to it I'm not gonna be here?"

"Counting on it, Rigatoni."

"How many times do I have to tell you?"

"Just one more."

"It's Ronzoni."

"The San Francisco treat."

"Jones, you're an idiot. What's going on here?"

"Bad doctor business. Lots of old people who are supposed to get money from a fund they paid into, but the doctor claims there's nothing wrong with them, so they get denied."

"Maybe there's nothing wrong with them. You thought of that?"

Ronzoni, champion of the rich and infamous of Palm Beach.

"I've got a university surgeon who says different."

Ronzoni was about to say something more when the horn on Dr. Wrexham's Porsche sounded like a foghorn sucking helium. The boom had lifted, and Wrexham was waving frantically for Ronzoni to get the hell out of his way.

I smiled. Ronzoni slid his car into Park and killed the engine. I stepped back so he could get out, then I followed him over to Wrexham's car. His gray, wrinkle-free suit was crumpled at the bottom of his jacket.

"Sir, can I see your license and registration?"

"What?"

"License and registration."

"I don't have time for this. First this guy, now you. I am a doctor."

"And I'm a police officer. So, sir, if you refuse to provide your license and registration, I will be compelled to draw my weapon and remove you from the vehicle."

Wrexham flopped across the console to reach his glove compartment and jabbed himself into the gear stick. He howled, and Ronzoni waited patiently. When the doctor handed the registration paper over, Ronzoni took his time reading like it was the Magna Carta, then repeated his request for the driver's license.

Once he had both, he wandered back to his car. In the normal course of things, he would run a check to see if the doctor really owned the vehicle and if he had any outstanding warrants or traffic offenses. But I could see Ronzoni from where I stood. He wasn't doing a damn thing other than sitting in his car wasting time.

I smiled at Wrexham, and the doctor snarled. We could both see his tee time sailing into the sunset. If he had a four-ball, he might be able to catch up to them on the course, but he was going to arrive in a mental state that was not suitable for a good round of golf. And if there was one thing a doctor hated more than a potential lawsuit, it was a poor round of golf.

When Ronzoni wandered back, he returned Wrexham's documents and asked why the doctor had called the station.

"He was sitting on my car."

Ronzoni glanced at me, then nodded. "Would you like to make a complaint?"

"Yes." Wrexham offered me a nasty smile, but I matched him with my best Tom Cruise grin.

No doubt this puzzled the good doctor, but I knew it involved Ronzoni returning to his car to get his clipboard so he could record the salient information in great detail, ensuring the doctor would be so late he'd be lucky to get in a bucket at the range and a glass of Chardonnay.

"I'll get my notepad," said Ronzoni.

"No, actually, don't bother," said Wrexham. "Forget it, it was nothing."

"Are you sure, sir? No complaint?"

"No. No complaint."

I could see Wrexham practically bouncing in his seat, agitated, but it was his lucky day having Ronzoni on the job—he hated paperwork more than crime, so he nodded and wished Wrexham a good day. The detective walked back to his car and then backed out of the way. I thought we might get the screeching of tires, but Wrexham had clearly decided such an act could only cause further delay. I walked over to Ronzoni as the doctor casually drove off.

"I wouldn't try it again," said Ronzoni. "Whatever you were doing."

"Nah, I got what I came for."

"In that case, get off my island before you cause any more trouble."

"Roger that, Detective."

As Ronzoni pulled away, I walked back to my car, then did as he instructed.

CHAPTER TEN

BACK AT THE OFFICE, LIZZY WAS CONCENTRATING ON HER SCREEN, AND Ron was nowhere to be found.

"How did it go?" she asked.

"In your research, did you ever come across the name Priestly?"

"Priestly? Yes, I believe I did." She brought up a note-taking app on her computer and clicked and scanned the screen. "Yes, he's the president of the Global Boxing Council."

"What can you tell me?"

"Hmm. Well, he's Canadian-born, was once a member of Boxing Canada, and was a representative on the Canadian Olympic Committee."

I smiled. "These Canadians, they're nothing but trouble."

"Careful, there's a few within earshot right now."

"I'm only concerned about this one. What else do you know?"

"He now splits his time between Toronto and the British Virgin Islands."

"Does he just?"

"Yes. Remember I said the GBC is based out of the BVI."

"I do. Let me guess: Priestly spends his summer days in Toronto and BVI the rest of the time."

"What makes you say that?"

"I'll bet dollars to donuts he's a snowbird. So what's his connection to the fund?"

"Who says there is any?"

"Dr. Wrexham."

"Did he?"

"Yeah, he told me to take it up with Priestly."

"I already told you you're not going to the Virgin Islands."

"All right, Mother, keep your shorts on. I'm wondering if he ever comes here. I take it they don't hold too many fights in Road Town."

"No, most of their events seem to be in the US or Mexico."

"Where in the US?"

"Florida."

"Of course. Do you know if we got anywhere with the Palm Beach PO box for the fund?"

"You mean like a street address? Not so far."

"Well, keep at it." I made for the door.

"Where are you going?"

"To see a man about a dog."

Lizzy rolled her eyes, and I walked out. In the Jeep, I headed down Route 1 until I got to Okeechobee Boulevard, then I began the long schlep west—such was the way of east–west travel in South Florida. I crawled along until I got to the wrong side of the turnpike, then traffic sped up just as I needed to go no further.

I pulled into the strip mall and around two sheriff's cars parked outside the Chinese restaurant. I stopped outside Sally's Check Cashing and Pawn. When I stepped inside the store, the little bell rang. The girl in the Perspex booth looked up from her phone with an expression that suggested she could cash a check or not; it wasn't going to be the highlight of her day either way. I waved and continued past as she shifted her attention back to her phone.

A pawn shop always reminded me of someone's garage—full of the stuff you collected through life that you didn't really want anymore—but without the musty garage smell. Sally was sitting on a stool behind the counter at the far end of the store, using a loupe to inspect gems like a jeweler.

"I'm loving those Patriots," he said to the gemstone as I approached.

"They say the Jets are in a rebuild."

"Aach."

"That's more rebuilds than a sandcastle."

"Aach."

He took the loupe away from his eye. "You come here to give me a stroke?"

"A winning season will do that."

"Then I'm safe, ain't I?"

"How are you, Sal?"

"I'm still ticking, kid, so it's all good."

"I see a couple PBSO vehicles outside the Chinese."

"It's what they eat when there's no donut shops around."

"Nothing to do with you."

Sal gave me his nicotine-stained grin. "Why would it have anything to do with me?"

I shrugged.

"So what can I do you for? You want an air fryer?"

"No, Sal, I don't want an air fryer."

"I'm getting drowned in the damned things."

"Why?"

"Who knows? Maybe people figure out they can cook oven fries in the oven."

"Genius. Actually, I was wondering what you knew about a guy called Priestly."

Sally pouted and pushed the solitary hair across the top of his head. "Rings a vague bell."

"Global Boxing Council."

"Yeah, right. What are you into, kid?"

I told him about Johnny Cabrini and the fund that wasn't funding anything.

"Good money in cases like that?"

"It's a favor for Mick. He's a buddy of this Johnny guy, and the guy is really doing it hard."

"Don't know many boxers who aren't."

"You know many boxers?"

"Not many good ones. But the GBC, I seem to recall them doing a fair bit in Orlando."

"Orlando?"

"That's what I remember, but my memory ain't what it used to be."

"Me either."

"You in a rush?"

"Not really."

"I'll make a few calls. You pick yourself out an air fryer."

Sally disappeared into the back room, but I didn't select an air fryer. Instead, I wandered over to a collection of musical instruments: a violin, several guitars, a tuba. I tried not to look at the instrument that had caught my attention, because it suddenly made me feel empty in my guts. I couldn't quite pin down why—a saxophone is not an inherently morose thing, unless played by a musician who makes you feel like your soul's being torn from your body. Like a persistent psychologist, the shining brass wouldn't let me look away until I had confronted why it had drawn me over in the first place.

This saxophone remained mute and mocked me with its silence. Mine, procured from this very store and now packed away in a box somewhere, was more than a twisted pipe with lots of holes and buttons. It represented moments lost, opportunities come and gone. I could always say that I played the saxophone because I had—a professional jazz musician had taught me enough to make the thing sound less than terrible.

At one point, I had thought about how life would look if I walked down that path—not all that different. I wasn't earning my living playing smokey clubs. In this dream I was still a PI who sat on a stool at Longboard Kelly's more often than a doctor would think was healthy, but I also hung with my musical friends, felt our common language over sips of brandy, and laughed as the trumpet player stole my solo right out of my lungs. But that dream had always remained exactly that.

There had been a time when I had dedicated my every waking thought to something. I didn't train at football or baseball because I wanted to; I did it because it was who I was right down to my bones. Like a node in a brain or a computer in a network, part of something larger in a way that I couldn't comprehend. When I retired I knew, like most professional athletes, that the thing I would miss most was not the winning or the losing but doing so with a group of people who were as consumed by it as I was. Folks referred to it as *camaraderie,* but it was even bigger than that. It was a connection to something so ethereal that it need not be explained.

Something I had and was now gone. Something I had searched for since and never found again. Something that I would probably continue to seek out even when I didn't know I was doing it, until I hit the realization once more that the connection was lost to me. That damn saxophone looked me in the eye, and I blinked first.

"You already got one of them," said Sally, his voice pulling me back into the room.

I spun around to face him. "What? Yeah. You find something?"

"My guys say there's a Priestly who promotes boxing out of Orlando. Very connected, so I'm told. I got you an address."

"That's great, Sal. Thanks."

"You all right, kid?"

"Sal, you ever miss the old days?"

"New York? When the mood strikes, sure. Why?"

"Wish I knew. Just wondering what I'm doing with my life, I guess. Stupid. In a pawn shop of all places."

"Most logical place in the world for it. This is a place for things that are left behind, so you're wondering about all those things you did as a young man, when everything was still possible."

"You ever do that?"

"I'm human, ain't I? But let me tell ya, it's sleight of hand. It's your mind playing games. Sure, I miss the old days, but when I do, it's the days that counted for something. I remember through rose-colored glasses, don't I? We all do. We don't reminisce the bad stuff, the days we hurt. Those damn northern winters. I'm telling you, it's a trick."

"I know. But I still fall for it."

"We all do. That's what they won't tell ya. But let me ask you, do you love your wife?"

"Of course I do."

"That's weak."

"With every fiber of my being."

"That's cliché."

I frowned at him as if I didn't know what he wanted from me. "More today than any other day, and every day in a different way."

"You pinch that from a song?"

"I don't think so."

"All right, then. You got friends?"

"Yeah."

"Are they good people?"

"You know most of them. Salt of the earth."

"Do you put money in the plate?"

"I don't go to church."

"Metaphorically."

"I have an autopay each month for Médecins Sans Frontières and St. Jude's."

"And have you tried to be your best self today?"

"I sat on a guy's Porsche and made him late for golf."

"Okay."

"But he wasn't a very nice guy."

"Then we'll go with yes. So I'm gonna quote Bull Durham: 'Stop thinking, meat.' You can't be a brain surgeon and bat .350 for the Yankees. It's a lie. Being a half-decent human being is hard enough. You got me?"

"Yeah, I think so."

"You got me?"

"Yes, Sal. I got you."

"All right. Now go do your thing, I got work to do."

"Thanks, Sal."

"And take an air fryer, will ya? I'm drowning in the damn things."

CHAPTER ELEVEN

Whenever I am feeling lost in the great cosmos of life and at
risk of being flung into the far reaches of a cold and endless
universe, I find the best approach is to recalibrate my equipment by
heading for the center of my own personal galaxy.

The winter sun had dropped fast and low, and the umbrella
shadows were long streaks across the courtyard, terminating at the
bar where I sat with Danielle, the Lady Cassandra, and Ron. Ron
and I gave up the stools shaped like our butt cheeks and moved out
to the flanks with our wives in between. The view was different but
no less reassuring.

Muriel lined up the drinks: beer, vodka tonic, French champagne, beer. The fact that Mick even had French champagne amazed
me the first time Cassandra ordered a glass. I had even asked Muriel
if the remains had been tossed out afterward for a lack of other
customers.

"Cassandra bought the bottle and gave it to a group of tennis
ladies in the courtyard when she left."

It wasn't exactly Robin Hood, but it was generous, and that was
the Lady Cassandra to a tee. She had a way of leveling me out,
getting to the core of a problem, and calling me on my baloney in

the nicest possible way. Plus she smelled good. Rich people usually do.

Danielle was smiling at me and pulling me toward relaxed when Mick came out from the bowels of the bar with a phone at his ear.

"Trouble," he said to me.

"What's up?"

"Johnny. Busting the place up."

Mick strode back inside and reappeared on our side of the bar.

"Whose place?" I asked.

"Tina's."

Danielle frowned as I slipped from my stool. "I'm coming," I said.

Mick didn't say no. Instead, he looked at Muriel, who said, "I got this."

I kissed Danielle and said I'd be back shortly. Ron asked if he should come, but I explained that a full army might feel a little intimidating for Tina and the girls, then I followed Mick out.

This time he drove. I had never seen Mick drive, but I knew his car from the lot: the massive Cadillac Eldorado convertible. It was Detroit steel from bumper to bumper and drank fuel like a thirsty dragon.

He cruised down to the Cabrini residence without speaking—I got the sense that half the reason Mick had a convertible was to minimize the chitchat while driving—and stopped in front of the house. As we crossed the lawn to the door, Tina was already opening it.

"Mick," she said.

"Okay?"

She shrugged. Mick stepped inside, and I followed, checking if Tina had any obvious bruises or abrasions.

All I saw was a living room in disarray. The sofa was askew, and a side table had been knocked over, with its lamp on the floor, its shade crushed. The wallpaper behind Tina had a hole in it—jagged and rough, and slightly larger than a fist.

"The girls are packing a bag," she said. "I can't do this anymore."

Mick looked crestfallen, as if he was somehow at fault, and his usual chatty demeanor eluded him, so I asked the questions.

"Are you sure you're okay?"

"No, Miami, I am not okay."

"I mean physically. Did he hit you?"

"No."

"The girls?"

"No, he'd never." She said it in a way that suggested she once believed it but was no longer sure.

"So you're leaving?"

"For tonight. I'll be back when the red mist fades."

"What happened?" I asked.

"He just lost it."

"Why? What made him so angry?"

"That's the problem, Miami. There's nothing. It just comes on out of nowhere. Used to be a funk, like a grumpy mood, and he'd go quiet or go out to the garage and stew. Then it turned into ranting about things, about people who were doing him wrong."

"Paranoia?"

"Yeah. Now he's screaming about me having an affair."

"Are you?"

"Excuse me?"

"Sorry to be blunt, but it happens. Living with him clearly isn't easy."

"No, it's not. But between picking up after an ill husband, working to pay the rent when he keeps getting fired, and looking after teenagers, when do you think this affair would happen?"

"It happens. It's not a question of blame."

"Well, not for me. Look, I love Johnny, but I don't love what he's become. It's not his fault, and I know that, but it is what it is. And now he's a danger to my girls, and I can't have that. I need to protect them."

"And yourself," I said.

"Yeah, that too. Listen, I need to pack some things."

"Do you have somewhere to go?"

"My oldest daughter lives with her boyfriend in Palm Beach Gardens. It's not a big place, but it will do in a pinch."

"Okay."

"Hopefully he's better tomorrow."

"Hopefully."

She moved toward the hallway, then turned back to me. "I want to help him, I really do. But the doctors say he won't get better. Maybe medication can manage it, but he won't get better, especially if he doesn't even take the meds and he keeps drinking. Taking care of our girls has to be priority."

"I get it."

She walked away, and I turned to Mick. He looked as lost as I had ever seen him, staring at the hole in the wall as if it were his fist that had made it. It was as if he felt responsible somehow.

"You got any idea where he might have gone?" I asked.

Mick nodded but kept looking at the hole, then he walked out the back door.

I followed him into the small, barren backyard, more weed than grass and in need of a mow, and stepped around a rusted-out grill and propane tank. Mick strode across to the garage and went in through a side door.

The space smelled of sweat, cheap liquor, and motor oil. The garage wasn't full of the detritus of life. There was very little in it. Some bags holding I had no idea what, and a row of steel shelves with a couple paint cans and a plastic tote. Against the wall was a camp cot, with a sleeping bag and pillow on the floor beside it.

Johnny Cabrini lay curled up on the cot, holding a bottle of whiskey like an infant with milk. Mick came closer, and Johnny stirred and came to.

"What?" spat Johnny.

"Brother," said Mick.

Johnny tried to get up suddenly but tumbled off the cot. He hit the concrete floor, cradling the bottle, keeping it from harm. He shook his head like a wet dog and used the cot to lever himself into a standing position.

His hair was a tangled mess, his eyes were bloodshot, and his face was in desperate need of a shave. Snot oozed from his nose. He was a man fighting his demons, and it didn't take a trained eye to know the demons were winning.

"Whadda you looking at?" he slurred.

Mick said nothing.

"Huh? What ya say? Cat got your tongue?" Johnny lifted the bottle to his mouth and made to take a long gulp, but the top was screwed on. He didn't seem to notice. He dropped the bottle onto the cot and stepped toward Mick like he was on a trawler being tossed around the Bering Strait. Johnny put his fists up in an approximation of a fighting stance.

"You can't have her," he said. "She's mine. You get me? Mine!"

Johnny took a long, loping swing at Mick, who didn't raise his hands; he just leaned back and let the punch pass lazily by his face. Johnny staggered, losing his balance for a moment, then looked back at Mick as if he forgot what he was doing.

"Time to go," said Johnny.

"Brother."

"Go! Go on. You go. They all are." Johnny sat on the cot, and the frame winced under the weight. His head wobbled and he blinked hard. "Time to go," he said again, and he curled up on the cot with the bottle beside him.

Mick and I stood in silence, breathing in Johnny's fumes and his sadness, until a guttural snore began rocking the cot.

Mick eased the bottle from Johnny's grip, then I led the way out of the garage and over to the driveway. Tina's car was gone. Bugs were raising a chorus in the still night. We stood there for a moment. I assumed Mick didn't know what to say about Johnny, because I didn't know what to say either. He wasn't much of a talker at the best of times, but now the silence seemed to envelop him.

"I'll get them the money," I said.

Mick nodded like this was the answer to everything, when we

both knew it was the answer to nothing. We liked to think that if we all had more money we could solve any problem, but we stood there dealing with the certainty that it was a lie. Money could tide Tina over, pay some rent, buy some food. Important stuff. But it wasn't going to right this wrong whether Johnny was a panhandler or a billionaire. The silence that engulfed Mick was the realization that he could tinker around the edges, but this was not something he could fix. I could see him questioning his value as Johnny's friend as a result. I couldn't read his mind on this, but I didn't need to. It was exactly how I was feeling about him.

After a few minutes, we walked to the car, and Mick drove us back to Longboard's. He parked but didn't get out.

"I saw a picture of you," I said. "At the Pugilists' Club."

"Yeah."

"Three young guys hanging off the ropes."

Mick nodded. "Another time."

"Yeah. You didn't get into boxing like the other two?"

"Too short, too slow."

"I wouldn't take you on."

"Good."

"Can I ask you something? I've known you a long time, but I've never heard you mention those guys or go drinking with them, and I've never seen them here at Longboard's."

Mick picked up a quarter out of the console and held it between us. He showed me the one side with an eagle on it, then he flipped it so George Washington was facing me. He held it there for a moment before dropping the coin back into the console.

"What's your point?" I asked.

"Same coin, but the sides never meet."

He got out of the car, so I followed as I considered what he'd said. Did he prefer to keep his work and private lives separate, or was it the old and the new, or did he just think that was how things worked out? I had no idea. Mick remained a riddle wrapped in an enigma covered in a burrito wrapper.

When we got into the courtyard, everyone was exactly where we left them, except my beer had disappeared. Muriel poured me a fresh one, and I sat beside Danielle.

"Okay?" she asked.

"Honestly, no. He's in a bad place."

"And his wife and kids?"

"They've gone to stay with other family."

"Did he hurt them?"

"No. No he didn't."

"Will he?"

I thought about the hole in the wall. "I hope not."

"That's not overly reassuring."

"No, but it's all there is. He's not in charge of himself when he's like this. Someone else is driving the bus."

"Maybe he needs professional help."

"He doesn't have any money or insurance to pay for that."

"You don't need money or insurance to be admitted to a psychiatric hospital. It's the Baker Act. If you believe you're a danger, or you're assessed as such, they have to admit you regardless of ability to pay."

"I'm not sure he's in a place right now to do that voluntarily, and he could argue he was drunk—which he is. Plus, he has a report from Dr. Wrexham saying there's nothing wrong with him."

"So we wait until he does something he can't take back?"

"No. Right now he's sleeping it off and his family is staying elsewhere. I think we have to wait until he's in a better frame of mind to talk to him about these other options."

"Will he listen?"

"I don't know. When I spoke to him the other day, he was lucid and apologetic about how his actions were affecting his family, so maybe."

"I hope you're right."

"So do I."

CHAPTER TWELVE

I LEFT EARLY THE NEXT MORNING AND HEADED UP I-95 BEFORE
switching onto the turnpike and branching out from Fort Pierce
toward Orlando. I felt a little like I was running away from the
problem of Johnny Cabrini, but the fact was I was best put to use
getting him and Tina some money than I was talking him into
psychiatric help. We agreed that Mick and Tina were the ones for
that job, and even then it was dependent on Johnny regaining some
control over himself. The fact that he had done so before was no
guarantee that he would again. The most important variable was
getting him sober.

I expected to get an update from Mick by the time I got to
Orlando a couple hours later, but I had heard nothing by the time I
pulled into the lot that surrounded the small business complex off
West Sand Lake Road.

It was one of those new-looking buildings with lots of reflective
glass and a fake lagoon out the back. Tenant directories were
becoming a thing of the past—I assumed for security reasons—but I
wanted to avoid the security desk, so I just continued to the elevator
as if I belonged in the place. My button-up shirt and chinos turned
out to be the perfect disguise.

Like in hotels, I assumed the suites were numbered according to their floor, so I got off on two and went wandering. Lots of heavy, closed fire doors and few people. The bathrooms were locked, and there were no communal spaces. It seemed like a stellar place to work, at least compared to a federal penitentiary.

I checked the nameplate beside each door as I passed by until I found one called Bruiser Promotions. It felt right. I tried the handle and found it open. Some businesses were worried about security more than others.

The office lobby was cramped, with two chairs in the corner and a reception desk. There were framed posters on every wall hailing events over what appeared to be about a thirty-year period. Most of the earlier ones were for big event boxing matches, and as time crept on it seemed that Bruiser Promotions had branched out into concerts and music festivals, many featuring acts from Mexico and South America.

The woman behind the reception desk, with her hair curled up her head like soft-serve ice cream, was not much more than a pair of eyes. Either she was sitting on a very low chair or the desk was built for a giant.

"Help you?" she said with a heavy accent that suggested English was not her preferred language.

"I'm here to see Mr. Priestly."

"Is he expecting you?"

"He certainly should be."

"Well, I don't think he's here right now. Can I take a message?"

"No. This isn't a phone call."

"Well, let me see if I can find someone to . . ." Her trailing off told me the plan was to find someone to help me out of the building. She walked off down the corridor to her left, where I could see a line of glass-fronted but dimly lit offices. On the other side of the reception desk was another corridor with offices bathed in a more natural-colored light, suggesting they had windows.

I took the corridor less traveled. Beyond the four sunny but empty offices, the corridor banked right and, I assumed, wrapped back around to the one where the receptionist had gone. In the middle of the horseshoe was a conference room with glass walls. I assumed that was where all the people were, but I couldn't tell for sure, as the drapes were closed on my side. That suited my purpose just fine.

I strode down to the end of the corridor and surveyed the corner offices. One had a nameplate that read *Breyer Priestly* and faced the parking lot. The other overlooked a pristine lawn and a lake with a water jet. The boss always takes the best view, so that was the office I let myself into. I noted the nameplate on the door: *Loman Priestly*.

It was a good-sized room, enough for a heavy desk and a casual meeting space with two sofas and a coffee table near the door. There were more posters: two heads glaring at each other as if one boxer suspected the other of a crime; a guy in an enormous sombrero with a title that simply read *Julio*; and several that advertised female singers dressed like they were Victoria's Secret models.

I settled into the sofa against the wall so I could see anyone who came in before they saw me. It took about twenty minutes before a man, whose cologne announced his presence ahead of his arrival, strode in. He walked directly to his desk and began tapping at his computer before he glanced up and saw me. He just raised a single bushy eyebrow, and I wondered if people regularly wandered into his office or if he was just one cool customer.

"You have ten seconds."

"And then?"

"I call security or I shoot you. Not sure which yet."

"Let's put a pin in those ideas, Mr. Priestly."

"You know who I am."

"I do."

"So who the hell are you?"

"Miami Jones."

"That supposed to mean something to me? You're not a fighter. You're too soft."

"Funny, I was thinking the same thing about you."

"Five seconds, and I don't think I'll bother with security."

"I represent Johnny Cabrini."

"Who?"

"Johnny Cabrini."

"Is he a boxer?"

"He was."

"Did I promote him?"

"Yes."

"Well, he couldn't have been much good if I don't remember him. I always remember the champs, but the losers ain't my concern."

"But they are, Mr. Priestly. See, Mr. Cabrini is owed money from your fund, and I'm here to collect."

"Fund? What the hell are you talking about?"

"The fighters' fund."

He leaned back and sucked in some air through his puffy, purple lips. "The GBC?"

"One and the same."

"Well, you're as dumb as a bag of rocks, aren't you?"

"You think so?"

"I know so, 'cause I got nothing to do with all that."

"Of course you don't."

"But if you knew a damned thing, you'd know that already."

"All I know is the whole thing is built like a house of mirrors, and when I see things that are deliberately complicated, I think there must be something crooked on the other side."

"You do all that thinking by yourself?"

"No, I got a team. Best in the business."

He spewed a phlegmy laugh. "At what?"

"Making a great deal of noise in the media about big guys ripping off the little guys."

"That must be terrifying. Look, Orlando—"

"Miami."

"Whatever. I told you, I don't have anything to do with that stuff, whether you like it or not. I'm a promoter, best in the business."

"Yeah, I'm sure Julio is a big deal."

"Over five million albums sold and plays arenas, twenty thousand strong."

That did seem like a pretty big deal.

"It's my brother that runs the Global Boxing Council, genius. Not me."

"And which office is he in?"

"He doesn't work here. The GBC is based in the Virgin Islands."

"And the ride-sharing app on my phone is based in the Netherlands, but the goose sitting on the golden egg is always in California."

"My brother is based in the BVI as well. Google it."

I surely would, and I wondered why I hadn't yet. Surely Lizzy already had.

"Well, tell him from me that Johnny Cabrini wants his money, and I'm coming for it."

"Do I look like a secretary?"

He looked like a pufferfish. "That's Johnny with a *y*."

I walked out before he could have the last line—or shoot me—and I didn't stop until I got to my car. I was on the road back to West Palm within a minute. It was a long way to go for such a short conversation, but I didn't blame Sally or his contacts. I had not been specific about which Priestly I wanted because I didn't know there were two. So now we knew. One was in Orlando and the other was based in the British Virgin Islands. That phrase—*based in*—was an interesting choice. It covered a fair bit of ground.

As I headed out of Orlando, I selected the Eagles live album on my phone and turned it up. I zoomed along the long black line thinking about how sometimes in life you swung and missed. People tended to get upset, to cause themselves massive amounts of stress, because something that they had tried hadn't worked as planned. A recipe went haywire or an outing was spoiled by rain or a sales pitch fell on deaf ears. Or they drove a total of five hours to have a two-minute conversation that seemed to achieve nothing.

But most people failed to acknowledge the math and philosophy at play—something all baseball players understood implicitly. The math said you swing more than you miss. A lot more. The best batting average in Major League Baseball belonged to Ty Cobb. He batted .366, which meant he got a hit 36 percent of the time he went up to bat. So the best ever didn't get a hit two-thirds of the time. When you factored in strikes and foul balls and other pitches that he didn't hit, Cobb's success rate was probably less than 1 in 10.

He failed 90 percent of the time and ended up being the best of all time. That was the math. The philosophy suggested that the 10 percent could not happen without the 90. Failure bred success as much as success did, as long as you didn't bathe in it. Edison failed to make a light bulb more times than most people would have tried, and then he didn't fail. I would bet all the sand on Hollywood Beach that Ty Cobb wasn't a Hall of Famer because he hit 1 in 10, but because he didn't let the 9 in 10 stop him from trying again.

The notion settled well with me as I cut through the long and lonely stretch toward Fort Pierce. Such thoughts and a little bit of Don Henley singing about wasted time helped me beat away the idea that it might have been exactly that.

I was pulling into Longboard Kelly's when my phone rang.

"Miami?"

"Tina. What's up?"

"I called to say thank you."

"For what?"

"Everything you've done."

"I haven't really done anything yet."

"But the fund."

"What about it?"

"They just called me and said they made an error and that Johnny was due a payment." She sounded like she had won the jackpot in the Powerball.

"How much did they offer?"

"Five hundred."

"Dollars?"

"Yes."

"A month?"

"No."

"First payment."

"No."

"So five hundred total."

"Yes." She sounded a little less excited now. "They say I have to sign an agreement."

"Tina, don't agree to anything and sure as hell don't sign anything."

"Why?"

"It's a bad offer."

"How do you know?"

"The first offer always is. This is just an opening gambit. We can do better."

I asked her to give me the name of the person who had called and their phone number, and I pulled a notepad from my console and scribbled it down.

"Fishook?" I said.

"Yes, that's what he said."

"Okay. We'll keep on it. We can do better, so remember, don't sign anything."

"If you're sure."

"Positive."

Before I went into Longboard's I called Lizzy in the office and gave her the info.

"His name is Fishook?" said Lizzy.

"That's what she said. Put the name and number together and see what it adds up to."

Lizzy ended the call, and I got out and wandered toward the courtyard and a well-earned beer, thinking that sometimes you have to be prepared to swing and miss in order to get a hit.

CHAPTER THIRTEEN

I didn't even get to sit down. I could see from Muriel's Wonder Woman pose—hands on hips, strong arms tensed—that all was not right with the world.

"What's going on?" she said.

"How do you mean?" I put my hands on the bar but didn't take my stool.

"Mick's being weird."

I was going to make a crack about Mick always being weird, but it felt wrong. She was talking about a different kind of weird.

"How so?"

"He's leaving again."

"Leaving where?"

"Since when does he tell me where he's going?"

"Now, you mean?"

"Yeah. He just asked if I was okay by myself for the night, but not in so many words."

"Are you okay by yourself?"

"Apart from the kitchen, of course I am. I'm usually by myself, or haven't you noticed?"

"Oh, I've noticed. Mick's usually in the back."

"Right. There used to be a time when he was always here, out in the back. Now he's heading off here and there, and he doesn't look himself, Miami. What's wrong with him?"

I smiled. "You worried about him?"

"Of course I'm worried about him, you idiot."

I dropped the smile. "It's this thing with his friend. A childhood friend who's in a bad way—depression and stuff—and I think Mick is trying to make up the difference because he doesn't know how to fix it."

"Can he fix it?"

"No. But that doesn't stop people from trying, does it?"

"You need to go with him."

"I need a beer."

"Miami, I'm serious."

"Okay. He hasn't left yet, has he?"

"No."

"So I'll ask him."

I didn't have to ask him. Mick came out of the back in a white tank-top undershirt and a stern expression. He rounded the bar but didn't break stride.

"Wanna know what Johnny's been doing with his life?" he said.

He didn't wait for an answer, so I didn't give one. It was the longest sentence I had ever heard from Mick's lips, so I was intrigued by that alone. I nodded at Muriel and chased Mick out into the parking lot. We got in the Eldorado, and Mick drove south. I didn't feel the impulse to chat and Mick never did, so with the wind flowing through my hair like a mutt leaning out the window, I sat back and didn't enjoy the ride.

Mick pulled into a building supply company in an industrial area near the Lantana airfield. A guy at the gate must have recognized Mick, because he waved us through, into a humongous lot, more for moving large machinery and heavy loads onto trucks than for parking, its perimeter lined with pallets of pavers and cinder blocks. The main building looked to be a warehouse, with a tiny parking lot in front of a people-sized door at one end and at the other, a double roller door that could accommodate a jumbo jet. One of the rollers was closed, and the other was halfway down and obscured by what had been erected in front of it.

A boxing ring—the real deal, with a lighting rig above it and speakers blasting music that I neither knew nor cared for. The ring was surrounded by folding chairs, about half-filled with people. My back-of-napkin math said the crowd could reach four hundred if every seat were occupied. Through a throng of people inside the ring—what were they all doing in there?—I could see two bare-chested men waiting in the corners, ready to face off.

Mick killed the engine, and we sat for a moment.

"You wanna share?" I asked.

"Johnny," he said, stating both the obvious and the minimum.

"Please tell me he's not fighting."

"Nup. License out of date."

"So?"

"Was supposed to be a cornerman."

"What exactly does a cornerman do?"

"Works in the corner."

This wasn't helping. "So . . ."

"He didn't show."

"Oh. So you're filling in?"

"Yep."

I must have known all I needed to because Mick got out of the car. I followed him across the lot and around the back of the folding seats toward the roller doors in the warehouse. The music stopped, and an announcer yelled into a superfluous microphone. He spoke each word separately with perfect diction and elongated the end of every sentence.

"Welcome to Fiiiight Niiiiiight, here in lovely downtown Laaan-taaaana!"

It was neither downtown nor particularly lovely. We were in the middle of a building-supply business, which I found a strange place to set up a boxing event. But I figured I'd cut the guy a break. He was imbuing all the pomp and circumstance of a world champi-onship fight into something that clearly was not worthy of it. Again

I thought about all those swings and misses. You might miss more than you hit, but that didn't mean you shouldn't treat every at-bat like the most important of your life.

At the large roller door, Mick met up with a guy who shook his hand and cursed—something about Johnny—then gave him a plastic pass on a lanyard. Mick uttered something, and the guy looked at me.

"Martín," he introduced himself, pronouncing it *Mar-teen*. "I'm the trainer."

"Miami," I said.

"You helping Johnny?"

"Trying to."

"Exactly. I can't keep giving him jobs if he doesn't show."

"Okay." I wasn't sure what it had to do with me. Martín handed me a lanyard like Mick's. I looked it over as they strode inside the warehouse. Attached to it was a poorly laminated, well-used pass, likely from a desktop printer like I had in my office, and the words *Lantana Building and Supply* were printed on the lanyard.

I heard the ding of a bell and glanced back to see the boxers in the ring dancing toward each other, but I didn't hang around for contact. I found Mick in front of a line of forklifts blocking access to the rear of the warehouse, where industrial shelving held I had no idea what.

Tight groups of people were huddled around boxers. Some were being strapped, and others were lying on towels on the floor, getting rubbed down. A few were in prayer.

Mick and Martín stopped in front of a man straddling a chair, rubbing himself with oil that made his skin shine. He was muscular but thin enough to blow away in a breeze. I hoped he was fast because I was afraid for him if he got hit.

Martín spoke to the boxer in rapid-fire Spanish, perhaps offering last-minute instructions. An official-looking guy came over to watch Martín wrap the hands of the boxer, who rested his arms on the back of the chair as Martín worked. He started with gauze around the wrist and up toward the elbow, then he wound it back down to the wrist. He then wrapped one layer around the hand but not the fingers. Martín took another roll of gauze and looped it around his own flat hand, about twenty-five times, to create a pad. He cut off the pad, placed it carefully over the boxer's knuckles, and continued the gauze wrap to hold it in place.

"What's that?" I asked Mick.

"Knuckle pad. Fills the glove."

Martín crisscrossed the hand like he was working on a mummy. When it looked like he was done, he was only beginning. Martín used some wide tape to wrap the wrist and hand over the gauze, getting the boxer to make a fist periodically to check it for fit. Next, he used a thinner tape for in between the fighter's fingers before creating a lattice across the whole thing to pull it all taut. Martín could have worked in an ER and saved a lot of lives.

The official moved over to watch a second contender going through the same process and glanced back as Martín did the boxer's second hand.

When he was finished, the official handed Mick some gloves. He fitted them onto the boxer's hands and tied them up tight like shoes he never wished to remove. Finally, Martín taped the laces down, and the official gave a curt nod and moved on.

"What's that about?" I asked.

"From the commission. Checks that the wraps are aboveboard."

I was going to ask what made a wrap belowboard, but I wasn't sure I would get an answer I would understand.

"So what exactly do you want from me?"

Mick handed me two sports bottles. "Fill with water. Between rounds, when I say *face*, shoot his face. Not the eyes. I say *drink*, shoot his mouth. Got it?"

I figured I could follow those directions. I went in search of water but found none. Before I made a run to the bathroom, I asked one of the many guys who were standing around with nothing much to do, and I was directed to an orange-colored drink cooler. I used the spigot at the bottom to fill my bottles and wondered if two would cut it. Boxers always looked so overheated, I feared I didn't have enough.

When I got back to Mick, the boxer was sitting quietly, staring into the middle distance, perhaps getting himself into the right mindset. I would have wanted some headphones and the soundtrack to *Rocky*, but to each his own.

The announcer outside declared the winner by TKO. I wasn't a hundred percent sure what that meant, but I recalled something about getting knocked down versus getting knocked out. I made a mental note to ask someone about that.

When our boxer sprang up out of his chair and started bouncing from foot to foot, I realized I was going into the corner for a guy whose name I didn't know. Martín threw several towels over each of his shoulders and led the boxer out toward the ring. Mick picked up a can cooler like he was off for a spot of fishing and followed, so I took my cue and dropped in behind them with my water.

We paused at the door of the warehouse, next to another fighter and his people, who all looked serious. There was no trash talk or banter; everyone was focused on their own job. I tried to get my head in the game, but it was hard to do when I didn't know a damned thing.

The ring announcer called out a name, and the other boxer walked forward with his team. I wondered if that made him the home guy and if our man was meant to lose, or if this was neutral territory and they were up-and-comers in a battle of wills. Then Martín started to move.

"In the blue corner, from Westgate, Florida, weighing in at one hundred seventeen pounds, Javier Guerrero."

The final vowel took longer for him to say than it did for me to walk from the roller door to ringside, but at least now I knew the name of my guy. Javier got into the ring and started bopping around as if he had just been fitted with new batteries. Martín eased in through the ropes, while Mick and I stayed down on the ground.

The referee brought the two fighters into the middle of the ring and spoke to them in a hushed voice. I looked around at the crowd, which had grown but not by much. It was the cocktail hour—not the time I expected two men to bash each other in combat. The sun was sinking, giving the place an eerie feel. The lighting rig above us cast colors that would be spectacular after dark but just now were washed out like an old T-shirt.

Martín and Javier returned to the corner and the boxer sat on a little stool. Mick stepped up but remained outside the ropes. He nudged his head to indicate I should do the same on the other side of the corner, so I did. Martín spoke again in Spanish to Javier, who cocked his head back slightly and opened his mouth like a baby bird. I read the cues and squirted a little water into Javier's mouth, which he sloshed around and then spat out onto my shoes.

Mick jumped down and I did the same, then Martín clambered through the ropes and down the steps. Javier popped up onto his feet. The bell rang, and he skipped toward the center of the ring.

The two boxers looked more like boys than men; I was pretty confident I could bench-press them both. They danced around each other and threw a few jabs, sizing each other up for a good minute. Then the guy from the red corner landed a left hook. Javier stumbled backward and woke up.

Javier rushed his opponent and started throwing wild punches. Most of them landed on the guy's gloves held high in front of his face.

It didn't look technical or composed. I could imagine seeing these moves outside a bar at 2 a.m. Javier must have run out of puff because he stopped flailing and took a quick step back to gather himself, and the two men resumed their dance until the bell sounded.

I hadn't noticed that Mick had removed the stool from the ring but he now replaced it, and Javier flopped down on it as Martín climbed back into the ring. Mick took something metal that looked like a small branding iron from his cooler of ice and held it below Javier's right eye as the trainer barked more instructions. The boxer opened his mouth, and I squirted some more water in, feeling like I was getting the hang of this cornerman business.

"Face," said Mick, and with a little more uncertainty I squirted water around Javier's face, which Mick mopped up with one of his towels. I mustn't have gotten it completely wrong because Javier didn't scowl at me. He just nodded at Martín until the trainer climbed out of the ring and the bell went off again.

The second round started like the first, dancing and feeling each other out, both men appearing light on their feet and in their bones. The battle edged toward our side of the ring, and then suddenly the opponent unleashed a flurry of punches all over Javier's torso—ribs and stomach and chest, the thudding sounds primitive and brutal, their deep resonance making my teeth ache.

Martín shouted something to Javier, but he didn't react. I couldn't blame him. I had taken a few body shots myself over the years, without the benefit of Marquess of Queensberry rules. I remember being astounded at how being hit or kicked in the belly could make my ears ring like a fire alarm going off in my head.

Javier launched himself into his opponent and wrapped his arms around him, preventing any more punches from being thrown. The referee stepped in and untethered them, then he pulled them into the middle of the ring.

"Box," he called out, and they resumed, but Javier looked spent.

The bell rang after a few soft efforts from both sides. When I got up onto the ropes, I was taken aback by Javier's face. It had developed a soft, papery texture that reminded me of the old guys in the Pugilists' Club. Mick held his metal tool on Javier's face and an ice bag on the back of his neck. I squirted some water into his mouth and on his face, but mostly I just stared at him.

He nodded to Martín as if all was okay, but his chest was heaving like his heart was clocking 200 beats per minute.

Mick removed the ice and said, "Body."

I directed some water onto Javier's chest, Mick wiped it up, and once more we got out of the way and let them do their thing. Mick put his ice bag back into the cooler along with the metal tool.

The next two rounds looked like an even contest to me, with

punches landing here and there, but mostly they circled each other and as they became fatigued, more holding on.

When the bell dinged after the fourth round, the ring filled with people. I sprayed down Javier's head. Martín removed his gloves and handed them down to a guy on the ground who carried them away to the warehouse.

The referee asked the two fighters to come to the middle of the ring, where they hugged each other. They were certainly brothers in arms, but I couldn't imagine ever wanting to embrace someone who had just attempted to punch my lights out.

The announcer called out the judges' scores and proclaimed Pedro Morales the winner. The man put his hands up in victory, then embraced Javier once more. While he did a victory lap around the ring to a smattering of applause, not unlike that from a golf tournament, we crawled out of the ring and back into the hole from which we had come.

Martín cut the wraps from Javier's fists and told him that it was a good effort. A guy dressed like a Vegas pimp—beige trousers and a shirt opened up two or three buttons too many —trotted into the warehouse to slap Javier on the back and say, "Okay, okay." Another man emerged from the office and handed the pimp an envelope. He slowly thumbed through the cash and handed some money to Martín, who shoved his cut into his shirt pocket. He then gave some to Mick. He offered me a look like I was the reason Javier lost.

"Okay?" Mick said to Martín.

"Sì. No problem. Tell Johnny to sort himself out." Martín shook my hand. "Thanks for your help."

I nodded but said nothing. I had performed tasks that had been perfected by monkeys at NASA, so I wasn't too ebullient.

"Next time," said Mick as he put his hand on Javier's shoulder. The kid nodded, but his expression said a next time wasn't such a great idea. He looked as close to dead as a healthy person ever did.

I followed Mick outside. The parking lot had filled up, and the crowd was growing. Evening gave purpose to the lighting rig and hid the industrial surrounds, offering an atmosphere similar to the

Vegas fights I had seen in passing on television. At least that was the effect if I squinted.

As we reached the Eldorado, Mick handed me a twenty-dollar bill. I looked at it for a moment like I had never seen one before.

"What's this?"

"Pay."

"For squirting water at a kid's face?"

He nodded and opened the car.

"Is this what you earn for this stuff?"

"You. Cutman gets thirty."

"So Johnny would have gotten twenty bucks for this?"

"Yep."

"Hang on. If I'm replacing him, who did you replace?"

"Dunno. Johnny was bringing the cutman."

"So he made two guys absent."

"Yep."

"No wonder Martín wasn't happy."

"Yep."

"Twenty's not a lot of dough for a night's work though, is it."

"Each fight."

"How many fights can a cornerman do?"

"Depends. One, maybe two."

"So forty bucks, tops."

"Double if you win."

"So you leave your own bar to make a lousy thirty bucks?"

"Not usually. I told ya, he wouldn't hire Johnny again if I didn't cover. You too."

"I don't need twenty bucks for that."

"Me either. I give it to Tina."

I handed the twenty back to Mick. "Mine too."

CHAPTER FOURTEEN

I woke up the next morning with a soft breeze flowing through the house. Danielle and I had enjoyed Mick's fish sandwiches when he and I had returned to Longboard's after the fight and then called it an early night. Danielle was now on the back patio, stretching or yoga-ing or whatever contorting one's body into a pretzel was called these days.

I made her a smoothie, which she took to the shower with her. When she came out, she was dressed to take on the world, and she left me at the kitchen counter with a kiss.

Sipping my smoothie, I thought about what I had seen the evening before. It was like the minor leagues of boxing—none of the pretense and flash of Vegas but all the sweat and hurt. I was familiar with the feeling, having spent six years in the minors and barely a glimpse of the show. I played my share of half-empty stadiums followed by cold showers in fleabag hotels. Those guys last night were paying their dues, doing the work to learn and maybe get their shot at something big—or at least indoor.

Ron was working on some kind of insurance case, having offloaded the task of tracking down details on the fighters' fund to Lizzy. I was considering going into the office to show some interest in what they were doing, even though we all knew I had none. My thought was interrupted by the siren call of my phone.

"Miss me already?" I said to Danielle.

"Of course," she said, not missing a beat in a way that I wished I could do. "But I was also listening to the PBSO radio on the way in."

"You listen to the sheriff's radio while you drive to work?"

"Sure."

"Okay." There was nothing else to say. Some people are trainspotters and some people are cops.

"Listen, you were doing something at this Pugilists' Club in Lake Worth, right?"

"Yep."

"They just called in a suspicious death at the club."

"Who?"

"They're not advertising that on the radio, MJ."

"Oh hell."

"You think your guy might have . . . ?"

"He wasn't in a good place, last I saw him."

"And he didn't show last night."

"Oh hell," I said again. "I gotta go."

I dashed into the bedroom, threw on some clothes, hopped across the living room putting shoes on, and returned to the kitchen for my keys and wallet. Despite rush hour being over, the morning traffic was heavy, but I knew that dead people didn't mind waiting.

I drove along 10th Avenue until I reached the strip of stores. Nothing looked out of place until I pulled into the rear parking lot, where a third of it was cordoned off with crime scene tape. Besides a medical examiner's van, there were patrol cars and an unmarked sedan parked askew in the way only cops and BMW drivers do. The focal point was the alcove that led up to the Pugilists' Club. I parked in the back near a news van, where people were setting up for the jolly overdressed folks on morning television.

The day felt cooler, as if the seasons had changed, to the extent they ever did in South Florida. Or maybe it was just the chill in my spine.

I slipped past a deputy talking with a reporter or segment producer and eased under the barrier tape. I recognized the detective standing with his hand in his suit pocket. He was talking to another detective I didn't know—she saw me coming.

"Sir, this is a crime scene," she said.

"Yeah, I saw the tape."

The detective I knew turned to me. "Jones? What are you doing here?"

"Kelty. I was out for a morning walk."

"That's gonna get you heaved to the other side of the line, regardless of who you're married to."

"I've been working with a client who is a member of the club upstairs."

"And you think he might be involved?"

"I'm concerned he might have harmed himself."

I could see the other detective was happy to kick me to the curb.

Detective Kelty was one of those guys who had been an old soul when he was a rookie graduating from the academy. He then spent thirty years waiting for his body to catch up to his attitude. He had gray hair when I met him and a slight paunch; his suit may have fit his shoulders but not his hips. I had never known him to break the law, but he wasn't a stickler for the rules either if it meant getting his job done.

"Miami Jones," Kelty said, pointing at me, "this is Detective Remington. Rem, Jones is married to one of our former deputies, Danielle Castle."

"Former?" asked Remington.

"She's with the Florida Department of Law Enforcement now."

Remington raised an eyebrow. I wasn't sure if she considered this a positive or otherwise.

"Who's the vic?" I asked.

Kelty shrugged. "Local ne'er-do-well. Minor dealer."

I let out a sigh. "Suspicious?"

"We're here aren't we?" said Remington.

"You got someone in mind?"

"More than that," said Kelty. "We made an arrest."

"What's your interest in this club?" asked Remington.

"Like I said, my client is a member."

"What's your angle?"

"My angle?"

"What are you doing for this client?"

"He's due some money from an injury fund that covers boxers, and they're saying he doesn't fit the criteria."

"Maybe they're right."

"I got a brain surgeon at the university says they're wrong."

"So what's that got to do with this club?"

"I was talking to other former boxers, looking for a pattern of denials."

"Did you find one?"

"I did."

"So all the members of this club are boxers?" asked Kelty.

"It's called the Pugilists' Club."

"And my gym is called Orange Theory," said Remington.

"Fair enough. I don't think it's exclusive, some members are just fans of boxing, but yeah, a lot of them are current and former boxers."

Kelty glanced at the darkened club upstairs and then at me. "You know the owner?"

"Maxine Mitchell."

"A woman?" said Remington.

"Yeah. They can do anything these days."

"Smart guy."

"Not according to my wife."

"I'll bet."

"Any link to Stone Mitchell?" asked Kelty.

"His wife. You knew Stone?"

"In passing. A few colleagues trained at his gym. You know the new guy?"

"Samson? Yeah, I met him."

"Thoughts?"

"Seems okay. Maxine said she'd known him all his life—he used to be a boxer too—and when Stone passed she sold the gym to him."

"That's what I heard."

"What's he got to do with all this?"

"Nothing," said Kelty. "In your travels, you hear of a guy called Johnny Cabrini?"

"Yeah."

Kelty scraped one shoe across the asphalt. "What'd you hear?"

"I'm gonna stop talking now."

Kelty frowned. "He's your client."

"Yep."

"Damn."

"Why?"

"We just arrested him for murder," said Remington.

I looked at all the cars and cops and crime scene techs, and the people watching and the news crews and the yellow-and-black tape reining it all in.

"You think Johnny killed your drug dealer?" I asked.

"We do," said Kelty.

"So who's this dealer?"

"We can't tell you that," said Remington.

"Okay. I'll see you guys around."

"Where you going?" she asked.

"To talk to the media," I said. "Get ahead of this thing. You know how it works."

"You're not on his defense team," said Kelty. "You said it was an insurance thing."

"That's right, Detective, I'm not."

"All right," he said. "You keep your mouth shut with the media and we'll share a little."

"That's all I want. I'm going to have to go and see his wife and explain what's going on."

Kelty jinked his head and led me closer to the alcove. I couldn't see much. The alcove was in shadow most of the day, but I did see a cloth over a body-shaped lump and a forensic investigator I knew.

"The ID on the vic says his name is Richard Whitecross," said Kelty.

"Doesn't ring a bell."

"Our database says he's a low-level dealer, mostly steroids and prescription meds, opioids, that sort of thing. A little fentanyl and meth maybe. Hangs around this area by all reports. Surprised you haven't seen him."

"I don't know what the victim looks like."

Kelty tapped on his phone and tilted it toward me: a photo of Richard Whitecross's driver's license. "Word is he goes by the name—"

"Ricky the Fudge," I said.

Kelty put the phone back in his pocket, and I could almost feel Detective Remington pulsing beside me.

"So you do know him."

"No. But you're right, I have seen him around. Here and outside Stone's—Samson's—gym. A trainer there told me he hangs around, and I saw him try to peddle his wares in the club the other night."

"That so?" said Kelty.

"She might be in on it, this club owner," said Remington.

"She's not in on it," I said. "Soon as she clapped eyes on him, she booted him out."

"So he's not popular at the club?" she said.

"How many dealers are popular in your neighborhood?"

She didn't reply.

I directed Kelty's attention to the alcove. "So you found Johnny here?"

"No. We arrested him at home. In his garage, to be exact. Make of that what you will."

I pictured the garage with its cot and rancid stench. "How did you place him here?"

"The cleaner discovered the body early this morning and called

911. We were here when the guy next door turned up for work." He jinked his head toward the payday lender on the right side of the alcove. "See the security camera?"

I hadn't noticed it before, but there was a camera mounted above the door to the store. It was targeted at the payday lender's vicinity but might have caught the area outside the alcove in its periphery.

"He showed us the video from last night," said Kelty. "The victim arrives and then your client. There's a fight and only your guy walks away."

"How did you know who he was?"

"Registration on his truck."

"So you went to his house."

"That's right. Got no one home, but the side door to the garage was open. We found him asleep in there. Can you imagine? Killing a guy and then going home for a nap."

"What did he say?"

"Not much, not yet. The tox screen will tell us what he'd been into, but the garage stank like a distillery. Is he a user?"

"Drugs? Not that I know of."

"But you can't say for sure."

I shook my head.

"And you were worried about him harming himself," said Remington.

I wished I hadn't mentioned that now, so I said nothing more.

"He went off the deep end," said Remington. "Drunk and drugged up. Then he had an argument with his dealer and took him out."

I couldn't argue, so I didn't.

"You say you know the wife?" asked Kelty.

"Yeah."

"She wasn't home last night."

I didn't want to say she was staying at her daughter's because Johnny had gotten violent, so again I said nothing. It was becoming a thing.

"You'll tell her?" he asked.

"Yeah, I'll tell her."

"All right. Let her know we'll be in touch."

"Sure."

Kelty and Remington moved away. I was about to leave when I noticed the forensic investigator near the ME's van. I wandered over.

"Lorraine Catchitt," I said. "Like with a baseball, not what's in a litter box."

The investigator spun around. She was wearing a full-body disposable coverall. The hood was pinched tight around her face, so she was nothing more than eyes, nose, and mouth. She smiled. "Jones, you remembered."

"It's hard to forget."

"What brings you out on such a fine morning?"

"Turns out the guy they arrested was a client."

"Nice."

"Not really. Kelty wants me to inform his wife."

"Classy."

"Can you tell me anything? I'd rather not go in blind."

"Looks like a fight. I'd say your man punched the victim's lights out and killed him."

"His punch or the fall?"

The plastic suit barely moved when she shrugged. "The autopsy will tell us more, but honestly, Jones, you punch someone in the head and they fall down and crack their skull, that's not really mitigating."

"But we're talking accident?"

"From what Kelty's saying, the guy might have been a user in a fight with his dealer, so maybe he didn't mean to do it. But maybe he did. Maybe he didn't like the guy and came to off him. That's not for me to decide."

"Me either. Thanks, Lorraine."

She smiled again, and I got the sense that few people in her line of work used her first name.

"Anytime, Jones."

I left her to her business, stepped under the crime scene tape, and walked back to my car. I was going to have to talk to Tina Cabrini, but first I was going to have to talk to Mick. I didn't relish either conversation.

CHAPTER FIFTEEN

Mick took the news stoically. I wasn't sure why I expected anything else, but I thought this might be the sort of thing to bring whatever played out as rage in Mick's head. Maybe rage was just a different kind of silence from happiness for him, and all the important stuff was going on behind the mask, hidden from view. I hoped not; no one could manage that kind of emotional range on the inside while showing nothing on the outside, at least not without doing some serious damage.

After a brief conversation that sounded a lot like two bulls grunting in a field, I asked Mick if he could help me find Tina.

"Yep."

I let him know what the sheriff's detectives had told me, that Tina was not at the house when they arrested Johnny, and I asked if he knew where her daughter lived. He hung up and texted me an address in Palm Beach Gardens. That could be thirty minutes in traffic from the club. I had no idea about Mick, as it suddenly occurred that I didn't know where he lived. This shouldn't have been a shock—he was the guy who owned my favorite watering hole, not my best man—but over the years we'd seen so much through the lens of Longboard Kelly's, he felt closer than that. Perhaps same coin, different sides.

I took off immediately. I wanted to be there before Mick. Not that he didn't care, but I wasn't sure how he would articulate the message. The traffic had cleared some, so it was only twenty minutes before I reached the interchange at PGA Boulevard.

Palm Beach Gardens might have been the mall capital of the world, there were so many of them; half the suburb was parking lots. I paid them no mind and followed my phone's dulcet tones to an apartment complex north of the Gardens Mall.

The place was called Gardens something or other, but I didn't get the reference—if you walked there, you wouldn't pass through a garden—but the development was nice enough: clean streets, tidy shrubs, and views of faux lakes.

The gatehouse attendant gave me some guff about not being on the list, so I told him some baloney about being welcome to pass on the details of her father being killed as an innocent bystander in a drive-by shooting. He likely decided it was better coming from me, because he lifted the boom without further debate. I parked on the street, which was often some kind of mortal sin in these gated communities, and waited for Mick. I passed the time picturing the gatehouse guy telling him he couldn't come in. Mick's response was sure to be less eloquent than mine.

Mick pulled up a few minutes later. He parked the Eldorado behind my Jeep, and I met him between the two vehicles.

"All right?" I asked.

"Nup."

We walked up the stairs to the second floor. Mick rang the bell. A man answered the door in a white T-shirt and camo pants. He looked a little like Desi Arnez Jr. with a crew cut. He didn't appear to recognize Mick.

"Help you?" he asked.

Mick looked at him like he was assessing the guy's weaknesses, but he said nothing. In a bar that was one thing, but in general society, that kind of staring was a touch creepy. I mentally patted myself on the back for not letting Mick do this alone.

"Is Tina here?" I asked.

"You are?"

"I'm Miami Jones. This is Mick. We're doing some work for her."

"Work? Like gardening or something?"

I had been called many things in my life, but this was a first.

"No. It's about Johnny."

The man nodded like he knew no good was coming of our visit, then he shut the door in our faces. I looked at Mick, who kept looking at the door. It opened again. This time it was Tina.

"Mick? Miami? What is it? What's wrong?"

Mothers and wives had an intuition about these things. Either that or they always assumed the worst.

"Are the girls home?" I asked.

"Yes, why?"

"You want to step outside for a sec?"

She did just that and closed the door behind her. "It's Johnny? What's happened?"

"Tina, he's been arrested."

She put her hands to her mouth to stifle something, and for a long moment she said nothing, just looked off into middle distance.

"We don't know everything yet, but the detectives are saying he was involved in a fight with another man late last night at the Pugilists' Club. The other man died."

"Oh no. It's my fault."

"No, Tina. It's not your fault. Johnny isn't well. You know this."

"But . . ."

"Do you want to go inside?" I asked. "I can help you tell the girls."

"Huh? No, no. I can do that. I just . . ." She moved to Mick and hugged him. It wasn't a lunge like she needed to be held more than anything on earth, more like she was thankful he had come.

"Mick," she whispered.

"Teens," said Mick.

Tina pulled away and wiped her face, but there were no tears. Johnny had been getting worse for decades. I figured she knew a conversation like this would come sooner or later.

"He was arrested in your garage," I said. "Were you home at all last night?"

"Yes, I collected some things for the girls, and some food and toiletries and stuff."

"But you didn't see him?"

"He wasn't there, no."

"Did you stay the night?"

"No, I went there after my shift, about nine thirty. I left close to eleven."

"And the side door to the garage was closed."

"Of course. Why?"

"Just trying to get a timeline of things. So you don't know where Johnny was last night."

"No," she said, also shaking her head. "What happens now?"

"He'll appear before the court in the next couple days, and then we'll find out."

"We don't have money for bail."

"The court will get into that. As and when, we can talk to a bail bondsman."

"But I can't even pay the rent, Miami."

"Okay. I'll ask my office manager to look into what services are available. But don't worry."

"Don't worry? Johnny isn't well. What bail bondsman is going to give him a bond when he can't guarantee he'll show up in court?"

"Sorry. I mean, we'll all do what we can. We just need to let this process work its way through."

"I don't mean to sound heartless, but what does this do to the fund money? They offered five hundred. I need that."

"I know it's hard, but don't take it. We can do better than that."

"But my rent."

"My office manager will look into what legal roadblocks we can throw up, see if we can slow that process down a bit."

"I need to get home."

"You might be better here with family."

"If I'm inside the house, it's harder for the landlord to change the locks."

"And the girls?"

"They can stay here for a few more days. It's better. I need to clean up the house, the garage. I don't want them reminded of their father's bad days. It's too hard on them already."

I nodded. Mick didn't take his eyes off her.

"Will you be okay over there by yourself?" I asked.

"You mean will I hurt myself because my mentally ill husband is in jail?"

"Maybe."

"Miami, I have held myself together for years now, all for my girls, and for Johnny too. I can hold on a little longer."

We agreed to keep in touch. She patted Mick on the shoulder like she was looking after him as well. As she made to open the door, I remembered I had one last question.

"Tina, was Johnny doing any drugs that you knew of?"

She frowned. "Dr. Abe gave him antidepressants. He took Advil a lot and sometimes OxyContin, I think."

"Where did he get the OxyContin?"

"I don't know. Dr. Abe, I guess?"

"He didn't take anything harder?"

"Just whiskey."

"Okay, sorry to ask. I'll be in touch."

She turned and pushed her way inside. I glanced at Mick. He looked the same. He might have been having a heart attack, or his team might have just scored the winning touchdown; it was impossible to tell.

We walked back out, but Mick didn't get into his car, so I stepped over.

"You okay?"

"I'll pay you," he said.

"What?"

"Get Tina her money."

"I plan to. This doesn't change that."

Mick sighed. It was so deep it lifted him up onto his toes. "I don't know law."

"What do you mean?"

"I need you to, you know. Navigate this."

I got his meaning. I knew the legal system better than he or Tina, and I had connections who knew even more. I also knew people inside the system who could provide insight into what would happen to Johnny during the whole process. It was a lack of understanding of the system that often caused the most stress for families.

"Don't worry about it, Mick. I'm on it, Lizzy's on it, Ron's on it. The fact that the fund didn't provide money might work in Johnny's favor now. It might be a mitigating factor—that he didn't get the help he needed."

"You think he'll get off?"

"I haven't seen the evidence, but it sounds like the sheriff's office knows he did it. This might not be about getting him out. It might be about lessening his sentence and getting him psychiatric care rather than just being tossed in a state prison for the rest of his life."

"That might not be long."

I said nothing for a moment. I wondered again what was going on in his head.

"Mick, do you have any idea where Johnny might have been last night?"

"Club?"

"The fight was at the club, but Maxine seemed pretty intent on not having him there when he was in a really dark place. I'll check it, but I think if he had been there when it was open, she would have sent him home. No, I'm looking for something else."

"There's a bar."

"Not Longboard's?"

"No."

Two sides, one coin.

"Give me the name, I'll look into it."

"He can't afford a lawyer."

"I know, Mick. The public defender's office is near mine. I'll go have a word. Will you be okay?"

Mick looked at me. "It ain't happening to me."

I had nothing to say to that. I wasn't qualified to get into Mick's lack of self-awareness or willingness to confront how things were affecting him. I left with the notion that maybe he was able to compartmentalize in a way that I couldn't. The whole train of thought made my head hurt, so I told him I'd see him later and headed for my office and a stiff drink.

CHAPTER SIXTEEN

THE STIFF DRINK WAS AN ESPRESSO THAT LIZZY WHIPPED UP ON HER NEW machine. It hit me like a bolt of electricity in a way that I didn't care for, so I walked the buzz off getting from my office over to the county court. It was a massive complex that made me reconsider our direction as a society every time I saw it.

The offices for prosecutors and defenders were in the same building off to the side. They had a constant energy about them, especially the public defender's office; there were always too many defendants and too few attorneys, too much at stake and too little money to fund the defense.

An appointment was usually necessary to get in to see the public defender. She was an elected official, and those folks were a different breed. She had to be part politician to even get the job but then had to do a job that was, in essence, set up to fail. The state funded both sides of the scales. Most cases that made it to trial only got there because there was enough evidence to convict, which meant the public defender's job was often to lessen penalties rather than to acquit. If the cops and prosecutors had done their jobs properly, the defender should always lose, because only the guilty should ever get to court.

I knew as well as anyone that this wasn't always the case—I had been accused of murder based on pretty flimsy evidence, but I comforted myself in the knowledge that the case never made it to court because it never should have. But because a lot of the cases that got approved by the state attorney's office for prosecution were slam dunks of a fashion, the nature of the relationship between both sides was often not adversarial but one of negotiation.

Lawyers also understood the word *adversarial* differently than the rest of us. It was a construct, a system where each side presented its case, and an impartial arbiter decided which argument had the most merit, given the laws and procedures of the system. It was no surprise that many attorneys were on the debate team in school. They had learned to argue a position, not to personally attack the other side.

Oftentimes both sides hammered out a resolution to a case before it ever got to court. Prosecutors would argue that the crime was this and that, and the punishment should be commensurate, and the defender would offer mitigation and counter-argument until they found a penalty that they could both live with. Politicians always wanted higher penalties, and defendants always complained their sentence was heavy-handed, so neither side ever left completely happy.

But this meant they all knew each other very well. I never had much cause to interact with the office of the public defender, but I had known the previous state attorney for the 15th Judicial Circuit better than I ever wanted to, and I hoped that counted for something.

The receptionist looked like her default response was no. She was taking calls in rapid-fire succession and spoke in an officious and curt manner. Working phones could do that to a human, especially when very few of the calls were to say *Hey, great job!*

Now between calls, she looked up at me.

"Can I get two minutes with her?"

The face she made was worth a thousand words, or even just one, but either way, it wasn't affirmative.

Then a flash of an impeccable suit strode by and stopped just on the far side of the security barrier. "You lost?" said a blond, broad-shouldered woman.

"Ms. Bakian," I said. I had to look up at her, she was that tall. She had the look of someone who had played volleyball in college.

"Miami Jones. Aren't you usually across the hall?"

"Not much these days."

"Right. Eric's moved on."

"Greener pastures."

"Is that what we're calling the state legislature these days?"

"Not personally."

"What are you doing here?"

"I had a question about a client. Just wanted some understanding of things to pass on to the family."

"We have a website, you know."

"I'm an old-school kind of guy."

"I've heard that about you. I've got a call in two minutes, so you have ninety seconds."

She used her card to get me through the barrier, and we headed for her office.

"How is Eric these days?" she asked.

"Eric Edwards is my wife's ex-husband, so I gotta tell you, we're not exactly golf buddies. But being back in private practice suits him, I think."

"Agreed. And your wife, she's with FDLE now?"

"That's right."

"Good. They need more women." She pushed open her office door.

"How's the new state attorney?" I asked.

"Like the old one. Passing through."

"Looking for greener pastures."

"Exactly."

"What about you?" I asked. "Ever thought about running for office?"

"I am elected, you know."

"I mean the legislature or even Congress."

"I've been in this job for twelve years, Jones. I would have looked elsewhere a long time ago if I wanted to. You have sixty seconds left." She smiled as she sat.

"I'm doing some work for a friend of a friend. He's entitled to some money from a health fund that's playing games. He was a boxer, has related injuries." I pointed at my head.

"Okay."

"He was arrested this morning for a fight last night—not the professional kind. The other guy died."

"That's not good."

"No. I just wanted to make sure he got represented."

"We don't go looking for work, Jones. The court appoints a public defender. But your client would have to be indigent, and if he's hired a private investigator . . ."

"A friend we have in common hired me, and I'm not getting paid anyway."

"You're not?"

"No."

She made a face like this meant something. "Okay."

"And the client is the definition of indigent. I mean, he's not on the street, but the landlord is trying to kick the family out. They don't have a bean."

"You say he got arrested last night?"

"This morning."

"So he'll have a first appearance, probably tomorrow. That's where the court will decide if a public defender is appropriate. But he'll have to apply for one. There's a fifty-dollar application fee."

"You have to pay fifty bucks to prove you don't have the money for a lawyer?"

"Go figure. But inability to pay the fee is not grounds to be refused representation. It's just then things take longer."

"I'll pay it."

"Okay." Bakian stood and opened her door and waved at a

woman sitting before a desk covered in paperwork. The woman came over.

"Elissa, this is Miami Jones. He's got a client who will have his first appearance tomorrow. Can you sort him out with the forms and so on?"

"Sure, Casey."

Elissa beckoned me to follow her back to her desk. Before I moved, Casey Bakian leaned into me. "She's good."

"Thanks for the help."

"It's what we do. And tell your wife to give me a call. We have a group for women in law enforcement she needs to be part of."

"I'll tell her. Thanks."

She closed her door as her phone rang.

I walked over to Elissa. "Miami Jones." I sat down.

"She said."

"And you are?"

"Elissa Croix, assistant public defender. So tell me your story."

I told her my story. About three-quarters of the way through, she started tapping on her computer and printing out documents.

"Fill these out and get them back to me today with a check. I'll drop in on his first appearance and have him sign them, then the clerk of the court will assess his status. What assets does he have?"

"He's got a car but not much of one. No cash. Works only sporadically. His mental health is shot. They're about to get booted from their house for not paying rent."

"Okay, so he should qualify. I'll ask the judge to assign me."

"Ask or tell?"

"You don't tell the court anything. That's why it's called a plea."

"Okay. And will he plea tomorrow?"

"No. That happens at the arraignment."

"When is that?"

"A few weeks, usually."

"And he'll be in jail until then?"

"The court may want bail at the appearance, or we can petition for bail once I'm appointed."

"This guy needs psychiatric help. Medication. Therapy and who knows what else."

"The county has people for that."

"I'm sure in jail it's top-notch care."

"You want better care, pay more taxes."

"Happily. Where do I sign?"

"When you vote."

"Okay. So will I be able to see him in jail?"

"You're not family?"

"No."

"Then, no. Family and legal representatives only for now."

"Listen, I'm already working for the family."

"How are they paying you?"

"They're not."

"So why are you helping them?"

"It's a favor for a friend."

"Really?"

"Yeah. You do favors for friends, don't you?"

"Sure. Go on."

"Well, since I'm already into it and they don't know the system, I could look into the case for you."

"For me?"

"Yeah. On behalf of our client."

"We have our own investigators."

"And I'm sure they're not overworked. Look, I'll do it pro bono. No cost to the people of Palm Beach. I'm licensed and everything."

"Will the defendant agree to this?"

"Sure. I'm working on his behalf right now."

She went to talk to a guy at a nearby desk. They both glanced at me as they spoke. Then she came back.

"Okay, you'll have to sign some paperwork to cover client privilege. You'll be subject to the same rules and regulations as our attorneys and paralegals. You can't talk about the case while you're drinking with your buddies."

I didn't think telling her it was my local barkeep that had hired me would help.

"Okay."

"Fill this out, and if the defendant agrees, we'll go from there."

CHAPTER SEVENTEEN

J̲ohnny C̲abrini appeared before the court at the county detention center the following morning. This was not the kind of building you just waltzed into. The public typically wasn't allowed in these sessions, but Elissa Croix got me in as her assistant. As a PI, I was already background-checked, so perhaps it helped some. The facility was run by the Palm Beach Sheriff's Office, but the staffing came from Humorless Incorporated. It was best to follow the process—do what you were told and accept that you were going to be made to feel like you had no business there, and having been inside, that you had no business being in society afterward.

Elissa led me to a small concrete room with rows of chairs occupied by people awaiting their first appearance.

She briefly spoke with Johnny, dressed in a blue PBSO-issued uniform that reminded me of hospital scrubs. As he listened he glanced at me with what looked like a mix of fatigue and sadness.

A court deputy called the room to attention, then explained the purpose of the appearance. He read everyone their rights as a group and arranged translation on the phone for those who didn't speak English or Spanish.

The magistrate ran through the appearances swiftly. When it was

Johnny's turn, the judge read the charges against him and asked if he understood them.

"Yes, Judge."

"I have read the arrest report and find probable cause. Do you have legal representation, Mr. Cabrini?"

"No, Judge."

"I see Ms. Croix in my court. Am I to take it you wish to apply for representation by the public defender's office, Mr. Cabrini?"

"Yes, Judge."

"Ms. Croix?"

"We have the affidavit of indigent status here, Your Honor." Elissa waved the document, but the judge didn't ask to see it.

"Very well. The court notes that Mr. Cabrini has accepted the public defender as his representation. Now, Mr. Bryant, the state is petitioning for a stay on bail?"

The state's representative stood on the other side of the tiny room. "Yes, Your Honor. The initial warrant was based on evidence of a fight, but the state has further evidence that Mr. Cabrini may be a danger to both himself and the public. The details are before you."

"I'm reading them. Ms. Croix, please join us."

Elissa stepped forward.

"Ms. Croix, do you have anything to add?"

"I haven't seen the documents, Your Honor."

"No. Well, that being the case, I am declining bail at this time, but I want a final hearing in five days to consider Mr. Cabrini's pretrial status. Okay?"

Both attorneys said, "Yes, Your Honor," like they were in an a cappella group.

"Mr. Cabrini, do you understand what is happening to you?"

"No, Judge."

"You are not being offered bail or release at this time. The crime we are dealing with is serious—a man has died—so we meet again in five days to hear from the state and from you to determine whether you can be released pending your arraignment and trial. Do you understand that?"

"Yes, Judge."

"Good. That is all."

The entire thing took less than two minutes.

Johnny sat again. The judge took another fifteen minutes to run through the rest of the appearances, then the session was closed and the defendants were marched away. I walked out of the mini courtroom with Elissa.

"That's it?" I asked.

"That's it."

"What about bail?"

"The state has opposed, so we'll have to make an argument otherwise." She held up some documents. "I'll review it."

"You headed back to your office? I'll walk with you."

She raised an eyebrow. "I have another appearance."

"Where?"

She pointed at a door down the corridor.

"How long will you be?"

"I don't know. Half an hour, less maybe. Why?"

I shrugged and she walked away. I leaned against a concrete wall and waited. I tried not to think about Johnny in his cell, but I wondered how many people around him were in as dark a place as he was. There wasn't always redemption in Shawshank.

About twenty-five minutes later, Elissa came out of the courtroom and stopped dead when she saw me.

"Are you stalking me?"

"I'm working for you."

"You have time to stand around doing nothing."

"I don't have to take on more clients than I can handle. Besides, waiting isn't wasted time." We walked out of the detention center toward the parking lot. "So you're officially Johnny's lawyer?"

"For this thing. Listen, what do you expect will happen here?"

"What do you mean?"

"This isn't Hollywood. We don't get a lot of happy endings here."

"I know. The cops seemed pretty confident he did it. What do you think?"

"I have no position on it. I haven't seen the evidence. The no-bail thing worries me though."

"Why?"

"The charge is second-degree murder, but it looks more like an accidental death in a fight. It's bad, but you're likely to get bail, even if the bond is huge and there are conditions. So if they're asking for no bail, it suggests they're not planning on negotiating."

"How can it be murder?"

"Second-degree murder."

"Whatever. It was a fight."

"So you say. But they seem to think they can make murder stick."

"Then our job isn't to clear him," I said. "It's to find mitigating circumstances, isn't it? To show it isn't murder."

"Is that what you want? To help a murderer?"

"Is that what *you* want?"

"My job is to ensure that everyone gets represented in court. We don't get to decide who does and doesn't deserve due process."

"You think he did?"

"I told you, I have no position on it. I haven't seen any evidence yet."

She stopped beside her car. I had forgotten where mine was.

"I want him to get the help he needs," I said. "And I want his family safe."

"Okay."

"So what about the evidence? We get to see it, right?"

"Who's we?"

"I signed a paper, didn't I? I'm with you."

"We will issue a discovery request to learn what they have."

"When do we see that?"

"Discovery materials? They have to be provided prior to trial."

"That could be months."

"That's right. But I'll go and talk with the assistant state attorney. See what they have before we do the bail hearing."

"They'll tell you?"

"They have to eventually," she said. "We share this stuff all the time because it usually shows guilt, and we use it as the basis for negotiation for a plea bargain."

"Like a guilty plea?"

"Maybe. Lesser charges for a shorter term and we don't bother going to court. The state loves to save the expense of a trial."

"I'll keep working on this fund thing," I said. "Apart from anything, his wife needs some money, but it might show that he tried to get help and was wrongly turned away."

"That sounds more like a civil matter, but everything helps, I suppose. We'll file for discovery and then see what we can get in the short term. But listen, Miami . . . is that your real name?"

"Real enough."

"I find it hard to address a grown man like that."

"It's from my university days, but think of it like a dog: you can call me anything you want, but I'll probably only respond to one thing."

"We'll go with Jones. And the thing is, discovery goes two ways. They have to disclose what they have, but so do we."

"We don't have anything."

"Have you learned anything prejudicial in the course of your investigation for them?"

"Like what?"

"Domestic violence?"

"I know he's lost his composure at times but—"

"Don't sugarcoat domestic violence, Jones. Losing your composure means you blush. It doesn't mean you punch someone."

"Okay, sorry. You're right. His wife has spent time out of the house when he drinks. I'm not aware that he's hurt her physically."

"Let's hope not. But are you going to dig up stuff that harms his case?"

"There's a chance he spends the rest of his life behind bars. How do we make it worse than that?"

"The prosecution finds something that ups the stakes, they'll ask for the death penalty."

"That can't happen. It was a fight."

"You weren't there, and you haven't seen any evidence. You have no idea what happened."

"Fair point. So I'll tread carefully."

"Do. I have some conference time now, but I'll go chat to the ASA later and see what he has."

CHAPTER EIGHTEEN

In the office, I found Lizzy standing on a chair replacing a light bulb. She stuck out a hand, and I helped her down.

"Why don't you let me do these things?" I said.

"Because I don't want to sit in the dark, waiting for whenever you might show up, and because men are not the only ones capable of—wait for it—changing a light bulb."

"Geez. I just wanted to know if you knew anything more about the fund."

"I know one thing. You met the brother in Orlando, right?"

"Loman Priestly, yes."

"So the other brother is president of the GBC. *Breyer* Priestly."

"Where do they get these names?"

"You're one to talk."

"Everyone's on me about my name today."

Lizzy pouted for me. "Anyway. Breyer is based in the Virgin Islands."

"The British ones."

"Yes, although they prefer to call themselves just Virgin Islands as opposed to the US Virgin Islands."

"Like there aren't enough place names in the world."

"Exactly. Your man is *based* there. But as president of the body, he has to be at many of the high-profile events in the US. Especially the ones on TV."

"I feel an event coming on."

"Tomorrow night there's something called a world middleweight championship. Apparently, it's a big deal."

"Where is this?"

"The Hard Rock Casino."

"Handy. How do I get a ticket?"

"That's your problem. It's sold out. And did you know it's almost a hundred dollars just to watch this thing on TV? Not to get in, just on TV?"

"I heard it's plenty."

"And that's after you already paid for cable."

"I don't have cable."

"You don't have a TV. But who pays for this?"

"People, I guess. It's supply and demand. The little guy always ends up paying. The house wins, every time."

"So what will you do about Breyer Priestly? Wait outside the stage door?"

"I got one or two tricks. Listen, you spoke to Tina Cabrini when you filled out the forms for the public defender."

"Yes."

"How was she?"

"Stoic."

"Like Mick."

"Him, I don't understand. Her, a little more."

"How so?"

"She's been through hell, is my guess. I get the sense that she really does love Johnny. They made a life together. It doesn't sound like my cup of tea, having a husband who gets beat up for a living, but God has a different plan for each of us."

"If you say so."

"I do. And she's living hers. I guess she takes that *for better or worse* stuff seriously."

"I'd say so."

"But it just means her heart has become a little hardened," she said. "She's giving what she has to give to her children and doesn't have much left for him or herself."

"I think you're right."

"How does it look for him?"

"Not great. He's going to do time—that looks pretty clear. So what we need to do is make a case that he goes to a facility where he can get treatment, not just the regular old slammer. If he goes there, I'm not sure things will turn out well."

"I'm not sure things will turn out well either way."

"How does that fit into your Lord's plan?"

"I don't claim to have all the answers, Miami. I just do what feels right in my heart."

"As good a plan as any. I'm going to go and update Tina. Was she at her house?"

Lizzy offered me a nod, and I left her to it.

I wasn't in any hurry, so I took it easy down to the Cabrini house.

I parked in front and turned off the engine. The neighborhood was quiet except for the distant traffic noise. I thought I heard a school bell that sounded more like a game-time buzzer.

As I walked across the lawn to the house, I noticed the side door to the garage was closed. The sheriff's investigators had done their thing and locked up after themselves, or perhaps Tina had closed it after she had cleaned up.

I knocked on the front door. Tina answered it in a T-shirt and jeans with a kerchief bundling her hair.

"Miami," she said, looking around. "Just you?"

"*Sans* Mick."

"I'm just cleaning up."

"Sure. I wanted to check in, see how you were."

"Come in. Would you like some water? I don't have any beer."

"Thanks, water's fine."

"Take a seat."

I looked at the hole in the wall, then focused on the tidy living room.

Tina came back in, handed me a glass of cold water, and sat opposite me on the sofa.

"Johnny had a hearing," I began. "He was denied bail, but they'll look at it again in a few days."

"What about moving him to some kind of hospital?"

"I think that'll be something the public defender brings up. She only just got appointed to represent him."

We both sipped our drinks.

"I got a letter from the fund," she said. "They confirmed the five hundred."

"Don't take it."

"The landlord says he's going to start eviction proceedings."

"Fine, let him say that. It costs him money to do it, so he might take his time. And even if he doesn't, even if he's on the courthouse steps today, there's a process. He can't just change the locks—that's illegal."

"But he can kick us out."

"Yes, in due course he can, but not over the weekend. But I'm working on something that I expect will see a better offer by Monday."

For a moment Tina stared at her sandaled feet. She had the look of a thousand thoughts pressing for immediate attention. I knew Johnny needed help with his issues, but I was growing concerned about Tina. Stoicism was all well and good, but there had to be a point where a person just needed to get stuff off their chest and out of their head. My friend and mentor Lenny Cox always said a problem shared was a problem halved. It was true for me. I had seen my fair share of troubles, and I had a whole gang to split my problems with: Danielle, Ron, Lucas, Muriel, Mick, Lizzy, and the Lady Cassandra. I didn't see anyone around Tina like that other than Mick. He was a good listener, but sharing pain with someone who was also going through pain had the potential to multiply the issues not halve them. I was prepared to be her sounding board, but we didn't know each other well, and she didn't seem inclined to open up to me.

"Tina, do you have someone to talk to?"

"About what?"

"Everything. All of it. I can see it's weighing you down. It's understandable."

"I'm fine. I just need to get through this, then things will be better."

I wanted to tell her that the thing she was trying to get through was life, and the thing after that was only better in theory and depending on your belief system. But she forced a smile and stood, and I said nothing.

She thanked me for stopping by and headed for the door, leaving me standing on the lawn with the feeling I was on a treadmill going full steam.

CHAPTER NINETEEN

Lenny always said that a tuxedo could get you into any room in the Palm Beaches. He believed in it so much he bought me my first tux, and it got me into a room where I should never have been. It was one of those tools in the bag that I rarely used—it got some pretty interesting looks on Singer Island or wandering around Little Havana—and I considered it the nuclear option in most cases.

This was one of those cases. But I also knew that while Lenny's rule held true, there was one thing better than a tux, and that was a tux and a ticket. I hit the phones and called everyone. I needn't have bothered. I should have just made the call to Sally my first and only call.

"I got you in," said Sally when he called back.

"How?"

"The usual way. I know a guy who knows a girl. One of my kids, his sister is the promotions manager at the casino."

Sally didn't have any children of his own, but over the years he had helped more at-risk youth than any charity I knew.

"Thanks, Sal."

"The pass will be at the promotions desk. Don't wear shorts."

"I'm all over that, Sal."

I got dressed at home.

"You look like James Bond," Danielle said, tightening up my bow tie.

"If Bond were a retired surfer."

"You could comb your hair."

I ran my fingers through my locks.

"Better," she said. "And sexy as hell."

"You think?"

"Try not to be too late."

"Why?"

She lifted an eyebrow, and I nearly didn't go. But she kicked me out the door with the promise that she would be waiting for me and my tuxedo when I got back. I wasn't sure if that thought was going to be a distraction or keep me as sharp as a tack.

I drove down to Hollywood and left my car with the valet in front of the casino. There was something strange about wearing a tuxedo in the middle of the day. With the tie done up, it was the promise of excitement to come, but with the tie undone, a sign of a night well lived. I wandered out of the sun and into the darkness of the casino, through the light-and-sound show of slot machines, taking in the people mindlessly tapping buttons and watching credits accrue or diminish on their playing cards. There were no handles to pull or coins to drop. The whole thing had all the romance of using an ATM.

After finding the promotions desk and retrieving my envelope as promised, I slipped the lanyard around my neck and checked the credential. Sally had delivered. It was an all-access pass for the boxing event at Hard Rock Live. Between that and my tux, I figured I'd get in wherever I needed to.

I walked to the rear of the venue where the theater was. An usher scanned my pass and told me to enjoy myself ringside, and I went in. The facility had been built to feel like a Broadway theater, with a stage at one end, bleachers along the sides, and seating across the floor leading to several balconies at the back. Only, for this event, most of the floor seats had been removed to accommodate the boxing ring. The top two balcony tiers were in darkness and out of use, the view from there blocked by the giant lighting rig above the ring.

I counted only three people in the bleachers and five on the lower balcony. The room had the echoey feel of a concert hall during the afternoon sound check.

Just along the main concourse, between the lowest tier of seats and the balconies above, was a pregame television crew. Bright lights shone onto a desk where four men sat, talking about the upcoming bouts. They were animated, shouting at each other despite the quiet, the way sports pundits do. It wasn't a conversation as much as a verbal barrage. They each wore a little wire microphone but also held a hand mic. It was the kind of redundancy the military always went for.

As I continued toward the ring, several ushers eyed my pass, but something about it told them all they needed to know because they offered me nothing more than smiles and nods. The setup was different from what I had seen on television. For starters, the ring wasn't in the middle of the room; it was close to the stage, with three rows of seats around it. A massive screen had been erected onstage, currently showing an ad for this very event. Yet another redundancy.

I was the only person in the room all gussied up until another tuxedo walked across the stage and down the steps. When he looked my way, I wasn't sure if it was a Brotherhood of Tuxedo Wearers moment, or if he knew he had my measure given his jacket was bright red and his hair had more product in it than a witch's brew.

He climbed up the ringside steps, and a roadie in black handed him a microphone. He checked a small card in the palm of his hand. The roadie then passed him a sports drink bottle, and he squirted something into his mouth like he was a quarterback about to call a play. He moved to the center of the ring as blue lights lit the canvas, then a spotlight clicked on, and he looked up at the balconies like a sunflower in the morning sun.

I followed his line of vision and spotted a camera mounted up on the second balcony. Having seen one, I then saw them all, hidden in the shadows at various angles.

The man in the red jacket touched his earpiece, then stood erect and lifted the mic to his mouth. "Laaaaadies aaaand gentlemen. This is premieeeer boxing by Liddo, in association with Bruiser Promotions and the Global Boxing Council. The first bout of the evening is a bantamweight contest between two up-and-coming challengers. In the red corner, John 'Sweet Talk' Spenceeeer."

Some smoke blew up on the stage. Lights flashed onto a boxer, who had emerged from the fog. He was ready to go—no shirt, no robe, fists firing like pistons. Music pumped around the venue as he eased down the stairs and onto the floor near me, followed by three cornermen. One of them pushed Spencer's backside as he clumsily got in through the ropes. He started shadowboxing and dancing around as if playing it up to a full house. A handful of people clapped, while the others looked at their phones. He finished his prancing and made his way to the corner farthest from me.

"In the blue corner, Bradley 'The Negotiator' Whitfoooord."

More smoke, and another boxer came out with his crew in tow. More dancing and shadowboxing and general apathy from the crowd, such as it was. Whitford came back to his corner, near me, and his trainer stepped in from the shadows and into the ring. I realized it was Harv, the trainer I had met at Samson's gym.

Harv gave his fighter final instructions, then climbed out through the ropes. As he did, he noticed me standing below, and I saw the recognition on his face. He nodded to me, and I returned the gesture, then he stepped down to the floor.

After the loud music, my hearing was super sensitive. As the fight went on, I picked up everything. There was no crowd noise to cover the sound of glove hitting body or head, or the *oomph* a boxer made as he threw a punch. Sweat exploded from their faces as a punch made contact with a chin or a cheek. By the end of four rounds, each man looked exhausted. Neither had struck the definitive blow, so it came down to the judges' decision, three men sitting on each side of the ring.

The announcer stepped up. "The winner by unanimous points decision: Bradley 'The Negotiator' Whitfoooord."

Harv's boxer shot his hands in the air like he was Rocky and then dashed around the ring waving to the crowd. I suspected it looked better on television where the background would be a blue glow. Here I could see him pointing and blowing kisses to absolutely nobody.

The music pumped again, and the boxers and their people climbed out of the ring. The music stopped, and the sound bounced around the room for a few more seconds before dropping into an eerie silence.

I looked around for Breyer Priestly. I thought the president of the whole shebang might be there for all the fights, but it was now clear that Priestly didn't spend his daylight hours watching the nobodies hit each other.

A few more people filtered in, and the ring announcer took some more water as the pundits up at the desk started yelling at each other about what the next fight might hold.

I wandered to the back of the theater, looking for a new vantage point on Priestly. I still didn't see him, so I stood in the concourse to watch the next fight. Another couple guys came out to batter each other, and as the fight drew to a close, I saw a familiar face at ringside, so I walked back down.

"Harv," I said.

"Hello, it's . . . "

"Miami Jones."

"Right. You were looking into that thing for Johnny."

"That's right."

"How's it going?"

"You haven't heard?"

"No. I been training."

"Johnny's been arrested. They say he killed a guy at the Pugilists' Club."

Harv shook his head. "That can't be."

"Afraid it is. You wanna grab a seat?" I pointed to the first row up at the concourse, where we could get a good view of the whole ring and not get hit with sweat.

Harv eased himself into a seat as if he had just gone a few rounds himself. He was no spring chicken, but he managed.

"How's Tina?" he asked.

"Keeping it together, just."

"You get any money for her?"

"Some. But we can do better. That's why I'm here. Do you know if Breyer Priestly comes to these events?"

"The president of the GBC? Sure, but he won't be at the undercard."

"Undercard?"

"At a big event like this, the fights go on for about five or six hours. What you're seeing here, during the day, is the undercard. Fighters who are up and coming, or not. Maybe headed down, in some cases. Limited TV and, as you can see, not many fans."

"I did notice. Is it usually like this?"

"Always. By the time the main event comes on later tonight, it'll be a full house."

"So I'm a bit early?"

"By about four hours."

"Awesome."

The ring announcer reappeared in his red jacket and called in the next fighters.

"Your guy won," I said.

"Yeah. He's a good kid. Not the hardest puncher but still a good kid."

It felt like an odd way to assess someone's character—either good or someone who punches hard.

"Does he have a shot at a title or something?"

"We'll see. He's not a contender yet."

"What does that mean, exactly?"

"You know boxers get ranked, right?"

"Yeah, but not how."

"Based on their wins and losses, the quality of their opponents—

that sort of thing. Once you get into the top ten rankings for your weight class, you officially become a contender. Then you hopefully start fighting other contenders to work your way up."

"So you have to get to number one as a contender to get a title shot?"

"Not necessarily. Once you're in the top ten, it also depends on your connections. If you have a good manager and you've got a record of attracting fans to the fights, you can jump the queue some."

"Seems like there's a lot of who you know, not what you know."

"Like life. Look at these two kids." He directed my attention to the ring, where two men were about to battle.

"These guys are lightweights, up to a hundred and thirty pounds. Neither are top ten yet, but the guy in the yellow shorts is a prospect."

"Why?"

"Fast feet, fast hands. See, some guys hit hard and can knock you out with one punch. But a guy who's fast and has good technique, good defense, he can avoid that big hit and get lots of smaller shots in, wearing his opponent down. It's like Johnny and Allan. Two good fighters but opposite styles."

"Really?"

"Sure. Allan—they called him 'Steamtrain Samson' because he came out fast and liked to run over his opponents. He was a decent mover but a big hitter. They called Johnny 'Slumber' because he would box his opponents to sleep. He wasn't such a big puncher and rarely knocked his opponent out. He won most of his bouts by technical merit or on points. He would just box away, score a point here, a point there, not often a big shot but a scoring shot. That was his problem."

"How was it his problem?"

"Johnny was a boxer's boxer, one for the aficionados. But most fans want to see big hits and knockouts—not too early, mind you; they want their money's worth. That's what they love. That's why Johnny was never a big-ticket seller. The fans who didn't really understand boxing found his style boring. Allan was a knockout guy. He sold tickets. You know about ticket sellers?"

"Yeah, Maxine explained it to me."

"You met Maxine? Good. She help?"

"In more ways than I know. She's good people."

"She is that."

"She said Johnny became a journeyman."

"That's about it. Because he was technically good but not a big hitter, managers could trust him to test their guys but not knock them out."

"Did he beat Samson that night?"

"The shot? Allan would have won on points, he was the more popular boxer."

"Fans like big hitters."

"You're getting it. But did Johnny put him down, or did he trip? Let me put it this way: I don't know what made him go down, but I know what made him not get up, and it wasn't a twisted knee."

The bell went off and instead of the usual delay, dancing, and feeling out the situation, the fighter in the red shorts went straight in hard, throwing punches like he was being attacked by invisible bats.

"You see that?" said Harv. "He's trying to end it early. Get one or two good shots in. Tells me he can't last."

"How long is this fight?"

"This one is eight rounds."

"Your guy only went four."

"Undercard. They go from four up to twelve usually, for a title fight. But watch, see the red shorts? He's already dropping his hands. That early barrage took his wind."

"He hardly hit the other guy though."

"Throwing air swings takes more energy than a punch that lands. Think about the physics of it."

I understood a bit about biomechanics from my pitching days, but I didn't spend a lot of time thinking about Newton's laws.

"If you hit, you transfer the momentum into your opponent, but if you miss, you have to arrest that momentum all by yourself or you fall over. Takes effort."

The bell rang and the fighters moved to their corners.

"Harv, did you ever see Johnny get into a fight outside the ring?"

"No."

"Never?"

"Never. Stone's rule, my rule. I don't allow it. All the fighting happens in the ring. That's rule number one."

"But he wasn't one of your fighters anymore. Not for a decade."

"If you're one of mine, you're one of mine for life. See, Miami, you gotta understand that a lot of the kids who come to me don't got a lot else going for them. They often don't have great home situations—there's money troubles, domestic troubles, single parents struggling through, doing the best they can. There's anger in those kids, and hitting a heavy bag is a great way to work that stuff through. You work out in my gym for a couple hours a day, you don't have a lot of energy left to get into trouble. But if you do, rule one is there. I tell 'em straight. You get into fights outside the ring, you're done. You're out. I don't tolerate it."

"Some must do it anyway."

"They do. And they get sent packing. I might give a kid a second chance after a while, but never a third. You either get it or you don't. So if fighting outside the ring is your thing, you never become one of my guys. Simple."

"And Johnny was one of your guys?"

"For sure. He worked hard. He did it right. He got a shot and it didn't quite go his way, but that's the game. But he learned rule number one. Even after my boys stopped training with me, they had that rule ingrained in them and they lived it. Now watch this guy."

Harv pointed at the ring, and the boxers came together. The fighter in the red shorts tried again to knock his opponent out with a bunch of haymakers. They all missed. After about thirty seconds, he ran out of energy.

"Now watch the guy in the yellow shorts. See, a smart boxer knows when to defend and when to attack. He goes on the back foot to make sure none of those wild swings hit, then when the puff is gone, he attacks."

Yellow shorts threw a series of jabs into the gloves and face, then he moved in and threw short hits into the body.

"See, he's smart. He's working his opponent into the corner, so red has nowhere to go."

Red shorts looked spent, then suddenly he used both his gloves to push his opponent's chest. Yellow shorts stumbled backward.

"Whoa," said Harv. "Can't do that."

The referee moved in and spoke to red shorts.

"He got stuck in the corner and couldn't fight his way out, so he just shoved his opponent out the way. Can't do that."

The boxers came together once again, and red shorts got in close, almost grabbing yellow shorts and shoving him into the far corner, but yellow shorts deftly stepped aside and clocked his opponent in the side of the head as he stumbled past.

"See that? Yellow shorts was getting pushed into the corner, but he's fast enough on his feet to avoid it. He doesn't want to get stuck in the corner. Limits his movement, prevents him from evading the big one. That's the only place red shorts is likely to win, and yellow shorts knows it. A smart boxer always avoids the corner. Even when it feels like a win, it's a losing move."

The bell ended the round.

"So about Johnny," I said, "what do you think would get him so worked up that he would go to the club after closing to meet a drug dealer and punch him dead?"

"He met a dealer?"

"Yeah. Ricky the Fudge."

"He killed Ricky the Fudge?"

"Yep."

"No great waste."

"Maybe true, but still manslaughter at best, possibly murder."

"Murder? How's that?"

"The sheriff seems to think Johnny may have gone there with the intent to kill."

"I don't see it. Johnny lived rule number one."

"Johnny wasn't well, Harv."

"I know, kid, but I still don't see it."

I wondered if he couldn't see it or if he just didn't want to.

"You ever hear anything about Johnny having a specific beef with Ricky?"

"Everyone had a beef with the Fudge."

"You didn't think much of him. It's not the same as killing him."

Harv shrugged and focused on the match.

"So, you ever hear anything between them?"

"Nothing really."

"Look, I'm on Johnny's side. I'm trying to find ways to make this less bad because it's never going to be good. But if the cops are going to find history, I need to know so I can find a way to explain it."

"All I'm saying is, Johnny knew rule number one."

"I get that."

"But there was a rumor."

"Go on."

"It was mentioned that the Fudge might have branched out to selling his drugs at the high school."

"Which high school?"

"The one around the corner from Johnny's house. The one his girls go to."

"You think his girls got into drugs and Johnny did something about it?"

"No. I'm saying it was a rumor. Hell, it wasn't even a rumor. I maybe heard it once."

"Where?"

"At the gym."

"From who?"

"I think Allan might have mentioned it, as in, if Johnny finds out, there'll be trouble."

"How would Samson know? Does he have kids?"

"Allan? No. But he has his ear to the ground, you know. A lot of locals come through the gym. But I never heard anything about Johnny finding out, and like I say, I only heard it the once."

The fighters came out for one more round. The guy in the red shorts wanted to wrestle more than box. He was spent. His defense was dropping, and yellow shorts was jabbing him in the face at will. I had to give the other guy credit though. Despite all the punches to his face, he didn't go down. He went in close to grapple and take time off the clock, but yellow shorts popped him with a left into his six-pack.

"Ooh," said Harv.

"What?"

"Liver shot."

Yellow shorts stepped back and threw a couple punches high that bounced off his opponent's gloves. Red shorts took a half step back, stayed in place for a second, and dropped to one knee. The referee came in close and spoke to him, then stood and waved his arms out wide. Yellow shorts put his arms up in victory.

"What the heck happened?"

"TKO."

"What?"

"Technical knockout. The referee called it off."

"Why?"

"Liver shot."

"That one to the ribs? It didn't look like anything." Yellow shorts was waving to the nonexistent crowd, but I was watching red shorts. He was still on one knee. A doctor had climbed in through the ropes to talk to him. "Maxine told me a liver shot was what did Samson in against Johnny."

"That's what they say. The liver is on the right side of the abdomen, down near the bottom of the rib cage. If a guy swings or opens up his right arm, a left to the body can hit it directly."

"But it's the liver, not the heart. He's still not up."

"Damage to the liver can sap the energy out of a guy, to the point where he can't even stand. If it's a good one, it can send the body into shock. That boy's going to be hurting tomorrow."

"Tomorrow? He doesn't look that good now."

After several minutes, red shorts was able to gingerly stand up, and he was assisted out of the ring. The ring announcer called the winner with a single fighter beside him.

I must have been shaking my head at the whole thing, because Harv said, "You're not a fan."

"Huh? Of boxing?"

"You don't think much of it."

"I've been punched before, and I don't really see the fun in it."

"You watch football?"

"Sure."

"You think getting tackled by those big boys is fun?"

"I played the game. I know it's not. But punching a guy's lights out is not the point of football."

"Agreed. I'm not gonna argue it ain't barbaric. But it's also pure. Mano a mano. One warrior against another."

"You can say the same thing about chess."

"You see chess getting kids off the street? Is chess getting them fit and healthy? There aren't too many fat boxers, you know. I get kids in my gym who eat nothing but fast food because the parent is working three jobs with no time to spare, and they do nothing but play video games. Six months in the gym they're a different person."

"I'm not saying these guys aren't athletes, Harv. That's one hell of a workout. But when I see Johnny Cabrini's kids fearing what their father might do to them, then I gotta ask whether it's worth it."

"Johnny isn't every fighter, kid. You're looking at the worst result and assuming everyone is like that."

"Maybe. But it seems to me that there are a lot of people making money on this at the expense of the athletes."

"Welcome to life."

We sat for a while, watching the light show on the ring, and then Harv asked me if I was staying for the main event.

"I'm staying until I find Breyer Priestly."

"Then you'll be here a few more hours." He levered himself up out of his seat.

"You not staying?"

"I've seen it all before. Take care."

"Thanks, Harv. Look after yourself."

He walked back around the ring and disappeared, then I checked my watch. I wanted to see Breyer Priestly, but I had had my fill of boxing for the day, so I decided to go for a walk.

I ventured out to the massive resort pool, put on my shades, ordered an Arnold Palmer, and sat on a poolside lounger in my tuxedo, waiting for the sun to set.

CHAPTER TWENTY

BY THE TIME I GOT BACK TO THE VENUE, IT WAS NIGHTTIME AND THE crowd had filled in. There was an audible buzz in the theater, and people seemed in good spirits. Not to my complete surprise, I was overdressed. People didn't dress up for anything anymore. Theatergoers wore chinos and wedding guests turned up in jeans or shorts. I was a casual dresser most of the time, but I really didn't see why we all had to wear leisure suits outside the house all the time.

The usher checked my pass and offered to walk me to my seat. The undercard bouts allowed for a guy like me to meander about, but at the business end of proceedings, I had a third-row seat on the right side. I thanked the usher, but I didn't sit.

The ringside seats were only half occupied as things headed toward the first of three fights on the main card—the final bout of the evening was for the world title. As people stood around chatting and looking wonderful, I wandered around the ring with my eye on the front row.

I didn't see Breyer Priestly. But I did see a seat bearing a placard with his name on it. I leaned over a judges' table against the ring, and while two people were talking I borrowed a marker. Then I sat down to wait.

Camera operators were moving around ringside, filming spectators. I recognized a guy from a nineties television show that I had never watched and one of the local news anchors. There was a couple that the camera guy kept drifting back to who might have been an actor and his supermodel wife, but they also might have been a local cosmetic surgeon and his test bunny.

The man in the red jacket returned, and I had to give him props for being the only person near the ring to be working the entire day. He was going through the running order with a man wearing a headset. My view was then blocked by an usher.

"Excuse me, sir."

I looked at him but said nothing.

"These seats are reserved."

"I know."

"Soooo, you'll need to find your own seat."

"I have."

The usher frowned and glanced at the two people behind him. One was a woman of roughly thirty and an older guy who I could have met in Orlando. He had his brother's eyes and nose, but his gray perm was all his own, a bold and interesting choice for someone not living in the 1970s.

"Um, sir, this is Mr. Priestly's seat."

I looked up at Breyer Priestly. He had matched me in wearing a tuxedo, but his jacket was purple velour, and he was totally rocking it. Beside him, I felt like a waiter in a French restaurant.

"I don't think so," I said.

"Yes, sir," said the usher. "There's a reserved sign."

"There is?"

"Yes, sir. You're sitting on it."

I leaned forward to reveal the sign. I had flipped it over and scribbled on it with a marker, so it now read: *Reserved, Miami Jones*.

"So it does," I said.

"Umm, sir?"

I smiled at him and then at Priestly, who didn't reciprocate. I didn't know who the woman was, but she seemed to find the whole thing amusing, which in turn seemed to sour Priestly's mood even more.

"I'll tell you what, why doesn't she sit with me, and Hugh Hefner can go play the slots?"

"Do you know who I am?" said Priestly. His Dr. Wrexham had used the same line.

"Bob Ross?" I replied.

"I'm gonna sit," said the woman, and she did just that, right next to me. She smiled, then looked up at Priestly.

He was obviously the head honcho of this whole rodeo, complete with prefight drinks in a luxury suite and front-row seats right where the TV camera would catch them. But right at that moment, he was a man who had just had his pants pulled down to his ankles, and he either hiked them back up and lost all dignity or he doubled down.

I gave him a third option. The way to save face. I leaned into the woman.

"It's okay. It's an old routine. We went to college together."

We had to be twenty years apart, but she giggled and said, "That's funny."

"Breyer, you old dog," I said as I stood. "It's been too long."

We shook hands with an audible slap like we had been on the wrestling team together.

"Give me a second of your time," I said, turning Priestly toward the ring and moving away from the woman. "Here's the deal. I'm going to leave here with a wink and a nod, and she's going to think you've got a sense of humor that we both know you don't have. But first I'm going to tell you that I know all about Fishook and your crumby fighters' fund."

"You're the buffoon that barged into my brother's office."

"Buffoon? That's a good word. I'm going to start using it more. And yeah, that was me. I know your brother spoke to you and you spoke to Fishook and he called Tina Cabrini and offered her five hundred measly dollars. These front-row seats go for what, four times that? So five hundred isn't going work, is it?"

"I don't know who you think you are—"

"Miami Jones. It says so right there on my reserved sign."

"Your client is a murderer. Yeah, I know he's in prison."

"Prison is where you go after you're convicted."

"Which he will be."

"Maybe. But that just makes it more important that his wife gets what she deserves from the fund."

"I am not involved in the day-to-day operations."

"But such an important guy like you can certainly make a recommendation. You know, that his case be reconsidered."

"Or what?"

"Three things. One, I tell the *Palm Beach Post* and local TV that we can prove boxers were cheated out of money they paid into a fund to help them when they got older. I have a university surgeon willing to confirm that not only do his tests show my client and others have boxing-related injuries, but that a hack with no neurology credentials denied claims from your fund. And two, I put a call in to Immigration and Customs Enforcement. You're a Canadian, right?"

"And British Virgin Islands. Dual citizen."

"Right, but not American. So you being at this boxing match as president of the sanctioning body would be considered doing business, which you can do on a business visa. But I know for a fact that there's an office up in Orlando with your name on it. That makes it a place of work, for which you need a work permit. It's a bureaucratic difference, I grant you, but one I assure you they take very seriously down there at ICE. One call and you get dragged out of here in cuffs and miss the big fight, and whatever you think is gonna happen with your granddaughter there."

Priestly pinched his lips together, and it didn't suit his hairstyle at all. "She's not my granddaughter."

"Glad to hear it. But the third thing I'll do is tell her about that funny time back in college during spring break when you and I met some girls who gave us a souvenir that itches like hell in the crotch when the humidity is up."

Priestly clenched his jaw.

"And if you're thinking to just tell me what I want to hear and then do nothing, remember that the first two things I mentioned don't go away so easily, and the third can be used to ruin a good time with your next prospect." I slapped his shoulder. "You feel me?"

"How do I know you won't talk after I've passed on the message?"

"You don't. But one of us is a stand-up guy who doesn't con invalids out of money they could use to pay their medical bills, and the other one is a piece of excrement that looks like Leo Sayer. So we'll go with me, you think?"

"I'll see what I can do."

"Good man." I took a step and turned so his date could hear. "Good to see you, Brey, you old dog." I gestured to the whole theater. "Great show. You always were the man." To the woman: "Nice to meet you, ma'am."

I walked up the stairs to the exit. I didn't need to see the main event. I needed my car. I needed to get home. My wife was waiting, and I was wearing a tuxedo.

CHAPTER TWENTY-ONE

I DIDN'T GET A LOT OF SLEEP, BUT SOMETIMES THAT MAKES THE NEXT DAY all the better. I had received a text message from Elissa Croix, so I left Danielle early and headed to her office. I turned up bearing bagels with cream cheese and lox as well as some decent coffee. Her building was locked up tight on a Sunday morning, so she let me in. It was dark and quiet, and the aura of disappointment and fear that pervaded the place seemed to have lifted for the day. She flipped the light on in her office.

"Don't tell me you don't do carbs or something."

"I went to school at NYU. I love a good bagel."

Score one, Jones.

She explained what she had as she spread some cream cheese on a bagel, scattered it with capers, and then folded lox gently on top.

"I spoke with the assistant state attorney on the Cabrini case. He sent over some preliminary discovery items. Mainly an evidence list and scene photos."

"Does it normally come in pieces like that?"

"It can. As they gather more, they send it over. That's why they usually wait until just before the trial, so they'll pretty much send everything in one go."

I picked up the evidence list. There was more on it than I

thought: personal items, things taken from the scene and from Johnny's garage, and his car.

"I haven't seen the video, but the ASA has. He says it shows the victim arriving shortly before the defendant. Then, after a short period, the defendant leaves, making some aggressive gestures as he goes."

"Gestures?"

"The ASA thinks he was shouting at the victim, as if telling him to 'cop that' or something like it."

"Something like it?"

"Yes. Anyway, he said there's no audio or a way to lip-read or even confirm that he spoke, so that's just the prosecution's spin on it."

"No video of the fight?"

"No. The attack, as he called it, was outside its field of view."

"I've seen the camera. It's over the shop next door, so that sounds right. What's your feeling?"

"It's a strong case, *prima facie*. But I think there's something he's not telling us."

"Like what?"

"Don't know. Just a hunch. Like there's something more, something in the works. My radar tells me they're working up to justify charges."

"What do you mean?"

"The arrest warrant was for second-degree murder. That's not uncommon. If they establish motive they can up it to murder one, or if necessary negotiate down to manslaughter. We would hope to do the latter. I think they're building a case for murder."

"How?"

"I don't know. It's a hunch and I could be wrong, but if they are, sooner or later we'll find out."

"When?"

"Probably at the arraignment."

"In a few weeks? Johnny needs help now."

"I'm going to petition for a psych review. If we can't get bail at the final hearing, maybe we can at least get him situated in a proper facility."

"It's got to be better than jail."

"Be careful what you wish for."

"So what do we do?"

"We can't worry about charges that haven't been established yet, so no point trying to disprove a motive that hasn't been presented. But we should look at mitigation. Gather anything that shows his deteriorating state of mind, especially clinically."

"You mean from a doctor?"

"Yes." She bit into her bagel and made an "mmm" sound that made her blush.

"I have the surgeon at the university researching the whole CTE thing. He says there's no doubt there's trauma and that it is boxing related."

"Can we get that in writing?"

"Don't see why not, unless there's some HIPAA thing preventing it."

"I'll get Mr. Cabrini to sign a waiver. You talk to the doctor."

As she took another bite, I picked up the folder with the crime scene photos. They weren't graphic enough to take my appetite away; most of the damage to Ricky the Fudge was internal. What stuck with me was the unnatural placement of the body. A living person doesn't lie with arms and legs akimbo; they position themselves. A dead person would drop as a function of gravity and momentum and the range of motion of their limbs. Ricky the Fudge looked like he had fallen down the stairs right through the door to the club, like a ghost. His feet were pointed toward the door, and he lay at an angle across the alcove, with his head toward the parking lot.

I didn't know Richard Whitecross, and I wasn't a fan of the way he had chosen to make his living, but I didn't care to look at the shell of what had once been a small boy with a toothy grin and hopes and dreams. I cared less for the idea that it had been my client who had ended his time on this ball of dirt and gas we call home.

I told Elissa that I would get onto the things we discussed and let her know, then I stood to leave. She eyed the box of bagels like a cat burglar looking at a diamond tiara.

"There are five bagels left."

"They said a half dozen was a deal."

"You don't want them?"

"Nah. You share them around here if you need the brownie points. If not, take them home. Enjoy."

"Thank you."

I walked out with just my coffee and walked over to my office, wondering if an assistant public defender made so little that free bagels were a blessing, or if she was just that New York.

I was sitting at my desk when I heard Ron roll in. He called out, "Good morning," so I did the same, then I heard the coffee machine click on. I had already satisfied my one-cup limit.

We convened at my desk. Lizzy took the whole rest-on-the-Sabbath thing pretty seriously, so I didn't ask her to come, but she volunteered to call in. Somehow she got us on a video call in her Sunday best, right before church. We went through what we knew and didn't know. The upshot of it all was that we now had two tasks: get Tina Cabrini some money from the fund so she didn't lose her house, and gather testimony on Johnny's mental health to both mitigate future charges and support the petition Elissa would file to get him the mental health treatment he needed while in custody.

"I can call Dr. Abe's office," Lizzy said.

"We need to get the waiver from Elissa first," I said. "Otherwise Abe won't be able to give us a bean. Can you call her paralegal tomorrow?"

"Okay."

"Then there's the fund. I've shaken the tree, so we'll see if that improves the offer. Do you have any more?"

"I tracked down the name *Fishook*. There's a company called Fishook Financial on the island. The mailing address is the same one as on the fund correspondence sent to the Cabrinis. There's not a lot of detail because it's a private firm, but I'm going to get into the state registrations and so on and see where it leads."

"I asked around," said Ron. "My data are more anecdotal."

"Always," I said.

"Yes, well, it seems Fishook specializes in handling portfolios for foreign nationals who winter in Palm Beach. Especially folks from the Caribbean and Central America."

"The British Virgin Islands?"

"Quite probably."

"Okay team, that's good work, but the clock is ticking. Johnny's next hearing is in a couple days and we need everything we can to make sure he gets into a psychiatric facility, not just the regular old cells at Gun Club Road. And Tina's facing eviction if we can't get her some money."

Lizzy left our call. Ron hit the phones and computers. I sat at my desk, reliving the image of Ricky the Fudge lying in the alcove. It gnawed at me. And I wasn't going to wait for the Office of the State Attorney for the Fifteenth Judicial Circuit to provide the evidence most damning.

CHAPTER TWENTY-TWO

I took the increasingly familiar route back to the Pugilists' Club. The hubbub was over, and the crime scene tape and onlookers and cop cars were gone. The lot was mostly vacant but I parked at the rear anyway and walked across the asphalt. The door to the club was closed, and the alcove was dark, so I couldn't see much of anything. It wasn't the movies—there were no chalk outlines on the ground. Law enforcement had more technology on their side than that now.

I wanted to see some of that technology. The evidence list from the state attorney's office included the surveillance video from the scene, and although Elissa had told me the defense would get access to it in due course, due course felt like a long time away. So like Ponce de Leon, I didn't wait for it to come to me. I went to the source.

I pulled open the heavy door at the rear of the payday lender and found a long corridor that led all the way to the front of the store. It was tight and as I walked its length, I assumed behind the wall to my right were offices and maybe a safe full of cash. At the front of the store, I found an empty lobby. The walls were covered in posters telling me that life would be better with a payday loan. Certainly paying for a car to be fixed so I could get to work might make life better, but these guys were suggesting that my next vacation should be funded with money I didn't have, and that didn't sit right with me. Besides, I lived in the vacation capital of the world, so where would I go?

There were four counter sections where a half wall was topped with Perspex, just like in Sally's pawn shop, but only one of them had an employee behind it. That guy looked bored out of his mind.

"Hey," I said.

"Morning." It was a good start, as I was expecting to be met with a grunt.

"Not too busy."

"We do payday loans—not many people get paid on Sundays. Regardless, it'll get busier after all the churches let out."

"You the manager?"

"Nah. He doesn't come in on Sundays."

"But you're the one who opens up."

"That's me. How can I help you?"

I stood outside the Perspex and looked at his button-up shirt and hairstyle that was messy but possibly on purpose. This was my guy. I didn't want the manager—they might be a corporate stickler for rules—but I needed a person with some level of seniority.

"I'm Miami Jones. I'm a PI working on behalf of the State of Florida's Office of the Public Defender." I minimized my role and expanded who I worked for because people tended to perk up at words like *State* and *Office of*. The guy didn't snap to attention, but he was listening.

"I'm investigating the incident that occurred next door."

"The dead guy?"

"That's right. Did you open up that morning?"

"Yeah. I showed the cops the video, and my boss sent them a copy already. You didn't get it?"

"The police are sometimes a little slow about passing things on."

"You're not a cop?"

"Office of the Public Defender. Part of the court. Separate from the police."

"Okay."

"So I'm trying to expedite the investigation. It would be a great help for me to get a look at the video."

"I don't know."

"You're under no obligation. I don't have a warrant or anything. I can just wait until the state attorney's office sends it to us, but that might happen after an innocent man goes to jail."

"I saw the video. He did it."

"I don't know. I haven't had the privilege, and you might be right. But I'm paid to check these things, and you'd be doing me a favor. Perhaps I can do one for you?"

His eyes narrowed. If I had been in a bank, I wouldn't have gone anywhere near the idea of bribing a teller for information. Banks got covered by federal laws and that was a whole other level of bureaucracy, let alone hurt. But this was a payday lender. It was basically loan-sharking as a franchise.

"I've got a break in five."

"How do you take a break when you're the only one here?"

He pulled out from below his desk a big red button attached to a cord. "If someone comes, they just hit the button. But no one comes. Wait outside the barbershop out back."

"Okay."

I went back down the corridor and out into the lot. I passed the alcove, but I didn't wait outside the barbershop. Instead, I walked to the end of the building. I had five minutes to kill and every bit of exercise added up to one more beer I could enjoy at Longboard's before my wife made me go running on City Beach. I shrugged involuntarily at the thought. Who was I kidding? She'd have me go running with her anyway, but at least she wouldn't make comments about the beer. Such were life's little tradeoffs.

The dollar store was still inviting me in, but I declined yet again. I strolled to the end of the strip and peeked into the area between the building and the cinder block wall along the side. There was a five-foot gap of wasted space, nothing but thirsty grass and trash. At the street end was an eight-foot-high wire fence covered in torn green plastic.

I walked back and leaned against the wall between the payday lender's back door and the alcove. The birds sang as if nothing had happened here. The sun shone on the asphalt, and the weeds coming up through the cracks in the pavement reached for the sky.

The door to the payday lender opened, and the guy was startled by me standing there. He shook his head and walked past me, down the sidewalk, and stopped between the alcove and the barber's back door. He gestured for me to join him.

"Sun too bright for you there?" I asked, nodding at where I had been standing.

"Think about it. We work with cash, so we're under surveillance all the time. I'm going to go to the trouble of stepping outside and then stand right under the video camera out here, am I?"

"I'm told the camera shows this spot."

"No. It shows the other side of that alcove, but not here, bro. We're good."

"Good for what?"

"You mentioned doing me a favor?" He held out his hand. It wasn't subtle. I knew I could get the video for free but I just didn't know when, and like those geniuses who slept in line to get the latest cell phone, I wanted it now. I took out my wallet and handed him a twenty.

He tilted his head and raised his eyebrows. I put another twenty in his hand. He didn't move.

"If I put something more in your hand, I don't just want to see the video. I want a copy of it."

"Bro, you think I'm gonna let you watch the video here? You not listening. They've got cameras on everything inside. Of course I'm going to send it to you."

"Won't the cameras see you doing that?"

"It's a download. I'll text you the link. You savvy with the internet?"

"Savvy enough." I took out another twenty, then put my wallet back in my pocket to say this was my final offer.

The guy shoved the money into his pocket and took out his phone. "What's your number?"

I told him and he punched it in with rapid-fire thumbs, then my phone bleeped and I saw his text.

"Download it right away. I can't guarantee my boss won't kill the link when he gets in tomorrow. Security, right?"

"Okay, thanks."

The guy walked back through the door he had come out of, and I walked back to my car. I got in and opened the text message. It was a web link, nothing more. I clicked an icon to forward the link and typed a message to Lizzy to download a copy first thing Monday. It took me a lot longer to type with my one pointer finger than the payday lender guy did with both his thumbs.

Almost instantly I got a text back from Lizzy with a thumbs-up emoji. Then I clicked the link for myself. I didn't want to download the video onto my phone, but I thought it might just play, and after a bit of buffering, it did.

It was hard to see everything on my little phone screen, but I got the gist of it all. The guy was right: I could see the sidewalk outside the building from one side of the payday lender to the near side of where the alcove was. But I couldn't see the pavement beyond the alcove or where I had been standing with the guy two minutes earlier.

The image was dark and gray—nighttime with one of those infrared cameras. I saw the section of the parking lot in front of the payday lender and a lighter gray across the right of the shot—light was likely spilling from the club above the barber. I used the little dot at the bottom of the image to fast-forward. It gave me a spinning circle as it played catch up, then showed the same scene. I fast-forwarded more. The gray turned to black as if the lights had gone out. Then I saw Maxine Mitchell walking from the bottom right of the shot as she came out of the alcove and headed to a car out of view.

Then there was nothing. I fast-forwarded again until I saw a person walking along the sidewalk at the bottom of the screen. It was a man, but all I could see was the top of his head. When he reached the sidewalk before the alcove, he looked around like a bad spy, and I saw his face: Ricky the Fudge. Ricky looked around once more, then disappeared into the alcove.

I advanced the footage again until I saw bright headlights. A car drove into the lot and parked in front of the payday lender, and the video went white. Then the lights went out, and the image took a few seconds to recover, like your eyesight moving from sunshine into a dark bar.

Next, I saw Johnny Cabrini walk from the car toward the alcove, talking to Ricky the Fudge, but the image was too small to lip-read. Johnny didn't appear stable on his feet, but he didn't stop moving. He stumbled right through the shot and disappeared into the alcove. For about thirty seconds, there was no activity, then Johnny reappeared. He backed out of the alcove, pointing and gesticulating to where I assumed Ricky now lay. I couldn't make out Johnny's face that well, but his body language said *rage*. Johnny took another step backward and stumbled and nearly fell, catching himself as he spun around. Then he went to his car, got in, and drove away.

I stopped the video and glanced in my rearview mirror at the building behind me. It was in reverse, but I could imagine everything. The hole in Tina's wall came to mind. It told me what Johnny was capable of. He might have been a good man, and he still might have his moments, but he was also now capable of bad things. When the ship captain lost control of the helm, perhaps the best move was to dock the boat. I hoped I could facilitate safe harbor for Johnny.

But it was nothing more than hope.

CHAPTER TWENTY-THREE

I spent the rest of the day at home thinking about collecting evidence. I didn't need to prove Johnny's innocence; I had to focus on finding evidence that mitigated the charges against him.

Lizzy texted to say she had downloaded the video and saved a copy to her hard drive. I was content with having seen it on my phone—a bigger image wasn't going to show another shooter on the grassy knoll—so my next move was to establish Johnny's fragile state of mind that night. And to do that, I needed to figure out where he had been before the video was taken. Mick had given me a possibility, but I still needed to speak to the right people.

In the meantime, Danielle and I took separate cars out to the island to join Ron and Cassandra for dinner at The Breakers. We sat at the Seafood Bar and watched the ocean go from blue to gray to black as the sun fell slowly behind us, eating shrimp tacos and drinking bubbles. It was good company in surroundings above my station, but I couldn't quite hit the mood. I kept wondering what Tina Cabrini and her girls were eating and drinking. I wasn't responsible for them or the position they found themselves in, but it gnawed at me all the same.

After coffee, Ron and Cassandra walked back to their oceanfront apartment, and Danielle drove home. I told her I shouldn't be long. I wasn't planning on making a night of it, but what I had to do had to be done late at night.

I drove down to Lake Worth Corridor and found a certain hole-in-the-wall. Mick had given me details for a local joint—a typical dive bar, with a low ceiling, stools bolted to the concrete floor, and some dark-wood booths in the back where the pool table was hosting a raucous game. The kind of place where a spilled drink would be washed away with a garden hose at the end of the night. The absence of carpet meant there was no stale alcohol smell. It was bleach and bathroom cologne all the way.

There were two guys silently watching West Coast football on a television above the bar, and at the opposite end, a bearded man sat with a melancholy expression, staring at a glass of amber liquor. I took a stool halfway between.

The bartender offered a nod. "What's your poison?"

"Beer, thanks."

"Coming up." He said it in a friendly way even though he didn't look friendly at first glance. He had a shaved head and tattoos peeking out from under his black T-shirt down both arms and his neck. He poured a beer without bothering with any guff, like asking what kind I wanted. One option took all the guesswork out of life.

He placed the beer on the bar in front of me and moved on. The melancholy guy had finished his drink. As he walked, the bartender picked up a bottle from the liquor collection at the back of the bar and poured the guy another shot, then turned away without a word.

"You work here most nights?" I asked when he came back.

"Every night but Monday."

"Day off?"

"Closed Monday."

I looked around the room. "Where do they go on Mondays?"

"God knows."

"Were you here last Thursday?"

"It wasn't Monday."

"Do you know most of your customers?"

"The regulars."

"You know a guy called Johnny? Johnny Cabrini?"

"I know you." He picked up a glass and started polishing it. I wondered what bartenders would do with their hands if they didn't have that to do.

"How do you know me?"

"I used to go to the baseball with my dad."

"That so?"

"Yeah. He lived in a retirement community up at Port St. Lucie. You were a pitcher for the Mets."

"That was a long time ago."

"Yeah. I've got a memory for faces."

"You a baseball fan?"

"Not so much. My dad was though."

"He's not with us now?"

"Nah. Lost him a few years back."

"Sorry."

"It's life, isn't it?"

I nodded and sipped my beer.

"What do you want with Johnny Cabrini?"

"So you do know him?"

"Didn't say that."

"I'm working for him. I'm a private investigator now."

"That right? Doing what for him?"

"He's been arrested."

"It happens." He moved to the beer tap and poured one, then he set it on the bar. A heavyset guy stepped up beside me, picked up the beer, and walked off.

"He's been charged with killing a guy," I said.

"Johnny?"

"Over at the Pugilists' Club. You know it?"

"I ride past it on the way to work."

"So I'm trying to confirm his movements the night of the fight."

"But you're not a cop."

"No. I'm working for Johnny's defense team."

"You don't think he did it?"

"It's pretty cut and dried that he did it, but we're trying to establish his mental state."

"Diminished capacity. You think it will get him off?"

"I don't think it's a question of getting him off, more about making sure he gets the help he needs."

"In jail? You ever done time?"

"No."

"It's not where you go to get help."

"That's why we're trying to get him in a facility better equipped for his, you know, issues."

"The nut house?"

"I don't think they call it that."

"You ever been?"

"In a psychiatric facility? No. You?"

"Nup, but I wouldn't want to, stories I've heard."

"Well, it's gotta be better than general population. So anyway. Were you here Thursday?"

"Yeah, I was here."

"Was Johnny here?"

The bartender looked at the ceiling. "Yeah, he was here."

"What time would you say?"

"Late. Got here maybe toward the end of the Thursday-night game, so eleven-ish. Left just after midnight.

"How was he?"

"Not in a great place, but lots of guys here like that."

"Aggressive?"

"Nah. Johnny wasn't usually like that, not here at least. He retreated into himself is more what I'd call it. Like I say, folks come here to do that." He nodded toward the end of the bar where the guy was still staring into his drink.

I sipped my beer. I knew the feeling. I had been down like that once or twice before, but it had ended differently. It felt like every time I fell, I was lucky enough to be caught. It had been the Dunbar family when I was a boy, and then Lenny, and then Danielle. And when I tripped, there was Longboard Kelly's. It wasn't the kind of place a guy was left to cry in his pretzels for long. Muriel would always let me drink my sorrows away if I felt the need, but the price was always working through my problems sooner or later. It was therapy at half the price.

"You know, now that I think of it, Johnny did get a bit worked up that night."

"He did?"

"Yeah. I remember now. He was sitting on his drink the way he does, and he got a phone call."

"A phone call?"

"Yeah. It got him all kinds of upset. Yeah, that's right. He wasn't in a great mood before, but this was something else. He started cussing and slamming his glass on the bar, you know, like something had really ticked him off. I was thinking about giving him his marching orders."

"Was he violent?"

"He was on the edge. One of the other customers came up to grab his drink, and they brushed shoulders—like barely touched fabric—and Johnny went off like the guy had knocked over his drink. I was going to tell him to go sleep it off before it got ugly."

"You were going to?"

"Yeah. I didn't 'cause he just upped and left. That was the last time he was in."

"Did you hear any of the call?"

"Nah. But I will tell you something, he knew whoever it was."

"How do you know?"

"I work in a bar. I see people having conversations. They talk differently to people they know."

"And he was doing that?"

"For sure. Real deferential."

I tried to think who someone like Johnny would be deferential to. A drug dealer? Was he in pain and pleading for some opioids? But why would such a conversation make Johnny angry?

As I thought about it, a woman came in alone and approached the bar. The bartender offered her a nod.

"Kelly," he said. "How are you?"

"Better, thanks, Dean."

"What are you after?"

"Just a beer, thanks."

"Good." He poured the beer and handed it to her. "Doing okay?"

"Yeah. I called her."

"You did? Good for you."

"We talked it through. We're going to have dinner later this week."

"Good."

"It's not fixed, but, like you said, at least I'll know."

"Better in than out, Kel. Momentum, that's all you need. One step at a time."

"Thanks, Dean."

"You bet."

The woman went and sat near the pool table, and I turned back to the bartender. He was pouring the guy at the end one more.

"You know your customers," I said as he came back.

"It's my job."

"Plenty of bartenders think pouring drinks is the job."

"Nah. If that's all it was, I wouldn't be here."

"You're good with people. You could be a therapist."

"I am."

I looked around the bar. I didn't doubt it. "No, I mean for real."

"Yeah, so do I. I majored in psychology. Florida State."

"Seriously? So why are you working in a dive bar?"

"I like it. I like working at night. And I prefer the people. They're, I dunno, real."

I looked at his bald head and his tattoos and felt like offering him an apology for something I never said, something about books and covers.

"Another beer?"

"One for the road. Can I ask you something?"

"As opposed to what you've been doing?"

"Yeah. How do they afford it?"

"Who? Afford what?"

"People like Johnny. How does he afford to drink here? He was struggling to keep a job and barely had a bean to his name. His wife is about to lose the house because they don't have rent money. So where was the money coming from? You're a smart guy. You watch and listen. Was Johnny doing drugs or selling them?"

"Doing them, I can't say. Probably. Painkillers, at least. But selling? Nup."

"So how did he afford it?"

Dean pulled down a bottle from the collection of liquor behind him. It was plastic and had a spout built into the top. He placed it on the bar in front of me. It was called Old Elbow and was pale amber in color. I picked it up and turned it over. The back label said it was 20 percent whiskey and 80 percent assorted distilled ethanol.

"What's assorted distilled ethanol?"

"You ever owned a lawn mower?"

I shook my head. "What's with the spout?"

"Easy pouring for shaky hands."

"And Johnny was drinking this?"

"Regularly."

"Do many people in here do that?"

"Enough for the boss to keep buying it."

"How much does it cost?"

"We get it at wholesale. A buck ninety a bottle."

"Two dollars for what, this is a quart?"

"Close enough. It's actually a metric liter."

"A liter? Where's it come from?"

"That's a need-to-know thing, and we don't need to know."

I wondered if cheap liquor was a mitigating factor in Johnny's case. I suspected not.

"Can I try it?" I asked.

"I wouldn't."

He seemed pretty serious about it, so I took his advice. Instead, I unscrewed the cap and took a sniff. The burning sensation removed hairs in my nose and lodged a headache in the back of my brain. It was somewhere between aviation fuel and mango.

I recapped the bottle, and Dean returned it behind the bar. I spent fifteen minutes drinking beer to take away the taste that had settled on my tongue despite not having taken a sip. When I was done I pulled out a twenty and laid it on the bar. Dean went to make change, but I told him to keep it. Most people would never come to a place like this, so they would never know the public service that people like Dean did for them. Keeping folks on an even keel helped us all, and although I had no plan to drop by for a drink anytime soon, I was glad such places existed. Not everyone could afford a leather couch in a Palm Beach psychiatrist's office.

I thanked Dean for his time. He nodded and moved on to help the next customer with whatever it was they needed.

CHAPTER TWENTY-FOUR

The next morning I was sitting in a little Cuban café on Gun Club Road, sipping a high-octane coffee, when Lorraine Catchitt walked in. The medical examiner's office was just down the street, on the same campus as the county detention facility, where Johnny Cabrini was being held. But there was nothing much of note around there, so I invited Lorraine for breakfast on her way in.

"Jones, get me one of those, stat," she said as she sat.

I ordered her a heart-starter Cuban coffee, and a chicken empanada and ham croquette for myself.

"You want something to eat?" I asked.

"Same."

The server left with a smile. Lorraine pivoted in her seat and hooked her bag across the back of her chair. In a white blouse and khaki pants, with a string of pearls around her neck, she looked different, but then most people did if they were normally seen in full-body coveralls designed to protect them from blood splatter.

"So you want to know about Cabrini," she said, getting straight to it.

"I'm working with the public defender."

"You think you're getting him off?"

"I'm not sure that's the objective. It looks more like a plea deal might be in the cards."

"At best." The coffee came, and she asked for a second before she even took a sip.

"So are we talking manslaughter?"

"I can't speak for the state attorney's office, Jones."

"Do you know Elissa Croix from the public defender's office?"

"In passing." She took a long drink of her coffee and shook out her shoulders.

"She's getting a vibe that the prosecution might be looking to up it to first degree."

"Hmm."

"What does that mean?"

"I can't do your job for you, Jones."

"I'm not asking you to. But what we're looking at is a fight gone too far. He might have killed the guy, but he didn't intend to."

"Croix gets to make whatever case she wants in court. I can't advise you on strategy."

"Can you tell me what's in the autopsy report? We'll get it eventually, but this guy's in a fragile state."

"You know what I always say? You don't like the view from your cell, don't get put in jail."

"As compassionate as that is, I'm just asking about something that we're entitled to know."

"Yeah, yeah." Two small plates of food landed on our table, and Lorraine attacked her croquette. "I like you, Jones. You're a good egg. So I'll tell you what's in black-and-white ink. The victim had bruising below the left eye consistent with being punched in the face."

"How many times?"

"Once."

"And that killed him?"

"Nope. Death was the result of a blow to the neck, right at the base of the skull."

"At the back of his head?"

"Yep."

"So what was the cause of death?"

"Asphyxiation."

"Huh?"

"He suffocated, Jones."

"Geez. How does that happen?"

"The blow severed the nerves between the spinal cord and the medulla oblongata."

"In English?"

"It severed his brain stem. The medulla oblongata controls many functions in the body, top among them the respiratory system. He lost the ability to breathe and developed hypoxemia—that's a lack of oxygen in the blood. In short, he suffocated." She picked up her empanada and bit into it. "These are so good. Have you tried yours yet?"

I peered down at my breakfast. I suddenly wasn't feeling very hungry. "Are you saying a sucker punch did him in?"

"Pretty much. But not any old sucker punch."

"Why?"

"The brain is pretty important, so the design really tries to minimize the likelihood of trauma. Usually getting hit in the back of the head gives you a headache, nothing more. When we see brain-stem damage from a blow, it's usually from the side. The impact causes a whipping action that damages one or more sections of the brain stem. But in this case, the blow was to the back of the head."

"But how is that not any old sucker punch?"

Lorraine sipped her coffee and shoved the rest of the empanada in her mouth. "It wasn't from a bare fist, and it wasn't from hitting the ground. The area at the base of the skull had been punctured—little dents—consistent with the use of something like brass knuckles."

"Brass knuckles?"

"Yep. But not any brass knuckles. Some are just like rings around the fingers, right? These had protrusions on them, like a diamond in a wedding ring, flat on top. They're not designed to hurt someone;

they're designed to severely maim or kill." She finished her coffee. "I gotta get going."

"Sure."

She looked at my plate. "You gonna eat those?"

"No."

"Mind if I . . ."

I didn't know how she stayed so trim. Maybe she had come from a workout, or maybe she only ever ate on someone else's dime. I called the server over for a to-go box and the check.

"You think the prosecutor will look for a more severe charge because of the brass knuckles?"

"They're illegal already, but your guy was a boxer. He was trained. He knew how to hit and where. If I were the prosecutor, I'd be arguing that a trained boxer who carried those kinds of brass knuckles to a fight fully intended to kill." She picked up her bag and the box of food. "And that's murder one, my friend. I'll see you 'round. Say hi to Danielle."

Lorraine stepped out of the café light on her feet like she was on her way home from the greatest date ever. I sat in place, feeling like my batteries had run dry. I had the check, but I needed to break my one coffee rule to wash away the taste of 80 percent assorted distilled ethanol that had returned to sour my day.

CHAPTER TWENTY-FIVE

I kept the murder thing to myself when I got back to the office. Lizzy had a whole presentation to go through, and I didn't need to distract her. The charges were largely irrelevant to the issues of the fighters' fund. Either way, Tina needed as much money as we could eke out of them because Johnny was not bringing home any bacon for a long time.

Ron and I took the sofa in my office, and Lizzy stood by the window with a whiteboard on which she had stuck several photos.

"Okay, so back to the beginning," she said. "The letters that Tina gave us, as well as the Global Boxing Council's website, make reference to what they call a fighters' fund." She pointed at a picture of the website with the words highlighted. "But I could find no evidence of such a fund anywhere in the United States or even internationally."

"Another name?" asked Ron.

"Getting there, Ron."

"Sorry."

"So using the name *Fishook*, I was able to cross-reference a number of databases and discovered a charitable foundation trust called the GBC Convalescence Trust. The documents show one Nolan S. Fishook as the trustee."

"Good fishing," I said.

"Oh, I'm not done."

"I didn't think so."

"The trust is a US entity with tax-free status. This means that it has to report to the IRS."

"Those returns will be public record," said Ron.

"Ron."

"Sorry, Lizzy."

"They are public record, and I have them. I then used data from the ABC—that's the Association of Boxing Commissions—to compile a dataset of GBC bouts for the past thirty years."

"Geez, Lizzy. You've been busy," I said.

"Yes, I have. And what I was able to do with these two sets of data was to calculate an approximate total purse for all the fights over that period. We know the standard GBC contract required twenty percent of the boxers' share of the purse into the fund, which we now know is really the trust. I used averages to allow for manager and promoter fees, which then gave me an approximate amount that should be in the fund now, minus disbursements plus interest, and allowing for the present value of money calculations, with a margin of error of plus or minus six percent."

"That's pretty impressive," I said. "There's just one problem."

"You have no idea what any of that means."

"You got me."

"That's why I have this chart. By my calculations, less than half the money that should be in the trust is there. Or, put another way, less than half the money that left the boxers' pay packet made it into this trust."

"Where did it go?"

"Good question, boss. It seems from Tina's records that after the promoter and the manager each get their cut, the rest is divided among the boxer, the cornermen, and the trainer if he was not one of the cornermen."

"Which he usually is."

"Thank you for that clarification. It seems that the money that doesn't go to any of these people is funneled to the GBC in the British Virgin Islands. According to IRS records, the funds going into the trust then come back to it from BVI."

"Why send money from the US to BVI and then back again?" I asked.

"Classic laundering technique," said Ron.

"You say that with too much confidence," I said. "You got a side hustle going?"

Ron smiled. "I read."

"There's another reason," said Lizzy. "The boxing commissions in various states require—I assume at the request of the IRS—that any benevolent funds for US bouts get administered in the US."

"That's some great work, Lizzy," I said.

"Thank you."

"So a bunch of the money goes missing, which makes these guys crooks. We might be able to use that. But the original problem is getting them to pay out. Are they ever doing that?"

"The IRS reporting shows an overview of disbursement numbers and claims approved. It makes no mention of claims denied because no money changes hands, and the cash is what the IRS is worried about. But there are certainly disbursements in the IRS records."

"So they do approve some?"

"Some, yes. Now here's the thing. This is not life-changing money. Based on this data, the average payout the trust made over the past decade is three hundred and thirty-one dollars per claimant."

"That barely keeps Tina afloat for a month," I said.

"And it's less than the current offer from Fishook," said Ron. "That's five hundred, right?"

My phone buzzed and I took a gander: the receipt of a text message. I studied Lizzy's whiteboard. "I need to check if that offer has improved since I met with Mr. Priestly." I looked at my phone again. "But first, the public defender wants me."

CHAPTER TWENTY-SIX

The receptionist at the public defender's office saw me coming. Maybe Elissa had left my name at the desk or I was becoming a known quantity. The answer to that question was not evident from her expression, but as I reached the security barrier, a tall, thin guy who reminded me a little too much of Eric Edwards attracted my attention with a wave.

"Miami Jones?" he asked.

"Reporting for duty."

He picked up a visitor's pass from the desk and smiled at the receptionist, who smiled back. Perhaps it was me after all. Then she took the next call and lost the expression faster than the eye could see. I took the visitor's pass and was shepherded through security. Eric 2.0 led me back to a small conference room that held the aroma of stale coffee and discarded skin cells.

"I'm Barry Schiff," he said. "Can I get you a coffee?"

After two Cuban coffees that morning, I didn't need caffeine, nor did I have high hopes for whatever had left the aroma in the meeting room, so I declined.

"Take a seat," he said.

"Sorry, who are you?"

"Barry Schiff."

"I got the name. I meant why are we talking right now?"

"Oh. I'm a paralegal here. I'm helping Ms. Croix with the Cabrini file."

"Okay, got it." As I took a seat, Elissa pushed in through the door. I tried to stand again, but the chair hit the wall, and I ended up doing a half squat. Elissa raised an eyebrow and waved me back down.

"Did you meet?" she asked.

"Of course," said Schiff.

"Okay, I have court in a few. What do we have, Barry?"

Barry opened a file. "The prosecution has provided initial discovery."

"Where is it?" I asked.

"Where's what?"

"The evidence."

"We don't get the actual evidence, Jones," said Elissa. "We can inspect it if we petition to do so, but otherwise we usually get photos and documents."

Barry held up the file. "Shall I continue?"

"If you think there's any point."

"We have the preliminary evidence list collected from the crime scene and from Mr. Cabrini's garage upon his arrest. We also have crime scene photographs."

"Does anything stand out?" asked Elissa.

"This." Barry handed her a document, which she silently read, then passed to me. It was a PBSO record of a call-out.

"What's this?" I asked.

"It's a record of a domestic-disturbance call against Mr. Cabrini," said Barry.

"Was he arrested?"

"No. It seems he had left the premises by the time deputies arrived."

"Who called it in?"

"It's right there."

"It says Antoinette Cabrini."

"His wife."

"Tina?"

Barry shrugged. "No formal charges, but officers recommended she look into a restraining order."

"Did she?"

"No record of such."

"So what does this mean?"

Elissa sat forward. "The prosecution will attempt to establish a record of violence that suggests Mr. Cabrini was capable of anything."

"He was a boxer—how hard will that be?"

"Out of the ring, Jones. I wasn't overly concerned by the charge of second-degree murder because I saw it as a bargaining position. We negotiate down to manslaughter. But the bail thing made me wonder. This gives me more pause. I think they might stick fast to second degree."

"But how? There's no intent, no motive. It was a fight."

"In the state of Florida, second-degree murder allows a charge for an unlawful killing when the act that led to the killing could be dangerous to life, and evincing a depraved mind."

"Evincing?"

"Revealing the presence of. But the key with this charge is that no intent needs to be shown. So they would argue that Mr. Cabrini was a trained boxer, he knew how to hurt and maim, and he should reasonably have expected danger to Mr. Whitecross's person. So all they need show is a depraved mind. His history of boxing together with the domestic disturbance offers a pattern of depraved behavior and disregard for human life."

"That's not Johnny."

"The prosecution will say the evidence shows it's exactly him. So we have to find evidence and a defense that refutes their theory. We need to show he didn't reasonably know that a fight would end that way. Start with his boxing record. None of those fights ended in death, did they?"

Barry shrugged.

"Not that I've found," I said. "He lost much more than he won."

"That's good," said Elissa. "We could argue that he didn't expect to win the fight. If we can show that, the state attorney might play ball on a downgraded plea bargain."

"On that evidence list, is there a murder weapon?" I asked.

Barry frowned. "You mean like 'item five: murder weapon'?"

"Something like that."

"It doesn't work like that. They don't have to tell us that an item might be the weapon used."

"They don't?"

"That would be divulging tactics," said Elissa. "They have to tell us they have it but not how they will present it. We have to work that out for ourselves. It's usually pretty self-evident if there's a gun or a knife. But in this case, there is no weapon—it was a fight. Why do you ask?"

"Do you have the autopsy report?"

"Not yet," said Barry. "The ME will send it to the state attorney when it's done, and they'll pass it on, or we can apply for a copy independently if we feel it's necessary."

"Again, why do you ask?" said Elissa.

"I have a friend in the ME's office."

"This friend is giving out confidential information to the public?"

"Well, first, it's not confidential. Autopsy reports are public record. Anyone can request one. And second, she was talking to a fellow investigator."

"Is there a brotherhood or something?"

"As someone working on behalf of the public defender."

"You haven't been deputized, Jones. There's no badge."

"You're not hearing me. I wasn't told anything that isn't in the report. You'll get it, you'll read it. And what you'll learn is that the victim died from a blow to the head delivered by someone wearing brass knuckles."

"Brass knuckles?" said Barry, flipping through his papers.

"That's bad," said Elissa.

"I didn't think it was good," I said.

"It's hard to argue 'no depraved mind' if you're wearing brass knuckles. Bringing them with you implies intent."

"Brass knuckles," said Barry. "They're listed here. Retrieved from Mr. Cabrini's garage at the time of his arrest."

Elissa rubbed her eyes. "Not good."

"Have you guys seen the video?" I asked.

"The surveillance video?" asked Barry. "We don't have it yet. It's on the list though."

"I have a copy."

Elissa dropped her hands to the table. "You have it? How?"

"I asked for it."

"From the state attorney?"

"No. From the store that owns the camera."

"Did you pay for it?"

"Don't worry about how I got it."

"You are representing this office."

"I know, and I'm getting the job done. Look, there's no chain of evidence on this. You'll get the version provided by the prosecution sooner or later, so let's call this a working copy."

"I don't have time right now to go through it."

"That's fine. I've got my office viewing the footage with a magnifying glass, but I think we should just check one thing. You have a computer we can use? The screen on my phone is too small."

Barry pushed his chair back and left then returned with a laptop. After receiving my email with the link, he opened it up. I moved around the table to better see his screen and told him to fast-forward until the action started. We all watched Johnny Cabrini walking toward the alcove.

"Where's the victim?" asked Elissa.

"Already in the alcove."

I was sure Elissa and Barry were taking in the big picture. I, on the other hand, was looking for something specific. We saw Johnny enter the alcove and then return to his car. Barry stopped the video.

"It doesn't show the fatal blow, but it places him there," said Elissa. "Combined with a murder weapon, that's fairly damning."

"But did you see what he had on his hands when he arrived and when he left?"

"No."

"Exactly. No brass knuckles."

"He could have put them on after entering the alcove and then taken them off."

"Maybe. But right after hitting the guy? Johnny's still fired up. You can see him yelling at Ricky as he leaves. Would he really have stopped to remove them that quickly?"

"I don't know."

"Neither do I. It's just weird is all. And if you were Ricky and you were there for a drug deal, and you saw a guy you know is a former boxer put on brass knuckles right in front of you, would you just stand there? That alcove isn't that big. Even if Ricky tried to run and Johnny stopped him, surely we would have seen something— Johnny stepping back or a flailing arm or something."

"That's all supposition. The prosecution has hard evidence." She shook her head. "You guys keep on this if you want. I have to get to court."

Elissa left the room without another word, and I sat down. Barry looked at me, then closed his laptop.

"Do you have the crime scene photos?" I asked.

He nodded and slid them across to me. I opened the folder and looked at them again. They didn't tell me anything new, but I wasn't used to thinking in a room that smelled like the inside of an IHOP coffee pot.

"Did you find anything else?" asked Barry.

"I found out where Johnny was before the fight."

"I'm not sure the prosecution even has that."

"I'm not sure they care. They've got their case right here. But I found out that Johnny was drinking at a bar and got a phone call around midnight. The bartender thought Johnny knew the caller."

"The victim?"

"Possibly, but he said by the tone of Johnny's voice, it was someone he knew well, and I don't know if Ricky fell into that category. He also said the call made Johnny angry and that he left straight after. The timing suggests he went directly to the club."

I spread the photos out on the table and started snapping them with my camera.

"I don't think you can do that," said Barry.

"Just for my personal use, I swear. As soon as the case is done, I'll delete them."

"I don't know."

"I want to think the whole thing through, and these may help, and I can't keep coming over here. Your receptionist hasn't taken a shine to me."

Barry didn't look convinced but said nothing more on it.

"So do you happen to have Johnny's phone log in your evidence file there?"

Barry flipped through and pulled out a sheet. "There's a download of the call log from his cell phone."

"Is that normal?"

"Pretty normal."

"What about Ricky's phone? Got that log? Let's see if Ricky called him."

"No. Nothing." Barry looked through his list. "I don't see Ricky's phone in the evidence log at all."

"So the victim had no phone?"

"None that the PBSO found at the scene."

"What's the number that called Johnny's phone around midnight?"

Barry looked the call log over. "There isn't one."

"What do you mean?"

"There's no call around midnight on that night. Nothing incoming or outgoing. Could the bartender be wrong?"

"Don't think so, he was a pretty switched-on guy. Doesn't make sense. Can you ask the state attorney's office if they have Ricky's phone and forgot to log it?"

"I doubt that, but we can ask. Why?"

"Because if they agreed to meet, then there was a mutual reason. Maybe that reason tells a different story than Johnny intending to commit murder."

Barry made a note and I stood. He walked me out and took my visitor's badge.

I wandered in the sunshine back to my office. Lizzy was standing in the front office again, looking at more paint swatches, which all appeared to be variations on white. I made no comment. At least they weren't coral.

"What do you know about call logs?"

"That's an odd question," she said.

"Someone called Johnny just before he left the bar for the club that night, but there's no record of it on the call log that the sheriff's investigators downloaded from his phone. So how can that be? Could he have another phone?"

"What was he, a spy?"

"No, but he appears to have had contact with a known drug dealer, so maybe he was dealing too?"

"Didn't you say he had no money? What kind of a dealer has no money?"

"A not very good one, or he was hiding it." My mind drifted back to the bar and the alcohol Johnny had been drinking. The thought alone made me almost gag. If he was only pretending to have no money, then that was Brando-level method acting.

"Maybe it's more simple than that," said Lizzy. "Maybe he deleted it."

I pondered that. He was drunk, had just been in a fight, and had gone home and collapsed in his garage. If he knew that he had killed Ricky the Fudge, would he have had the presence of mind to delete the call from his phone? To do that and leave the brass knuckles right next to his cot?

"It doesn't matter anyway," said Lizzy. "Even if he deleted the call from his phone, there would still be a record of it with the cell phone provider."

"You're right. It would be on his bill."

"If he gets a bill. Some people go paperless and pay automatically online. It might even be a prepaid phone, so there is no bill."

"How would we see that online record?"

"If he had an online account, you can just log in. But you would need to get his username and password, and he's in jail."

I nodded. "I need to speak to Tina."

CHAPTER TWENTY-SEVEN

I returned to the Cabrini house. Tina was dressed in a shirt with a logo for a chain pharmacy.

"I don't have long," she said. "Gotta get to work."

"No problem."

She let me in, and I noticed that the room not only looked orderly but also smelled better. I glanced instinctively at the hole in the wall and saw a picture hanging there.

"The landlord will never fix it," she said. "And if he kicks us out, he'll use my deposit to pay for the repairs anyway."

"I know a guy who can fix that."

"I don't have any money, Miami."

"Don't worry about it."

"Don't worry about it?"

"I mean with fixing the wall."

"I got another call."

"From the fund? How much?"

"A thousand. I was going to call back on my break and say yes."

"That's it? Geez, that Priestly's a real philanthropist."

"You got him to double it, so I'm grateful."

"Don't be grateful yet."

"I just want this done."

"I know, Tina, but you also need to start preparing for a life where Johnny doesn't bring in any money."

She led me into the kitchen and leaned against the sink. "I've been living that life for years."

"But this time he won't be around at all."

"You're saying he's guilty? That he killed this person?"

"I'm saying the evidence suggests he'll be found guilty of something. He may even end up pleading guilty in return for a reduced sentence."

"Why would he do that? Aren't you innocent until proven guilty?"

"Yes, unless you confess or enter a guilty plea. It might ensure that he does his time in a facility that can take care of his mental health needs."

"You mean the nut house."

"I mean a secure hospital. He's increasingly a danger to himself and others, you included. You know that. There are places where he can serve time without it being a regular jail, where he'd just go downhill."

"So how do we get him in this place?"

"We have to show that he is of diminished capacity, that he already had these health issues. We get testimony from Dr. Abe, for instance. We show that the death was accidental."

"Of course it was accidental."

"That's perhaps not what the prosecution will present."

"Why? How?"

"They have a police record of a domestic-disturbance complaint from you against Johnny."

"That was nothing."

"It's an official record that the prosecution will say shows a pattern of behavior."

"It was just the mood swings. Johnny left to cool off, and the deputy asked should it happened again if I had somewhere to go. I told him my daughter's place. That's why last time I didn't call anyone. We just left and went to Sofia's."

"Well, it's evidence that can paint a certain picture, so we have to paint a different one. I found out where Johnny was that night: at a bar called The Copper Kettle. Do you know it?"

"No."

"It's between here and the club. Lake Worth Corridor. Anyway, the bartender says he saw Johnny take a call that agitated him, and he left, presumably to the club. But there's no record of such a call on Johnny's phone log."

"Maybe the man at the bar was wrong."

"It's possible but unlikely. He had a good memory of it."

"Was it this man, Ricky?"

"Maybe. That's what I'm trying to find out. Do you guys have an online account for your phones?"

"No."

"Do you get a bill or are they prepaid?"

"Prepaid. From the drugstore where I work."

"Are they on the same account?"

"They don't work like that. Each phone is separate. Johnny had his phone for a few years first because he got calls about work. I didn't need one because I was at home, but I got one when I started working."

"How do you refill the credit?"

"I buy it at work. Five bucks a time. We just keep the minimum on there in case of emergency."

"I understand. So has Johnny ever mentioned this guy Richard Whitecross?"

"Who?"

"Ricky the Fudge. That's his nickname."

"No."

"Something got Johnny all worked up about this guy. There was a rumor going around that he was dealing drugs at the high school."

"Our girls' school?"

"Yes."

Tina sighed. "Johnny maybe mentioned something about that. A drug dealer was hanging around the school and something needed to be done."

"Something like what?"

"He didn't say, but I thought he meant like call the police."

"What about the girls? Have they ever mentioned anything?"

"They don't do drugs. They're good girls."

"I don't doubt it, but they don't have to be using to hear things. In schools the walls have ears."

"No, they never said anything about it. Listen, I have to get to work."

"Of course. I'll walk you out."

She collected her bag and keys, and we walked across the grass to the driveway. Before she unlocked the car, she paused.

"Is Johnny going away for the rest of his life?"

"I don't know, Tina. I really don't. But it would seem he's going away for a long time. Why?"

"That thousand. I really need it, Miami. My girls are losing their father, and I can't let them lose their home as well. I got a letter from the landlord saying he's starting eviction proceedings. The fund guy said I could have the thousand by the end of the week. All I need to do is say yes and he'll send me the papers. I told the landlord, and he said he wasn't stopping the process, but he would if I gave him the thousand on Friday."

"Okay, Tina. Leave it with me. I'll go and collect the papers personally."

CHAPTER TWENTY-EIGHT

The offices of Fishook Financial were in an upscale suite on Royal Palm Way in Palm Beach. The building's tenants list read like the most likely to create a Ponzi scheme. Import–export, accounting, finance, hedge funds. Businesses most of us rarely had cause to use but that were of vital importance to the well-heeled of the island.

The vacuous marble glistened in the lobby, and my shoes squeaked as I crossed to the elevator. I preferred to take the stairs as a rule but they were locked from the outside, so I did it the old-fashioned way and got the elevator.

I found the office I wanted and pulled hard to open the door but it didn't budge. Then there was an electronic buzz, so I pulled again, and voilà. I didn't see the point of the lock if they were going to buzz me in sight unseen anyway.

"I'm here to see Fishook," I said to the receptionist. Lizzy had mentioned Fishook's first name, but I couldn't remember it. *Moron* was all that came to mind, and that really didn't feel right, although with what people named their kids these days, it was a possibility.

"You are?" asked a blond-haired woman with an eighties do. It seemed my childhood was repeating on me like a bad burrito.

"Jones."

She used her headset to announce my arrival—no one picked up a phone anymore—then stood up.

"Follow me."

We walked about twenty paces. She knocked on the door, and someone said, "Come."

The woman opened the door and said, "Mr. Jones."

I stepped around her and into the office. It wasn't anything special. Room for a decent-size desk but no meeting table or sofa. Ron would have hated it. My office across the bridge was bigger, and I probably paid a quarter of what this guy coughed up in rent. Such was the glamor of a Palm Beach address.

"Nolan Fishook," he said from behind his desk. As we shook hands, I repeated in my head *Nolan, Nolan, Nolan*. I feared it wasn't going to stick. *Moron* was going to be hard to dislodge.

"Miami Jones."

He gestured for me to sit.

"So, you are here on behalf of Mr. and Mrs. Cabrini."

"I am. They have authorized me to accept an offer of five thousand dollars."

Fishook looked like he was about to choke. "Umm, sorry. I believe the figure discussed with Mrs. Cabrini was one thousand."

"No, that was the lowball, embarrassing offer you put to her. Not really a discussion."

"It's too much. You misunderstand the nature of the fund."

"To help boxers with medical issues post-career. That's Johnny Cabrini."

"That's debatable," said Fishook, in a voice that had suddenly gotten an edge to it. "Our doctor has confirmed that Mr. Cabrini does not fit our criteria, and I also believe he is now in prison, so I'm not sure the fund can help a felon."

"He's in jail. He won't be in prison unless convicted."

"Nevertheless."

"Nevertheless? Okay, let's look at what you have. A series of blanket denials from a doctor who has no qualifications in neurology. We, on the other hand, have testimony from a university researcher who is not only a world expert on the effects of combat sports on the human brain but is also a neurological surgeon. Yeah, that's a brain surgeon. He says Mr. Cabrini's issues are a direct and demonstrable result of a career as a GBC boxer. His expert opinion is that Mr. Cabrini not only qualifies, but he is the poster boy for who the fund is meant to support. I also have a well-known litigator on call who is willing to work pro bono to take this case to court. It's going to cost you tens, maybe hundreds of thousands of dollars in lawyer fees alone."

I sat back and tried to keep my face from breaking out in the smuggest of grins. I didn't have a lawyer on call, but I wasn't in court and I wasn't on the record.

He straightened his tie, and his shoulders lifted with a big sigh. "The agreement is a no-fault, no-return contract with a nondisclosure addendum. The claimant and his wife are both forbidden to discuss the nature of the agreement with anyone. *Anyone.*"

"I'm sure you have a boilerplate ready to go," I said. "Why don't you fill it in and sign it? I'll take it to my client, and this will all go away."

Fishook picked up his desk phone and asked someone to amend the GBC fund agreement in the name of Johnny and Tina Cabrini for the amount of five thousand dollars. Then he listened for a moment.

"Yes, Delia, I said five *thousand.*" He hung up and straightened his already straight tie. "What's your cut?" he asked me. "Thirty percent?"

"Nothing."

"What?"

"It's a favor for a friend."

"A favor?"

"Yeah, it's where you do something for someone with no expectation of anything in return."

"Yes, I do favors all the time."

"No you don't. Quid pro quo is not a favor. Issuing a marker to be cashed in later is not a favor. You expect something in return, even if it's down the line. I don't. The Cabrinis don't owe me a damn thing. That's a favor."

"Those kinds of favors don't buy caviar."

"Got that right. But you do end up with good people to share a beer with later. I'll take that over eating caviar with people who'll backstab me when my usefulness runs out."

"Is that what you think?"

"Actually, no. I take it back. I wouldn't eat caviar, period. Salty fish eggs? Seriously? I'd rather have one of Mick's grouper sandwiches."

"Who's Mick?"

"The architect of your demise."

He didn't seem to know what to do with that information. I sat back and waited, not taking my eyes off him. Fishook tried looking at his computer screen and was getting fidgety. Then Delia returned with the documents. Fishook looked them over. He handed them to me to check the names and the amount, then I gave them back.

"What?" he said.

"You need to sign."

"I sign when I get them back."

"You sign now to show Mrs. Cabrini you're serious."

"And how do I know she's serious?"

"Because I'm wasting my afternoon in your office rather than enjoying a drink with a bunch of fine people who would rather eat one fish than ten thousand eggs."

He groaned but pulled a pen from his breast pocket and signed the document. He shoved it toward me, and I took it with a smile. I stood and opened the door before turning to him.

"I'll be back."

CHAPTER TWENTY-NINE

I enjoyed my evening with people who didn't eat caviar. Mick served us falafel wraps, which I was dismayed to find out contained no fish or meat. Danielle assured me they would be fantastic. I acquiesced, but they turned out to be a revelation. Who knew garbanzo beans were so versatile?

We stayed for a couple beers, but there was a cloud hanging over Longboard Kelly's. I had a text message to meet Elissa Croix the following morning for a visit with Johnny Cabrini.

After a fitful sleep, I arrived early at the detention complex on Gun Club Road. I saw families with little children lining up outside like they were going to the movies, and I thought of Johnny's girls and whether they had been to visit.

Being legal representatives, we were expedited through the metal detectors and X-ray machines. I carried no bag or briefcase, nothing more than a manila envelope, but that somehow made me suspicious, so I was patted down. Elissa and I were then led to a concrete room that was painted in a color Lizzy would have called *beige sadness*.

About five minutes later, Johnny Cabrini was let in by a guard from another door. He didn't look happy to see us. *Indifferent* was the word that stuck in my mind. He sat at the table opposite us. The guard stepped outside but kept watch through the glass.

"How are you, Mr. Cabrini?" asked Elissa.

"Doing okay."

"Are they treating you well?"

"I guess."

"Do you have any medication, Mr. Cabrini?"

"Nup."

"I have requested access to the medication prescribed by Dr. Abe. I will ask about it again."

"Okay."

"We are preparing for what is called your final hearing, although it's not really final. At this hearing, the judge will determine whether you are eligible for bail and will set a date for your arraignment. You will not enter a plea at that time. Do you understand?"

"Sure."

"You know Mr. Jones?"

"Yeah. You're getting money for Tina and the girls."

Elissa looked at me.

"That's right," I said. "But I'm also helping to look into your case here. Can I ask you some questions, Johnny?"

"Nothing better to do."

"How much do you remember about the night in question, at the club?"

"Nothing."

"Nothing at all?"

"Nup."

"You were at The Copper Kettle that night."

He nodded without conviction. "Think so."

"The barman, Dean, he remembers you."

"Dean. Good guy."

"Yes, he is. He said you got a phone call just before you left the bar. Who called you?"

"I don't remember."

"Try, Johnny. It might be important."

"I said I don't remember, damn it!"

Elissa tapped her hand on my leg under the table.

"Okay, Johnny," I said. "No problem."

"Sorry," he said. "I'm sorry."

"It's okay."

"I don't remember. I was drinking."

"Don't worry. Do you know what you're charged with here?"

"I killed a guy."

"Do you know who?"

"I don't remember."

"Do you know a guy called Ricky the Fudge?"

"Ricky the Fudge. Yeah, I know him. He hangs around."

"It was him."

Johnny looked me in the eye for the first time. "I killed Ricky the Fudge?"

"That's what they're saying."

"I don't think the world will miss him."

"Maybe not. Do you remember where he sold?"

"Everywhere around town. He hung out at the gym, sometimes the club, but Maxine didn't like him being there."

"Did you ever buy from him?"

"I don't do drugs."

"What about pain meds? Opioids?"

"Nup. Not from Ricky."

"What about the school? Did you ever hear about him selling drugs at the high school?"

"Nup. I don't remember hearing that."

"Okay. I just need some personal details to help access the records that Tina's going to need. Do you mind if I ask?"

"For Teens? Go on."

I asked him the questions that Lizzy had written down for me: middle name, first street he lived on, first pet, that sort of thing. It seemed his long-term memory was better than his short-term.

"Do you need a social security number?" Elissa asked.

"We have it on the fund documents. I think we're set."

"Why do you need to know my mom's maiden name?"

"We're just trying to get the best possible outcome for you."

He let out a sound that was half cough, half laugh. "There's no good outcome for me. You don't think I know that? The evidence you say they got puts me in the slammer forever."

"We're working on that," said Elissa. "The likely charges come with a long-term sentence, but there is a lot of difference between a first-degree murder conviction and a guilty plea with diminished capacity. We're trying to have you serve time in a facility that will help with the issues you're having."

"It doesn't matter," said Johnny. "I'm either in some psych ward drugged up to my eyeballs so I don't hurt nobody, or they toss me into the general population with all this anger that's only getting worse—eventually I'm gonna poke the wrong bear and that will be that."

"We're trying to get you treatment, Johnny," she said. "Just hold on."

He blinked hard like he wasn't listening anymore, then looked me in the eye again. "You gotta help Tina and the girls. That's all that matters."

"Johnny, I have an agreement with me. The fund has offered five thousand dollars."

"Five grand? So I was worth something after all. How does she get it?"

"You sign this and I'll collect a check and get it to Tina."

"Give it to me, then."

I removed the document from the envelope and showed Johnny where to sign. Elissa handed him a pen. He scribbled his signature and gave her back the pen. For a moment he stared at the page, maybe at the amount. A smile appeared in the corner of his mouth as if he felt he had finally done something good for his family. Perhaps he thought it was a king's ransom. It would certainly keep Tina afloat for a while. But I couldn't help think of Fishook and his caviar and how he could pay that much for a room with a view at The Breakers for a single night.

I took the contract and slipped it back into the envelope as Elissa put her notes away. We all stood. As she made to get the attention of the guard, I remembered I had one more question.

"Johnny, do you own brass knuckles?"

"Are you kidding? They're illegal, and on a boxer they're considered a deadly weapon." The guard opened the door and moved toward us, and Johnny put his hands behind his back for the cuffs. "Besides, Stone always taught us to handle things like real men, with gloves on. Keep the fights in the ring. That's the rule."

As the guard walked him out, I let out a breath I didn't realize I had been holding in.

"You okay?" Elissa asked.

"I don't know how you do it."

"Because if I don't, no one will. And I don't want to live in that world."

She led me toward the exit. I couldn't wait to feel the sunshine on my skin.

CHAPTER THIRTY

Out in the parking lot, Elissa and I split off just as my phone rang.

"Miami Jones," I said.

"Jones, this is Barry Schiff, public defender's office."

"You just missed Elissa."

"It's you I was after. When you guys are done, can you drop by the office?"

"On my way. Will you tell Elissa?"

"She has court."

"All right then, see you in twenty."

I parked near my office and walked over again. The extra miles were earning me kudos, but I feared Danielle would not give credit for work she couldn't verify. I repeated the process at security: got my visitor's tag and gave another smile to the receptionist that was not reciprocated.

Barry led me into the same coffeepot-scented meeting room.

"So the police found Richard Whitecross's car."

"I didn't know it was missing."

"It wasn't at the scene. It looks like he parked a couple blocks away from the club and walked."

"What sort of car?"

Barry looked at his documents. "Honda Civic. What difference does that make?"

"Explains why he walked over. No drug dealer worth his salt is going to roll up in a Civic."

"He left his phone in the car. The PBSO think so he couldn't be traced back to the club."

"But he was."

"Perhaps he didn't intend to die there."

"I like the way you think, Barry. So what does all this mean?"

"We have a call log from Mr. Whitecross's phone."

"Aah. And?"

"Calls all night long, but none to or from Mr. Cabrini's phone."

"Damn. Could he have deleted it from his call log?"

"It's possible, but why delete that one and not the others?"

"Good point. But is there a way to check?"

"The call logs from the provider can be subpoenaed."

"Will the prosecution do that?"

"I doubt it. I'm not sure it suits their case to keep digging. They know they were both there, and they'll hypothesize as to why in front of a jury. They don't need it."

"It makes no sense. If they didn't call each other, how did they both come to be there?"

"Unless someone else called them."

"I'll say it again, Barry: I like the way you think. Can you cross-reference the calls on both logs and see what they have in common."

"It'll take a long time for the whole history."

"Don't care about the whole history. Let's start with that night."

Barry put two sheets side by side on the table and ran his finger down one of them. He was done in a minute.

"I was wrong," he said. "It didn't take long. Mr. Cabrini didn't make many calls or get many, and Mr. Whitecross made a lot of calls but only to two numbers."

"Johnny's wife said they only used the phones in emergencies, to save the credits."

"Well, that makes my life easy. There's nothing in common here."

"Not one number?"

"Nope."

I sat back to think. We were getting nowhere. Then I had a thought.

"Maybe the number in common is the missing number from Johnny's phone."

"So?"

"So that would be a call just before midnight. Did Ricky get a call then?"

Barry checked the papers. "Yes, yes he did."

"From who?"

"It doesn't have a listing here, just a number. I'd have to look it up in the reverse database."

"There's a quicker way. Tell me the number."

I tapped the digits into my phone as he recited them, then hit the little green phone icon and waited to learn something.

"Pugilists' Club," said Maxine Mitchell.

"Maxine," I replied, my mind spinning in all directions. "It's Miami Jones, from the other night."

"I remember you, Miami. How's Johnny, do you know?"

"I just saw him. He's doing as well as can be expected under the circumstances. Maxine, I wanted to ask you about the night Ricky the Fudge was killed."

"Horrible business. Not a nice boy, but still."

"Yeah, I know. But on the video from the store next door, you appear closing up and leaving the club at about eleven thirty p.m. Is that about right?"

"Eleven twenty I would say. We close at eleven thirty, and I've usually cleaned and done the register, so it takes about ten to fifteen minutes to finish and lock up. I remember that night was quiet—no one was there at that time, and I'm not pouring anything for a walk-in at that hour, so I closed up about ten minutes early."

"Okay, so you locked up."

"That's right. Why, pet?"

"Just trying to get a timeline. You're saying no one was there when you left?"

"Nobody."

"And would anyone have come later? A cleaner or anyone?"

"No. I do a wipe-down before I leave, and the cleaner comes in the morning. She found the body, remember? Poor thing."

"Yeah, that's right."

"What's up?"

"Nothing. Just putting all the pieces together. We're trying to mount some kind of defense for Johnny."

"It's a shame what's happened to him, Miami. A real shame. If there's anything I can do."

"Thanks Maxine. I'll let you know."

I ended the call and looked at Barry. "That was the owner of the club. Whoever called Ricky was inside the club when it happened. After the owner had locked up and gone."

"This person was hiding in there?"

"Maybe, but I gotta tell ya, there's not a lot of hidey-holes in there."

"And you're sure it wasn't her?"

"She's on the video, leaving exactly when she said she did."

"So who was inside the club?" Barry asked.

"That, Barry, is one question."

"What's another question?"

"Did the mystery person in the club call Johnny as well?"

"We'll have to subpoena those records."

"I have another plan, Barry, my man. I've gotta get to my office."

CHAPTER THIRTY-ONE

I burst into the front office like a rhino.

"Miami!" screamed Lizzy. "You scared the daylights out of me."

"Every office I go to these days has to buzz people in. You think we need that?"

"Only to stop you."

"Okay. Are you busy?"

"I don't get paid to lay on the sofa."

"Can you help me with something? I need to get into Johnny's phone records."

I strode into my office and turned my laptop on, then I pulled out the paper on which I had written the answers to Johnny's personal questions.

"Don't do it online," she said. "There might be authorization that needs to be sent to the phone to set up an account."

"So how?"

"The old-fashioned way."

The old-fashioned way involved me waiting on hold for thirty minutes. The Muzak was worse than the silence, but eventually someone answered, and Lizzy coached me through what to say.

After giving their rote spiel, the customer service rep asked who they were talking with.

"Johnny Cabrini."

"Thank you, Mr. Cabrini. How may I help you today?"

"I've left my phone at someone's house."

"That's a shame."

"It is. I went to a party, you know, and I forgot it."

"I see."

"So I know who probably has it—it's a friend of a friend—and I could call him to ask him to bring it with him so I can get it. But the thing is, his number is *in* the phone and I don't know it by heart."

"Do you have online data backup on your plan?"

"No." I was pretty sure Johnny was not paying for any bells and whistles. "But the thing is, I remember the person called me to invite me to the party, so his number will be in my call log."

"I see, but that is also on your phone."

"Right, except you guys must have a record?"

"Yes, we probably do. I'm going to have to ask you some verification questions."

"Of course. Ask away."

"The phone number?"

I recited Johnny's number.

"The last four of your social?"

I gave the last four digits of Johnny's social security number.

"For security purposes, what was the first street you lived on?"

I told the agent what Johnny had told me.

"Great. And finally, what plan are you on?"

"Prepaid."

"Yes, and how many credits were on your last refill?"

I looked at Lizzy, who made a face like this question was above her pay grade. Then I remembered something Tina had told me.

"Five dollars," I said. "We keep the minimum on there for emergencies."

"Yes, that is what I see. Now let's check your records. When was the call in question?"

"Thursday night, just before midnight."

"Just before midnight . . . Okay, there's only one number here. Do you have a pen?"

"I do."

I didn't, but Lizzy did, so she wrote down the number. I thanked the rep, and she invited me to stay on the line for a brief survey, asking me to give her five stars if she was helpful, so I did just that.

By the time I was done with the survey, Lizzy was back at her desk looking up the number. I walked over, and she frowned.

"What?" I asked.

"A prepaid cell."

"So no name?"

"No. Just your garden-variety drugstore cell phone. Could this Ricky guy have had two phones?"

"Possible but unlikely. He's got a lot of calls on his log, so why have a second phone? But there is a way to find out."

"If you call it, they'll know it's you. Caller ID."

"Don't care. Do it."

Lizzy placed the call, then hit the button on her desk phone to put it on speaker.

"The voicemail box for this user has not been set up."

"Well, we know one thing: it wasn't from the club. So that's two mystery callers."

"It's a Palm Beach area code, if that helps."

"Only if we door-knock a million people—hang on." I took out my phone and called Barry Schiff.

"Barry, I've got the missing number from Johnny's call log."

"How did you get that?"

"If you want to enjoy your hotdog, don't ask how the sausage gets made, Barry."

"Okay. Give it to me."

I gave him the number and waited.

"No dice. That's not Whitecross's number, and it's not in his call log."

"Damn, I thought that might be something."

"We'll keep at it."

"Thanks, Barry." I hung up and shrugged at Lizzy.

"Sorry," she said.

"Not your fault. It was a damned good idea. I didn't think a good Christian like you would commit fraud like that."

"I didn't. You did."

"Good point. Identity fraud is easier than I thought."

"You should change the password on your bank account."

"*Danielle* isn't a good password?"

"Save me. Maybe this will cheer you up."

"Go on."

"I know you already got the money for Tina."

"Not yet. Just signed the docs."

"Well, I did some more digging on this fund and Mr. Fishook. I searched the usual databases, and then I trawled social media platforms and so on."

"Okay."

"I found an old post from a woman who was a former employer of Fishook Financial."

"Tell me more."

"There was nothing on her public profiles per se, but I used her username to link her to accounts on several anonymous bulletin boards."

"You're like a one-woman online cookie."

"I'm just glad you know what a cookie is. Anyway, on these forums, she was talking positively about her new job, how happy she was to be working somewhere that had its stakeholders' best interests at heart."

"And?"

"And she compared it to her old job, where they routinely denied every claim. There was then a chain of comments about companies that did this. She mentioned in a comment that she worked for an injury fund and that she had documents that showed they always denied claims and fudged the numbers to line the pockets of the people behind it."

"Fraud. You kind of already established that, didn't you?"

"I established it, but I couldn't prove it. This person is claiming she has documents to prove it. She kept records in case they fired her, but in the end, she left because the place made her sick."

"You said *she*. You know who this person is?"

"I know who she is, I know where she works, and I even know where she lives."

"You got all this info online?"

"Yes."

"That's a little scary."

"Isn't it though? Imagine what you could do with millions of dollars in technology and a lack of scruples."

"Okay, so what do we do with this information?"

"I don't know," she said. "Something though. It's not your job to take these guys down, but we can't do nothing knowing what we know, can we?"

"No, Lizzy, we can't. Sick people are being cheated. I mean, no one should get cheated, but when you're sick and down and have nowhere else to go, that's too much."

"I agree. So what do we do?"

"Well, we tread carefully. If proving anything depends on this woman, we need to know if she has something useful and that she's prepared to help before we out her as a whistleblower. Because, Lizzy, the whistleblower rarely gets a medal."

CHAPTER THIRTY-TWO

Thinking about prepaid numbers made me think of Ricky the Fudge and all his calls to just a few numbers. I wanted to know if Ricky really was selling drugs at the school and if that could be used as a motive against Johnny. But more than that, the number of loose ends in this whole business was starting to get in my craw.

I had seen Ricky the Fudge at the gym and the club. If I plotted that on a map, the gym was on Forest Hill Road at the top of a square, and the club was near the bottom of the square on 10th Avenue. The right side of the square was the freeway, and the left was North Military Trail.

It was a territory like those of the door knockers of old. Ricky was in the people business, like an old-time encyclopedia salesman. And like such a business, his wasn't some online lark nobody understood; it was an intentional enterprise done by hitting the pavement and being where the customers were. And if there was one rule of sales, it was that the territory must be worked. Or perhaps the sales must go on. Fact was, I had never worked in sales, so I had no idea what the number one rule was, but I was confident that a drug business—low level or otherwise—was not going to leave a territory unstaffed.

I drifted down past the club and saw no one loitering with intent the way Ricky the Fudge had. It was probably too early in the evening for that crowd, so I drove up toward the gym. I didn't think parking in front of the strip mall was smart, so I stopped a block away and walked over.

The noise coming from the gym was the sound of hard luck and trouble. I glanced in through the open door to see the place packed with athletes stretching and hitting heavy bags. Few words were being spoken against the throb of large fans trying to drive expelled air out the door.

As I stood at the entrance, I noticed the familiar repose of a body leaning against a wall. I did a double take before convincing myself that it wasn't Ricky the Fudge. This kid couldn't have been more than twenty, but he had the same wispy frame as Ricky. He was biting his fingernails in lieu of a match, and he looked more like an adolescent with acne than a rat man.

I took a single step toward him when I heard someone yell, "Hey, you!" I shot around to see Allan Samson quickly coming at me from the parking lot. His gait was off, as if he had a bad hip—or, as I recalled, a bad knee.

For a moment I stiffened until I realized he wasn't making a beeline for me. His target was fingernail boy. The kid bounced from the wall and stood erect without the slack arrogance of his predecessor. The new hire always took time to learn the customs of the workplace.

"You, get out of here! You hear me? You wanna piece of me?" Samson was getting closer to the kid, who must have decided that this role wasn't in the employee manual, so he took off. He did the stiff-legged walk of a guy trying to look like he wasn't running.

Samson just stepped onto the sidewalk and watched the dealer escape, then he turned toward the gym and saw me.

He didn't speak until he got right in my hemisphere. "I know you."

"I get that a lot."

"You're Mick's pal."

"That, not so much."

"You looking for a workout?" He jutted his chin toward the gym.

"I try to avoid getting hit in the head as much as possible."

"How's that going for you?"

"Still happens more than I would like."

"You come in, you might learn something."

"I don't doubt it."

"Or you can take it out on a heavy bag. They don't usually hit back."

"Tempting."

"Spend an hour a few times a week with me and you'll never get that beer belly."

I took that as a suggestion that I didn't have one now, which was a win in my book.

"Like I say, tempting."

"Well, I'm not gonna make you do it. You know where the door is."

"You know Johnny's in jail."

"Course I know. We all know."

"Just thought you might be concerned."

"I grew up with Johnny. He's like a brother. But I can't do nothing to fix what he's got."

"It didn't happen to you."

"I didn't go as long as Johnny. He went too long."

"And now his brain is turning on him."

"Sad but true."

"What about his friends?"

"What are you getting at, pal?"

"You banned Johnny from the gym, probably the only place he ever felt at home."

"I didn't ban him. I told him to take a break. I can't have guys coming here starting fights. It's rule number one."

"All fights in the ring."

"Yeah, that's right."

"Stone's rule."

"It certainly was. Now it's mine."

"But you broke it."

"What?"

"I heard you got into a bar fight and busted up your knee while you were in rehab. That's what ended your career."

"You know plenty."

"I do."

"Then know this. I did break the rule, and exactly what Stone said would happen did happen. I messed up my chance of getting another shot. And Stone banned me from the gym for six months after. Then he came to my house and brought me back. Said I learned my lesson. And he was right. I did. Now it's *my* number one rule. So when Johnny came here in a bad place and wanted to take on anyone in the parking lot, I told him to clear off. I would have brought him back in, eventually. Still will, if I get the chance."

"I don't like those chances."

"Is Tina okay?"

"She's doing it hard, but she seems tough."

"She is. She'll get through."

Samson saw me glance down the sidewalk, but fingernail boy was gone.

"You know that guy?" he asked.

"I think he's Ricky the Fudge's replacement."

"I think so too."

"I'm going to have a word with him," I said.

"Why? This ain't your hood."

"No, but it's Tina's. It's the girls'. Anyway, I'll see you around."

"Come by for a workout. I promise no one will mark you up."

"Maybe I will."

As he went inside, I jogged up to the road to see if I could spot the new salesman but no luck. I wandered along the top of my theo-retical territory square and then hit the corner and turned down the side along North Military Trail. I couldn't imagine the job was to just wander the perimeter. There were probably way-stops where Ricky had loitered and where the new guy would too. Maybe he had a map like the one they give when you tour the homes of the stars in Hollywood. Maybe there was an app.

I was considering going back for my car to drive a zigzag through the area, when the new guy walked out of a KFC, licking his fingers as he headed toward the middle of the square. I gave him some space and followed.

Tailing someone alone is hard. A single tail is easy to spot. The late, great Lenny Cox had shown me that. But he had also taught me that most quarries were oblivious. This kid was wandering around whistling Dixie, so I could have gone shoulder to shoulder and he wouldn't have noticed.

He wandered into a subdivision of low-slung houses surrounded by miles of hurricane wire fencing. The guy walked right up to a house with two gleaming pickups in the driveway and went inside. I settled against a tree to wait. Maybe he needed the bathroom and didn't like fast-food restaurant toilets, or maybe he needed a pep talk from the sales manager.

Fifteen minutes later, he came out with a bit of pep in his step, so I wondered if he had sampled a bit of the company product while he was inside. I didn't know much about the drug business, but I suspected if they had a rule number one, it was *don't sample the merchandise*.

The kid wandered south, toward the bottom of my territory map and the Pugilists' Club. As he got to 10th Avenue, I quickened my pace and closed in on him. I appeared at his side as he neared the strip where the club was. He nearly jumped out of his skin, and I realized he was wearing earphones. Lenny would have loved this clown.

"What the hell you doing, Hoss?" he said.

"What did you call me?"

"Hoss."

"What are you, a *Bonanza* fan?"

"What?"

"Forget it. You the new guy?"

"Maybe. Who are you?"

"I'm a trainer for a major-league sports franchise."

"You are?"

"Sure. I need painkillers. Lots of them."

"Lots?"

"Lots."

"Don't you got a doctor?"

"Doctor doesn't give enough. I've got boys in pain, real pain. You feel me, *Hoss*?"

His head was bouncing up and down like a toddler needing the bathroom. He could see a bulk order materializing from the suburban darkness.

"Wait, if you was for real, you wouldn't say you was from a major sports franchise."

"I didn't tell you a team, did I?"

"No."

"No, right. So I want the same deal as the last guy."

"The last guy?"

"The one you replaced."

"Oh, Ricky."

"That's him. You're taking his patch, right?"

"Yeah, I'm acquiring his territory."

"Are you doing the school too?"

"What school?"

"The school on the other side of Military Trail."

"No, man. My territory is east of Military." He said it like he was an Avon rep.

"So no school? I thought Ricky did the school."

"Did you know Ricky, Hoss? He didn't do no school."

"Are you sure? He might have been doing it on his own time. Expanding his territory."

"You don't get it, Hoss. You seen Ricky?"

"Of course."

"He's got that face."

"Kind of devious-looking."

"Yeah, you can say that. A face like that hanging around a school wouldn't last one afternoon."

"Maybe I'm wrong."

"You wrong all right. When Scotty deals in a school, he don't get some creepy-looking dude. He hires a student, you know?"

"Makes sense."

"Now, what you want?"

"You got opioids?"

"We got what you want."

"Five hundred."

"Five hundred. Whoa. I don't carry that kind of merch."

"How many you got?"

He pulled a bag from his pocket and counted its contents. "Seven."

"That won't do. Tomorrow night, can you set me up?"

"Think so."

"Don't let me down, uh . . . what do I call you?" I asked.

"Gary—um, no, George."

"George?"

"Yeah."

"You curious, George?"

"What? I guess."

"Good. Now be a good little monkey and meet me tomorrow at the back of the gym. You got me? I'm counting on you."

"Wait. How do I know you're not a cop?"

"Do I look like a cop?"

"Yeah."

"How?"

"You're old."

I was loving this kid. "I'm not a cop, George. I promise."

"I don't know."

"If I were a cop, I couldn't lie about that, could I?"

"No. You got a wire?"

"You want me to take my shirt off, George? It's cold out here."

"Yeah, take off your shirt."

I unbuttoned my shirt and showed the drug-dealer-on-training-wheels my chest. I was going to need a *Silkwood*-level shower when I got home.

"Scotty's gonna think you're a cop."

"Ask Scotty, does a cop make a bunch of small buys before setting you up?"

"Yeah."

"I don't care about that. I want what I want, and if you can't deliver I'll find another street to walk. Okay?"

"All right, Hoss. Nine tomorrow night."

I walked away sure that I was dealing with an amateur-hour operation. Probably some bored middle-class kids who thought they were in the movies. Real dealers didn't put people that stupid on the street.

But I was convinced of one thing: Ricky the Fudge was not dealing at the school. If Johnny had heard that rumor, it was wrong. And I now had all kinds of doubts about him hearing it at all. Which only served to confuse me more.

I wandered back to my car and drove toward home. As I cruised up the quiet freeway, I called Detective Kelty.

"Jones, I'm watching *Wheel of Fortune*."

"Sorry, Detective. Just wanted to let you know I just set up a drug buy for five hundred opioid pills."

"You ill, Jones?"

"No. I thought you might have a colleague who works that sort of thing."

"Of course I do."

"Jot down the where and when."

"Okay, shoot."

I gave him the buy at the gym and the address of the house. "Nine o'clock. I won't be there, but tell your guy to tell George that Hoss sent him."

"Hoss?"

"Yeah, just go with it."

"I'll pass it on. He might want to call you."

"You got my number. Enjoy the Wheel."

By the time I finished the call, my car was practically on autopilot as it homed in on Blue Heron Boulevard and the subdued lights of Singer Island.

CHAPTER THIRTY-THREE

THE WHISTLEBLOWER'S NAME WAS MARJORIE CARTWRIGHT. SHE NOW worked in Miami for a billionaire's foundation, an organization designed to help with global problems, like water quality and food scarcity and diseases like malaria. When I called her and explained what had happened and what Lizzy had discovered about the fighters' fund, she was not eager to get involved. I saw her point. Like I had told Lizzy, the whistleblower rarely got a medal. Big government and big corporations that did things the wrong way never wanted to be exposed and often undertook smear campaigns against the whistleblower. And once that can was opened, the person's life was rarely the same.

I resolved to not push Marjorie into anything she didn't want to do. I didn't need to take down the fund or stop Fishook and Priestly from doing what to me looked like money laundering. My job was to get Tina Cabrini and her family some cash. That was it. The rest was outside my mandate.

But I couldn't live with that. After Marjorie declined to meet, the whole thing started to eat at me. I was a big believer in what the United States offered to people who wanted to work hard and succeed. I had no problem at all with an immigrant who arrived with a nickel in their pocket and holes in their shoes becoming a millionaire and their kids becoming billionaires, even though those millions would probably elude me. I worked hard, too, but there was always an element of timing and luck and working hard on the right thing. If someone cracked that code and became successful, then I applauded them.

Unless they cheated. People who got good at that game developed a taste for winning, and some of them decided they were then above the rules, or they became powerful enough to rewrite the rules in their favor. Those people kept me up at night.

Then Marjorie Cartwright called back and said she wanted to meet. I had to be at Johnny Cabrini's bail hearing later that day, so she suggested we connect in the morning, about halfway between West Palm and Miami at the Isle Casino at the Pompano Park racetrack.

The slot machines were flashing and bleeping at a smattering of bored patrons as I walked through the casino midmorning. I found Marjorie sitting in a booth in a restaurant made out to look like a Jewish diner in New York City. She was tapping her fingers on the table with a coffee cup in front of her.

"Marjorie?"

"Miami," she said with a muted smile.

I ordered a coffee, and we talked about traffic until it came. I took a sip and nearly burned my lip.

"I was surprised to hear back from you," I said.

"You weren't going to keep calling?"

"Sorry, no. I figured you had your reasons, and I get that."

"I didn't want to. I still don't."

"So why are you here?"

"People are getting hurt. They're paying money in, and when they get old and need it, they're not getting it back. It's wrong."

"I agree."

"So I talked to my boss."

"Your current boss?"

"Yes. I figure it's going to come out if I go whistleblower on this thing, and it might embarrass the foundation I work for now."

"You like it there?"

"I love it. We're doing important work with good people. But I don't want to hurt that work by doing this. So I talked to Mark."

"Oh, you mean the ultimate boss, your billionaire boss?"

"Yes. He doesn't work with us every day—he's very busy, as I am sure you can appreciate. But yesterday he was in the office, so I decided that if he didn't like it, I wouldn't do it."

"He didn't mind?"

"He said I had an obligation to do it. You spend your whole life looking for a job like this, to work for someone like that. He said my job was solid, that he'd put it in writing, and that he had media resources I could use if they tried to bad-mouth me."

"Nice guy."

"He is. Not everyone cares for him—he's rich, right? Some people don't like how he got there or they're jealous, but I love what the foundation tries to do."

"In that case, we owe him a debt, and you. So what can you tell me?"

"Okay." She took a deep breath. "I worked for Fishook Financial for two years. I have an NDA with them, but Mark says it won't matter with whistleblower laws in place."

"My people tell me that an NDA can't force you to break laws or require your silence when laws are broken."

"That's what I understand. So anyway, I can't speak to the money that was supposed to come in—I didn't have anything to do with the boxing side of it—but the numbers your office shared with me show that only half the money made it into the fund, which doesn't surprise me. If they were skimming off the end, they were probably skimming off the top."

"So they *were* skimming?"

"I'm not sure you can call it that when most of the money disappeared. It was like the fund members were the ones skimming—that's how little got paid out."

"Explain that to me." I sipped my coffee and didn't burn myself.

"So you know that the fund is technically based in the US because of commission rules, right?"

"Yep."

"Well, the boxers who paid into the fund, or at least thought they were, fall into two categories: internal to the US and external. Nationals and foreigners. Or more specifically, those under the watch of the IRS and those not. So the basic plan was that all requests for funds in the US were denied. We had a form letter that went out right away. Didn't even look at the case details."

"Do you have a copy of that letter?"

"I do. If someone contested the denial—and you would be shocked at how few did—we would refer them to our doctor."

"Wrexham."

"You know him."

"I've had the pleasure."

"So he would see them, and after the appointment, we would send another denial."

"Based on his diagnosis?"

"Based on nothing. I never saw a diagnosis. We just got told who had an appointment, and we sent a denial letter out, saying the doctor found no issues covered by the fund."

"Did this worry you?"

"You're wondering how we even let it happen? At first, I didn't know. We were letter stuffers, more or less. It could have been that these people legitimately were not covered. But after a while, I realized that I never sent out a letter of approval. And I never mailed a check, not until someone complained a lot about the diagnosis or asked what the reason for the denial was. Eventually, it felt dirty. That's why I started keeping copies of things."

"When I started making noise, they offered five hundred."

"That's pretty high. But here's the thing: the fund has to report to the IRS, and those reports are public record."

"That's how my colleague found all this out."

"Right, but she only knows the half of it. See, the trust can't show zero disbursements. That wouldn't pass muster with anyone.

So they have to show money going out and record a number of disbursements—a number, but not who received it."

"Right, it was a total I saw."

"Exactly. Now, if the IRS were to call, the trust would need to have records of who got that money, right? But as I said, there are people the IRS can reach and people they can't. So inside the US, the only claims that ever got funded were the loud ones, the ones that complained, and they were very few. There were a lot of hoops to jump through to get to that point. Then the trust would finally cut a check and require an NDA, so they wouldn't spread the news about how to get money out of the so-called fund."

"But you're saying the number of payments was not properly reported to the IRS?"

"Not a fraction. But if the IRS came calling, the trust could show the right number of payments going out because most of those went to boxers outside the US."

"Where the IRS can't tread."

"Not so easily. Laws and treaties are tightening up, but this scam has been running for thirty years."

"So what happens?"

Marjorie tapped her fingers on the table as if she was nervous about crossing a line. "As I say, the majority of the disbursements listed on the IRS documents went to boxers outside of the US. The GBC had plenty—it's pretty big in Mexico and South America. In these countries, a larger number of requests for funds seemed to be approved."

"Seemed?"

"It wasn't done by me or my colleagues. We just got the approval and the amount of payment to update the records. I never saw a check, and I don't know who sent them out."

"Why separate that?"

"Exactly. We were told the office in BVI handled the foreign processing, but that didn't feel right. The money had to come from the US trust, and our mail was as good as the mail in BVI. But one day, a list of recipients and the amounts due ended up on my desk."

"An error?"

"I'd say so. Because I just did what I did. I cut the checks, maybe a dozen of them, and then I mailed them. I even went to the post office myself because I didn't regularly send mail overseas."

"Okay. What was the problem?"

"Not long after, one of the checks came back—return to sender. So I followed up, to make sure the person got their money, right?"

"Of course."

"But the person who was supposed to receive the payment had died."

"Damn. That was only a matter of time."

"It was, but not the way you think. Because the next check came back, and the next. Eight of the twelve, in fact. All returned to sender. And none of the twelve was ever cashed."

"Why?"

"Because all the recipients were dead."

"They all got a payment and died?"

"No. They died and then got a payment."

My brain finally caught up with what Marjorie was telling me. "They were sending disbursements to boxers who were already dead?"

"No. That was an accident. I wasn't supposed to get that sheet. They were listing dead boxers as recipients and then sending the money to their own accounts."

"Can you prove that?"

She handed me a bundle of papers. "There's a list of boxers and the dates they were supposedly sent money. I've checked. All those men were dead before the issue date. I called the first ten or so, and the families knew nothing about any fund or trust sending money. Your office could confirm the rest, if you want."

"Where are these men?"

"Mostly Mexico, some in Brazil, and a handful in Central America."

"Where the IRS can't see."

"Right."

I sat back in the booth and looked at Marjorie. She was an ordinary person with a conservative haircut and a basic blouse and skirt. The pearls around her neck were the only bit of bling about her, and even they were understated.

"I feel terrible about this," she said.

"Why?"

"I should have stopped this years ago. I tell myself I didn't know how, but I didn't even try. I just left and found a better job."

"That's not your fault. That's how these guys work. They disempower you. You feel like there's nothing you can do, that the system is against you, because they are the system. But the thing is, they're not the whole system, just a broken part of it. Good people have the ability to create better systems if they try. The hardest part is believing that we can."

"What will you do with all this?"

"Full disclosure, I am married to an agent of the Florida Department of Law Enforcement. I plan to show it to her and send it where it should go."

"What if they do nothing?"

"That's not an option now. My wife won't let that happen."

"They might force her. They might disempower her, as you say."

"She's funny like that. She's one of those people who gain power from fighting the system. She's been doing it all her life, as have you, I'm sure. And I can be fairly tenacious at times too. But you might be required to testify at some point."

"I'm okay with that. As I said, I'm lucky I've got a good boss."

"A good boss makes all the difference."

I thanked Marjorie for her time and told her I had to get going to see my client in court.

"I hope he gets what he's earned."

"I think he already did. Now it's time for him to get something better."

CHAPTER THIRTY-FOUR

I ARRIVED AT THE DETENTION CENTER FOR JOHNNY'S HEARING A LITTLE late, so I eased quietly in through the door and found that the court was running behind schedule. Elissa Croix was waiting at the back. I offered her a nod, and she mouthed the word "fifteen." As I waited I saw Johnny sitting among the men in blue uniforms that reminded me of hospital scrubs. He didn't acknowledge me.

The deputy called the court to order, and the judge proceeded to run through his docket. It was pretty much all the same thing—applications for bail that had been deferred from the first appearance. The four men before Johnny were all denied.

Johnny moved to the lectern, and the assistant state attorney read from a document. The judge, looking down at a page in front of him, seemed to be following along with his own copy. The state argued that the attack was violent and purposeful and that with Mr. Cabrini's history, he was a danger to both himself and the public.

The judge looked through the document. "I tend to accept your argument. Ms. Croix?"

"Your Honor, the defendant has ties to the area and a family home. He has no previous record of failing to appear."

"I don't think that's the issue, Ms. Croix. The issue is his conduct, should he be released on his own recognizance. There is an open domestic-abuse complaint here."

"There were no charges, Your Honor."

"I can read, Ms. Croix, but what I see concerns me. I am declining bail at this time and ordering a psych review. You may petition the court again at the arraignment."

"Thank you, Your Honor."

"Mr. Cabrini, you will be held in custody until your arraignment, which is on demand. That simply means the date has yet to be set by the court. Do you understand?"

"Yes, Judge."

"And I have ordered the county to have a doctor evaluate you, to make sure you get any treatment you require. Have you been the subject of a psychological evaluation before, Mr. Cabrini?"

"Yes, Judge."

"Okay. Ms. Croix, you have something more to offer?"

"My client has a prescription for medication from his treating physician, which does not appear to have reached him."

"The court will direct the sheriff's office to ensure that Mr. Cabrini has access to his meds as required by the prescription."

"Thank you, Your Honor."

"Anything else?"

Both attorneys shook their heads.

"Next."

Elissa had to appear for another client, so I waited until he didn't get bail either, and then we left together.

"Is that normal?" I asked as we walked into the parking lot.

"What?"

"Those hearings are like cattle sales."

"Too many crimes and too few resources to process them."

"It doesn't seem right."

"Not getting due process would be not right."

"The judge read priors for almost all those guys. So they've all done time?"

"Not necessarily. They've all been found guilty of something.

They might have done community service or paid a fine, but some will have done time."

"Is the system really working if it's like a revolving door?"

"No, it's not."

"How do you stop it?"

"I don't. You do."

"How do I do that?"

"You vote, you advocate, you stop complaining when you pay your taxes. You tell the people who run the system that tinkering with detention is like shuffling deck chairs on the *Titanic*. The boat's already going down because the problems are happening *way* before these people end up committing crimes."

"When is it happening?"

"When parents can't afford to feed their kids because eight bucks an hour working for a billion-dollar company doesn't pay the rent. And paying more than you can afford in rent to a corporate landlord with ten thousand units in its portfolio is good business in the short term but terrible in the long run."

"Is it the landlords' fault that their tenants don't have good jobs?"

"Yes, it is. Yours too. Economics 101. Supply and demand only works when everyone has equal access to information and resources and education. But when a corporate giant gets assessed on nothing but quarterly earnings, then the public is left to cover the cost. We need better corporate citizens."

"You sound a bit like a socialist."

"I am. So are you. So is everyone in this country."

"I don't think many people will agree."

"You ever driven on I-95?"

"Of course."

"Then you're a socialist. You didn't pay to use that road. Have you ever watched football at a big stadium? Socialist. Most stadia are built with major public funding. You put gas in your car?"

"I pay taxes on that."

"More than you know. Energy companies get tens of billions in direct federal subsidies, and most of that money goes straight onto their bottom line. And at the same time, schools have to act like food banks and provide breakfasts and lunches to kids who would literally eat nothing that day if not for those meals. Imagine if the government funded farmers to grow broccoli and apples and they became cheap enough for everyone."

"You can't tell farmers what to grow."

"We already do, Jones. We subsidize corporate agribusinesses—they get more billions to grow corn and wheat, so that's what they do. There's so much corn we can't eat it all, so they invented corn syrup just to use it up. They make plastic out of it. It's not a question of being socialist, Jones. You already are, at least a little. And you want it that way. Societies have to be or they just don't work. We need to combine resources—roads, schools, all the things we have to share. It's just a question of what we share and how. It's not about preventing people from building great businesses or owning their homes—those are things that made this country great—but so did neighbors helping neighbors. When a troop of New York firefighters flies to California to help fight wildfires. When people in Michigan drive truckloads of water they bought at Costco to Louisiana after a hurricane. If people want to pursue the almighty dollar, I say go at it. But read what it says on the damn dollar bill before you start. 'E pluribus unum: out of many, one.'"

She took a well-earned deep breath.

"Sorry," she said, moving a strand of hair from her face. "I didn't mean to rant. But when you don't ever have to look at the other side of the coin, you start to believe it isn't there. I see the other side every day."

Elissa clicked her remote and opened her car door. "We're just better together than not. That's all I'm saying."

I said nothing. I watched her drive away, thinking about two sides of a coin. Again. That was going to keep me up nights.

CHAPTER THIRTY-FIVE

I SPENT THE AFTERNOON ROASTING A CHICKEN. I HADN'T INTENDED TO, but I desperately needed to focus on something other than coins and jails and fraud for a few hours, plus I happened to drive by a Publix at that exact moment. I put some potatoes and brussels sprouts and onions in the roasting pan and tucked garlic and rosemary under the skin of the bird. The house smelled like a great restaurant by the time Danielle walked in.

"Delivery?" she asked.

"Cheeky. I cooked."

"Smells great. Is it ready yet?"

"Forty-five minutes."

"Awesome. Time for a run."

"It might be less."

"It'll be fine. Get your shoes."

We jogged down our street and out around the bars and beach stores and over the dunes at City Beach. There were clouds in the sky, but only enough to give the postcard definition. Danielle led the way along the sand toward the thin end of the island, and I dropped in behind and watched her move. She was a natural, fluid runner. I was built for throwing things very hard.

We didn't go all the way to the state park, Danielle's concession to dry, pasty chicken. She didn't stop at the volleyball courts on the way back, instead pushing on down the road to home. The chicken was not the only thing cooked by the time we got back. I wondered if I should take up Allan Samson's offer and go in for a boxing workout.

"Feel better?" she asked as I turned into a pool of sweat on the pavement.

"Why do you do this to me?"

"Because I want you around for a lot longer, Miami Jones."

I removed the chicken, tented it in foil, and ran through the shower. As I carved and served dinner, I told Danielle about my conversation with Marjorie Cartwright, the potential whistleblower.

"Does it sound like something?" I asked.

"It sounds very much like something. She's claiming dead people are the recipients?"

"Lizzy's checking a sample of the list to confirm, but that's what Marjorie says. So is that an FDLE thing?"

"In the first instance, we can certainly look into it. But it might end up being FBI, especially if the money is going abroad."

"Turf war."

"This isn't the movies, MJ. If they're in the best place to investigate or the likely crimes fall under federal jurisdiction, then I'm happy for them to have it. There's plenty of crime to share around."

I thought about the small courtroom at the detention center. There *was* plenty to share around there. I put a plate in front of Danielle on the kitchen counter and walked around to join her on the other stool.

"What would happen if you took a look and found something?" I asked.

"If we felt there was a case or even probable cause for further investigation? We'd apply to the court for a warrant to seize information: documents, computers, that sort of thing. We'd want to freeze all accounts associated with this trust and maybe everything associated with the financial company administering it. That would require more proof, but it could be done."

"But if the accounts were frozen, Tina wouldn't get her money."

"It might hurt her but help thousands of others. And she might get some money eventually. If a crime was proven, the court could appoint a trustworthy administrator to handle the functions of the trust and disperse the funds."

"But there's nothing to stop the GBC from continuing to do it since they're based in the British Virgin Islands."

Danielle was chewing, so I waited. "Didn't you say the athletic commissions required a convalescence fund to be administered in the US?"

"That's true, but it doesn't help any boxer outside the US."

"You can't save everyone. The GBC might decide to play it clean."

"The only way that happens is if there's a spring clean of the deadwood at the top."

"To mix a metaphor."

"So I can help some but not others, and I can help many at the expense of my current client."

"Let's start by giving me what you have, and I'll pass it on to the right people. They'll need to verify a few things before they make any moves. And they'll want to talk to your whistleblower."

"She's up for that. I think, in a way, she's been waiting for this day."

I was sitting on the patio later, watching the lights twinkle across the water in Riviera Beach, when my phone buzzed.

"Detective Kelty," I said.

"Just thought you'd want to know, the drug boys just brought in a tidy haul from your distribution center. Arrests aplenty."

"Good work."

"The guys said to drop by for a beer sometime. Looks like you made friends in the drug squad."

"A life goal fulfilled."

"Yeah, whatever."

"They pick up the kid?"

"If you're talking about a knucklehead referring to himself as

Curious George, then, yes. His arrest gave them probable cause to enter the house. Nice, neat package."

"Glad to be of service."

"Anyway, *Family Feud* is coming on."

"They still do that show?"

"I think these episodes are from the eighties, but who remembers the answers from the eighties?"

"Not me. Enjoy."

I hung up and smiled at Danielle. "Another happy customer."

"You're making friends all over town. How long do you think that will last?"

"It's gotta end sooner or later."

CHAPTER THIRTY-SIX

Lizzy and I spent the next morning chatting with Agent Rowan Dorcas, a colleague of Danielle's from the FDLE who dealt with financial crimes. Lizzy's highlight was when Dorcas called her research "stunning work." He said he would keep us in the loop as things moved forward.

I dropped Lizzy up in West Palm, then turned around and headed back south to Lake Worth. I was struggling to understand how to really help Johnny Cabrini, because I couldn't get my head around what had actually happened. Had he heard about Ricky the Fudge selling drugs at the school? And if he had, where did that rumor come from? I was convinced after talking to Curious George that Ricky the Fudge was not the guy to be selling Adderall at a high school. And Johnny had been adamant that he didn't have brass knuckles—the kind of denial that came from a deeply held value, the sort of thing he would never even need to think about— yet the weapon had been found with him in his garage.

I decided to end where it all began. I drove to the strip of stores and parked in the lot behind. The three businesses on the ground floor were all open for business, but the club wasn't yet, and the door to the stairs was closed. That was how I wanted it.

After walking across the lot in the afternoon sun, I stood in the parking bay that was approximately where Johnny Cabrini had pulled up in his car, directly behind the payday lender's rear door and in the eye of the camera. I walked toward the alcove as Johnny had and imagined Ricky the Fudge standing there, waiting. He would have been almost impossible to see at night with no lights coming from the windows of the club above.

I reached the sidewalk and checked the video on my phone. It was the last point where the camera caught Johnny before he stepped into the alcove. He had no brass knuckles on yet, but he had to know Ricky was there because Johnny was talking to him at this point. I stepped into the alcove and glanced toward the payday lender. I couldn't see the camera.

I had been a pitcher in the pros and a backup quarterback at Miami, and I had seen enough film of myself to know that I had developed a twitch somewhere along the way. I would kind of half roll my right shoulder, like a spasm, right before I wound up for a pitch. In football, I did it when I was standing in the shotgun, just as I finished the count and called for the center to snap me the ball. I did it every time and still did today, even if I was just tossing a ball back to some kids at the beach. It was muscle memory in its purest form.

Johnny was a boxer, and even if he hadn't fought in a decade, he had trained so long that he would have muscle memory too. The first thing he would do, if he even sniffed the likelihood of a fight, would be to assume the boxing stance, putting his left foot forward until he was in a three-quarter position, not side-on but far from open to his opponent.

I took that stance and looked at the crime scene photographs on my phone. Lorraine Catchitt said that Ricky had suffered bruising to the left side of his face under the eye, which was consistent with a punch from a right-handed person. I did a bit of shadowboxing and threw a couple left jabs. They weren't particularly strong punches, coming in with core strength and not a lot of shoulder. Positioning punches, feeling out punches. A jab didn't feel like the thing to leave a decent bruise.

I rebalanced myself, then I swung another punch. This time I threw a right cross from back near my shoulder and extend out, finishing across my body. As I did it, my body rotated, my hips snapped like a golfer in a swing, and my right foot thrust forward as I stepped into the punch. That one scored.

In a real bout, I probably would have gotten clocked on the chin in return, but I had no opponent, and neither did Johnny. Ricky the Fudge wasn't a challenge to a pro like Johnny. But my punch would have connected on the cheekbone and left a good mark, a real shiner.

I studied the crime scene photos again. Now I was in the middle of the alcove, where Ricky was at best recoiling back against the door, or at worst falling to the ground face up. I pictured Johnny backing out of the alcove from this spot, cussing as he came into view of the video camera.

That accounted for the bruise on Ricky's face, but it didn't account for what Lorraine had described as a sucker punch: a hit from behind, the brass knuckles making contact with the base of Ricky's skull. I moved around the space, putting myself into different positions to try throwing such a hit. I couldn't make it work. I was tripped up every time by the way Ricky had been found: splayed on the floor with his feet near the door and his head toward the sidewalk end of the alcove.

I found only one position consistent with that hit: Johnny maneuvering himself around his opponent, ending up against the door—the one place he couldn't freely move, where his punches and his feet were restricted. Then I remembered something Harv the trainer had told me: a good boxer gets his opponent into a corner and goes to work, but he also guards against getting put into the corner himself. Johnny was a good boxer. Not great, but good. He knew his craft. He fought in almost a hundred professional matches. He knew how to not get stuck in a corner. And he certainly wouldn't give up a position of strength to move into a position of weakness.

The fight sequence made no sense. Johnny's training wouldn't have let him do it, even drunk. That was muscle memory—repetition drilled into the subconscious.

I stood with my back against the door to the stairs and looked at the picture of Ricky's body, lying where I stood. I imagined sucker punching him. Such a punch was not a little jab; it was a full-body effort, enough to rupture the nerves connecting the brain to the spinal cord. But I kept banging my elbow on the door. I moved farther out and repeated the motion, but now the body would have fallen partially outside the alcove. We would have seen it on the video. I moved back farther and swung, hitting my elbow on the door again. I needed another six inches to make it work. I just needed . . .

I needed the door to be open.

Then it dawned on me. The call to Ricky's phone had come from inside the club after Maxine had locked up and gone home. So either someone was up there when she left, or someone had arrived between the time she left and Ricky arrived.

But I had watched the video, as had Ron, Lizzy, Barry Schiff, maybe Elissa Croix, and probably some folks at the state attorney's office. No one else had arrived. No one had gone inside. If they had, we would have seen them. The video saw all.

I stopped breathing as the thought hit me like an uppercut. The video didn't see all. I stepped out of the alcove and moved to the side, against the wall. Right where I had stood when the guy from the payday lender took my money and emailed me a link to the video. The guy didn't want the video cameras inside the store to see him taking the cash. He didn't want the video camera outside to see him take the cash. He said right where I stood was beyond the range of the camera.

I edged along the wall away from the alcove, then I edged back along the wall. I could see the side of the camera but not the lens. And if the guy from the payday lender was right—and I was confident he had seen the angle plenty of times to know—I could keep sliding along the wall and around into the alcove without being seen by the camera.

Somebody was inside the club during the fight. Somebody had called Ricky from there and probably Johnny too. Johnny had hit Ricky and then retreated from the alcove, yelling at him to stay away from the school. Then somebody else had come through the door to the stairs and sucker punched Ricky the Fudge.

I felt a rush of adrenaline as I realized Johnny didn't kill anyone. It wasn't mitigating circumstances; he was flat-out innocent, not of assault—I was sure he had hit the rat-faced kid—but he wasn't guilty of murder or even manslaughter.

My adrenaline then plummeted just as suddenly. I had no proof. It was all just theory. Good, solid theory in my opinion, but certainly not admissible in court. I stepped back out into the sun. The flaming orb was dropping toward the horizon, the afternoon growing late and beckoning the evening. The shadows grew longer across the lot. I scanned the area.

If someone had killed Ricky, then they had also left without being seen. I kept my back against the wall and slid along, away from the camera. By the time I got to the barbershop, I knew I could walk normally. As I wandered toward the dollar store, I opened the video on my phone once more and noticed the range of the picture. The shot captured the lot straight out from the payday lender all the way to the rear. Nobody could leave the lot that way without being seen. I kept walking until I reached the end of the building.

The space between the building and the cinder block wall went out to the main street. A person would have to climb over eight feet of hurricane wire to get in and out. Far from impossible. I had gotten into my share of baseball games that way as a kid. But it was risky, climbing out onto a public road, even at midnight.

I turned back. Option two was a five-foot cinder block wall. Easy doing and easy hiding. I put my phone in my pocket and went for it. I could almost vault the thing. I pulled up and almost Fosbury-flopped right over the bricks and onto the dirt on the other side. A shorter guy or someone less athletic could have hoisted themselves up into a seated position and then swiveled around. The thought made me look along the top of the wall, at the cap blocks, the top pavers that gave the wall a finished look. They were covered with years of dirt.

Except near where I had come over. There was a circle of disturbed dirt.

I took a photo, then turned away and made my way through the foliage. The leaf litter underfoot was moist. I pushed through branches and came out into another parking lot.

The building up ahead had a newer prefabricated design, with the middle section higher than the ends. I could see the side window of the store at one end was papered over as if it were vacant. I had no idea what business was in the middle, but it had a large roller door on the back, likely for deliveries. As I walked closer, I saw there was another business at the far end. Another rear door. And above it, another surveillance camera.

The door beneath the camera was locked, but access to the street was on that side, so I walked around to the front. It was a family-owned convenience store, the kind of place that wasn't part of any chain or franchise. I went in with the ring of a little bell.

The store was packed to the rafters with stock. It was like one of those New York City bodegas, where much of the merchandise was so high on the shelves that the store provided a hook on a long pole to get stuff down. I got the scent of coriander seed and cumin.

The guy behind the counter was an Asian man about my age. He offered me a half smile as I approached.

"What time do you guys close on Thursdays?"

"Eleven."

"You got video surveillance?"

"Why, you gonna rob me?"

"No, sir. I'm from the office of the public defender."

"You got ID?"

I pulled out my PI ID card, which I never showed to anyone.

"That says you're a PI."

"I am. I'm investigating for the public defender. You hear about the dead guy on the next block?"

"Yeah, I don't like that."

"Me either. So you got surveillance video?"

"Yeah."

"I saw a camera in the back."

"Yeah."

"Does it run after you close?"

"Twenty-four seven."

"Would you mind if I took a peek at the video for that night?"

He looked me up and down. I got it. He was a businessman, and in this case, he held all the cards. Supply and demand. Not like the goose at the car wash. This guy had what I wanted, and he was the only show in town.

I already had my wallet out, so I took a twenty and held it out to him. He frowned at me.

"What do you want?"

"To see the video."

"Okay. What's with the twenty?"

"To see the video."

"You trying to pay me to see the video?"

"Well, yeah."

"You don't pay me for that. I want you to find these guys. I don't want crime in my neighborhood."

I nodded and made to put my money away.

"You want to buy something, that's different."

"You show me the video, and I'll think about my shopping list."

He seemed satisfied with that plan. He took me to a back office and woke up his computer.

"What's the store next door?" I asked.

"Bed shop. Closed down. Bad for business. Makes the place not look good."

He clicked on his video app and found the night in question. I asked him to start it at closing time. The video showed the section of the rear lot behind the store. I saw the man sitting before me come out and throw trash into a dumpster. Then nothing.

"This is your store?" I asked.

"Yes."

"Long hours."

"Yes."

"You work hard."

"Better than staying in North Korea."

I couldn't argue with that.

Each time he tapped the space bar, the video advanced by thirty seconds. We kept seeing nothing. Then around 11:20 p.m., something flashed on the screen. He jumped back in time a minute.

A car cruised in behind the shops and stopped. The lights were killed, but no one got out for a few minutes. I half expected to see the car start rocking, as whoever was inside got amorous, but instead, a man got out and walked away from the camera out of view.

"Damn," I said. "Did you see him?"

"No."

"Damn."

"Don't worry."

"Thanks."

"No, I mean, don't worry. I have another angle." He pulled up the view from a second camera. He explained that it was situated in the same place as the first, but it was a wide angle of the entire parking lot. He forwarded the video to 11:20 p.m. This angle didn't show the car stop behind the store, but it did show the man walking across the lot toward the cinder block wall. He pushed into the foliage I had just come through and disappeared.

"He's gone," said the store owner.

"He'll be back. Can you go to just after midnight?"

As he tapped the space bar, I asked him what his name was.

"Kim," he said. "You?"

"Miami."

"No."

I smiled. "Yeah, I know."

"Really, your name is Miami?"

"Yes."

He smiled. "My son's name is Miami."

My jaw hit the floor. "Are you serious?"

"Serious. He was born in Miami, three weeks after we came to the United States."

"And you named him Miami?"

He nodded proudly.

"I like that," I said. "I'm not the only one."

"No."

"Does he live there?"

"No. He's in Chicago. At medical school. He will be a doctor."

"Damn. A doctor. You must be proud."

"You ever have a dream that you dream so hard you know it will come true?"

"Yeah, I know that dream."

"Did it come true?"

I thought about getting to play baseball and football at Miami, about playing in the minor leagues. I never made the majors, and I lost my parents and my mentor along the way. But I found Danielle, and I found Ron, and I found my Longboard Kelly's family.

"Yeah, it did."

Kim nodded. "Mine too."

He slapped the space bar a few more times, then I watched the man come back out of the bushes. The video said 12:44 a.m. The man walked like he was injured, as if he had maybe tripped when climbing over the wall. He went across the lot and out of view.

Kim quickly switched back to the first video and forwarded it to 12:44 a.m. We watched the back of the store and the car. The man clicked his fob, and his lights flashed. As he pulled the car door open and the interior light came on, he glanced around, looking in the direction of the camera.

"You know that guy?" asked Kim.

"Yes, Kim, I do."

CHAPTER THIRTY-SEVEN

I didn't climb back over the cinder block wall. I couldn't do it with the bags full of merch I had picked up from Kim's store. I walked along the street, past the closed bed shop, the hurricane wire fence, the dollar store, the barber's, and the payday lender.

After dropping my purchases in my car, I looked back and noticed the door to the stairs was open. I walked over and up the stairs to the club. That door was open, too, but there was no humdrum of conversation or televisions in the background. I stopped at the entrance and looked inside.

The folding chairs lay on the tabletops where the cleaner had mopped the floor that morning. There were no customers, nobody sitting in chairs by the window or at the bar. There were a couple of kegs near the door. Coming or going, I wasn't sure.

Maxine Mitchell came out from the back room with a clipboard, checking the liquor stocks behind the bar. I didn't want to give her a heart attack, so I knocked on the doorjamb before walking in. She gave me her tight smile as I crossed the floor.

"You're early," she said. "Hard day?"

"For some." I leaned against the bar and looked around the room.

"If you're looking for someone, they're not here yet."

"I like watching bars open. It's like seeing a sunrise. Nothing but possibilities."

"You're a strange duck," she said.

"Am I?"

"Definitely. I like strange ducks. You want a soda?"

"No, I'm good."

"So you came up here to watch me work?"

"Not exactly. I saw the door open. I was wondering about Johnny."

"Wondering what?"

"You told me about him and Samson and Mick, as boys."

She looked over at the photo of the three boys leaning on the ropes. "Yeah."

"They grew up together," I said. "Inseparable."

"Yep."

"Then a promotor put two of them together in a fight for a title shot."

"It happened."

"How often did two fighters who fought each other remain friends?"

"I don't know. But Johnny and Allan were all right after."

"I got it from a good source that Johnny definitely won that fight but that Samson was more likely to win a title. He could sell tickets. That's important, right?"

"It is."

"So the guy less likely got the title shot and muffed it, and the guy more likely lost an unlucky one then got drunk and busted up his knee."

"That's about it."

"Is it though? Because something doesn't add up."

"What's that?"

"Stone's rule number one."

"All fights happen in the ring."

"It's like gospel around here."

Maxine leaned her elbows on the bar. "It was. It is."

"I agree. It's ingrained in fifty-year-old men who learned it as teenagers. Which makes me wonder."

"Wonder what, pet?"

"Why would one of your boys—Stone's boys—on the cusp of success, break that golden rule?"

"You mean Allan?"

"I do mean Allan. He was a ticket seller. Seems unlikely that one lucky shot ended his career. I could see that of Johnny. He never filled the halls, he never got the crowds in. So much so that he became the other guy, the opponent, the journeyman. But Samson? The knee injury in the fight didn't end his career. Everyone says so. They tell me he did rehab, was on the way back. I can't believe a big hitter who got backsides in seats doesn't get another shot. Maybe the next shot. Johnny didn't win a title, but maybe Samson could."

Maxine picked at the grout between the tiles on the bar.

"But instead he broke Stone's rule," I said. "A rule as ingrained in all of them as breathing."

"He got drunk."

"He wasn't the first guy in the world to get drunk, nor the last. Not even the first around here, I'll wager. But he broke the rule. Why?"

Maxine focused her attention on the grout.

"Why did he break the rule, Maxine?"

She looked up at me. The tight smile was gone. "Because of Tina."

I nodded. I didn't know for sure, but once I saw Allan Samson's face in Kim's video, I started getting a tic in my pitching shoulder. I tried to listen to my tics.

She sighed. "Tina and Allan stepped out together."

"Stepped out?"

"You know what I mean. They were an item. Tina had been around the boys for years. And they were young and they became a thing. It happens."

"Yes, it does. But . . ."

"She left him."

"For Johnny."

"Yes."

"Because he got a title shot and Samson didn't?"

"That's what we all thought. That's when it happened."

"Samson's in rehab and his girl leaves him for his best friend?"

"I know."

"So Samson gets drunk and fights."

"You can understand why."

"Not really. See, I know a little about muscle memory. About learning things so deep that you can't defy them. I can try not to breathe, but it doesn't work. I can try to throw a ball without wriggling my pitching shoulder, but I can't. To stop it, I have to think so consciously about it that I can't throw properly. That's how these guys think about this damned rule. So Samson broke it, and he fought outside the ring. I figure to do that, he has to work so hard to forget about the rule that he's not switched on for the fight."

"You think a lot," said Maxine.

"It comes with the territory. I have to read between the lines because people often don't tell me the whole truth. What is the whole truth, Maxine?"

"You know what it is. Tina left Allan and Allan took it hard. After the title-fight loss, Johnny went to him to make peace."

"And they fought again."

She let out a long breath. "Yes. They fought again. And Allan lost again. Really did his knee in. Johnny felt bad about it, but what was done was done. Those boys could forgive a fight, but matters of the heart? That's something else."

We stood at the bar in silence for a while before I moved things along.

"Do you open up every day, Maxine?"

"If we open, I do it."

"No one else?"

"Nope."

"What about closing?"

"I've had some of the guys do that over the years, but all they need do is pull the door closed at the bottom."

"They have keys?"

"No. That door is self-locking."

"Anyone else have keys?"

"No. Just me."

"Has it always been like that?"

"Always." She moved along the bar, opened a drawer, and lifted up a large ring with about twenty keys on it. I didn't know what people had all these keys for. I had one for my house and one for my office. Even my car started with a button.

"You've got a lot of keys."

"I should get rid of some of them, but I just got used to carrying them. They remind me of Stone."

"Your husband? Why?"

"We had the same keys. Actually, some of these are for the gym. I should probably go through them and give them to Allan. I don't really need them."

"Samson has a big key ring just like that."

"Yeah. That was Stone's. When I sold the gym to Allan, I just handed him Stone's keys. I don't even know what half of them are for, maybe lockers and storerooms. No idea."

"You had the same keys as Stone?"

"Yeah. In case one of us ever needed to cover for the other. You know."

"I do. So Stone had a key to this place?"

She stopped and thought about it a moment. "You know, I think you're right. He would have."

"And that key would be on the ring you gave to Samson."

"I suppose it still would. Not that he needs it. He probably doesn't know what all those keys are for either. You think I should ask for it back?"

"Not right now," I said. "But I could ask him when I see him."

"Yeah, whatever. If you don't mind."

"I don't mind."

I glanced out the window. There were things I wasn't ready to share with Maxine. That I had seen video of Samson sneaking toward the club after it closed, that someone had called Ricky the Fudge from inside the club shortly afterward, and that Samson had fled the scene after Ricky was dead.

And now I had a motive, and it had nothing to do with boxing. The end of a boxing career was one thing—and I knew about not quite making it to the top in your chosen sport. But like Kim's dream, I knew things could work out for the best despite that. I got the sense that Allan Samson had done okay. He wasn't a world champion, and he would always have those *what ifs* in his mind when he lay awake at night. But he was also the owner of a gym that took at-risk kids off the streets and gave them purpose and hope. He was the center of a community, heavily involved in the sport he loved. He might not have known it, but he was the descendent of Stone Mitchell, carrying on his legacy, imbuing young men and women with Stone's rules, rules that would hold them in good stead for the rest of their lives.

The motive I saw was the oldest one in the book. It seemed hard to believe that three decades down the track that motive still burned in him, but it was obvious to me that it did.

Maxine said she was just going to collect some bottles from the back. I said I needed to make a call. I walked to the far corner of the room and looked out at the sunny day. I must have been just above where the payday lender guy and I had discussed getting the video, where Allan Samson had slid into the club sight unseen.

"Office of the public defender, Barry Schiff speaking."

"Barry, Miami Jones. Do you have the photos from the Cabrini discovery?"

"And good afternoon to you."

"Sorry, Barry. I do hope you are well and that prosperity rains down upon you."

"Well, thank you. The files are locked up. What do you need?"

"Did the investigators take photos of the arrest scene, the things they found there?"

"Probably."

"Can you see?"

"One sec." He put me on hold, and I glanced back to watch Maxine straightening bottles of liquor behind the bar. Then Barry came back on the line.

"Okay. Yes, there are some pics. The cot, the garage, and so on."

"Is there a photo of the brass knuckles they found?"

"Hmm. No, no, yes. Yes, there is a shot of them. Although there's just one. Is that a plural like a pair of scissors?"

"It is, Barry. A set is one item because it covers multiple knuckles."

"That makes sense."

"What do they look like?"

"How does one describe brass knuckles? They're a brass color?"

"The rings, Barry."

"There are four rings attached side by side, and there's a bigger space at the bottom where the hand goes through, I guess."

"No, the hand wraps around the bottom part and it tucks into the palm. But I'm asking about the rings, where the fingers go through. What do the tops of the rings look like?"

"Like rings. Like wedding bands. I don't know how else to say it."

"That's the way. They're smooth and rounded, no protrusions?"

"No."

"Nothing sticking out that might rip or tear or dent?"

"No."

"Okay, thanks, Barry."

"Sure, happy to help."

I ended the call and said goodbye to Maxine at the bar. She gave me her tight smile again.

"I gotta get going," I said.

"Me too. Got customers soon. There's a pay-per-view tonight."

I was about to slap the bar as my farewell when my phone rang. It was Longboard Kelly's.

"Muriel?" I asked.

"Mick."

"Mick? What's up?"

"It's Johnny."

I looked up at Maxine. "What about Johnny?"

"He's dead."

CHAPTER THIRTY-EIGHT

MAXINE TOOK IT HARD, BUT SHE WAS A TROOPER. SHE'D LOST THE husband she had spent a lifetime loving. I suspected everything after that was a dull jab in comparison. I wanted to stay with her, but I feared there were other people taking it harder.

I drove to the Cabrini house. It was only five minutes away, but it felt like forever. I knocked and Mick opened the door. He didn't look good, at least to the trained eye. He more or less looked like his normal self: set jaw, stoic expression. But his eyes betrayed him. There were no tears there, but they were rimmed red with fear and uncertainty.

My first instinct was to hug him. I wasn't sure it would go over well, but I couldn't think of what else to do. I needed a hug, and I didn't really know Johnny Cabrini. But he was like a brother to Mick. I wrapped my arms around his solid frame and felt his stubby limbs go around me for a second or two. Then he banged my back with his fist and we both let go. He diverted his eyes to the house and cleared his throat like he was going to speak, but he didn't.

Tina and two of her daughters were on the sofa, hugging so tight they were almost one entity. The girls were weeping, and their eyes suggested there had already been heavy sobbing. I figured there was more of that to come. Tina's demeanor of control had cracked. Tears welled in her eyes and silently ran down her cheeks. I waved gently. She looked at me but gave no response.

I turned to Mick. "What happened?"

"Dunno."

"How do you know about Johnny?"

"The jail."

"The jail what?"

"Called."

"What did they say?"

"He's dead."

"How?"

"Dunno."

"They didn't say?"

"Nup."

"Who called?"

"Chaplain."

The front door burst open. The boyfriend of Tina's oldest daughter came in followed by a woman I assumed to be the daughter.

"Mom?"

"Sofia, honey."

Sofia ran around us like we were furniture and dropped into her mother's arms. The boyfriend stood uncomfortably looking at Mick and me.

"What happened?" he whispered.

Mick shrugged.

"I'm gonna find out," I said, stepping past the boyfriend and walking outside to make a call.

"Office of the public def—"

"It's me, Barry."

"Miami. I just locked the file away."

"I'm not calling about the file. Have you heard anything about Johnny?"

"Anything like what?"

"I'm with his family. Tina got a call from the detention center chaplain saying Johnny was dead."

"Oh no."

"You haven't heard?"

"No. We're on the list of people who have to be told, but we're not that high on it. Family is number one."

"All they know is he's dead, nothing more."

"Maybe that's all there is to say? I don't know."

"Okay."

"I'm sorry, Miami."

"It's not my husband."

"Pass on our sincere condolences."

"Thanks, Barry."

I hung up and made another call.

"MJ, how's things?" said Danielle.

"Not great."

"What's happened?"

"Johnny Cabrini is dead."

"Dead?"

"Yep."

"How do you know?"

"The jail chaplain called the family."

"I'm so sorry for them."

"You and me both, but they don't know anything."

"I doubt the chaplain gets into detail. Do they have support?"

"The family is here. Do you know anyone who might know what the hell happened?"

"I'll call you back."

I stood outside by myself to gather my thoughts. I understood Mick's sense of helplessness. There was nothing I could do to make these people feel better. I could give them information if I got it, but that was putting a Band-Aid on a bullet wound.

The sun had dropped away and had left the yard in darkness. I watched a woman walking a dog as if nothing else in the world mattered. Everything I knew and didn't know rolled around my head. Johnny was dead. Fishook was committing fraud. I had a contract for $5,000 in my possession. Johnny hadn't killed Ricky the Fudge. A family's life was in ruins. Why?

When I stepped back into the house, Mick was near the picture covering the hole that Johnny made. The boyfriend was in a chair, and the three sisters sat together on the sofa.

I found Tina in the kitchen. She was wiping her face and trying in vain to keep it together. She took a deep breath. That was as good a sign as any.

"I had to call his mother," she said.

"I'm sorry."

"She's in a VA home. She doesn't know who Johnny is."

That didn't feel like the worst thing at that moment. "Did the chaplain tell you anything?"

"Johnny passed away. That's it. He didn't know what happened or he didn't say. He said the sheriff would contact me with more. The sheriff. Is that right? He was in jail."

"The sheriff's office runs the facility he was in. My wife used to be a deputy, so I asked her to see if she can find out anything more."

Tina nodded but said nothing. Perhaps she didn't care. Perhaps she would later.

"I don't know what we'll do now," she said, now shaking her head.

"All I can tell you is that you do one day and then the next."

"Have you lost someone?"

"Both my parents. I was in middle school when I lost my mom."

"Sorry."

I shrugged. "You don't need to hear any platitudes from me, but I'll say this: I didn't think I was going to ever get through it. But other people saved me. People will offer help, and you'll be inclined to send them away. I get that compulsion. But don't. You don't have to have a house full of people, but let them help, however they can."

"I won't even *have* a house soon."

"Tina, I got the fund to agree to five thousand dollars."

Her eyes went wide, as if she was seeing a sliver of hope, then her expression dropped.

"The universe hits me again," she said.

"Why?"

"I bet there's no way they'll pay a widow. The agreement was with Johnny, right?"

"Yes."

"And he's dead. He can't sign anything now."

"He signed it already."

"What?"

"I visited him with the public defender. He signed it. I have a signed agreement."

"Will they pay it now that he's dead?"

"A contract is a contract." I wasn't so sure about that. I was glad I had made Fishook sign in his office. It would make it harder to contest. But contest it they might. So I needed to move quickly. Deaths in custody rarely made the news, so Fishook might never learn about Johnny's passing, but I didn't want to give him the chance.

My phone rang. "I should take this." I stepped out into the backyard. There was only residual light from the house, and all I could hear was the murmur of insects in the grass.

"What do you have?"

"Nothing good," said Danielle.

"Tell me."

"This is all unofficial, right?"

"Sure."

"It looks like there was an altercation."

"What sort of altercation?"

"A fight, MJ. It looks like Johnny started a fight with an inmate who had been an associate of Richard Whitecross."

"Johnny fought one of Ricky's gang buddies?"

"I don't know if Ricky was in a gang or not, but Ricky was allegedly mentioned."

"So what happened?"

"They were pulled apart, and Johnny was sent to his cell. He was found an hour later hanging in there."

I felt the air leave me. For a moment I forgot the process, then that damned muscle memory kicked back in and I breathed.

"Johnny took his own life?" I asked.

"It looks that way."

"How does this happen?"

"It happens, MJ. It shouldn't but it does."

I said nothing.

"I'm sorry, MJ."

"Yeah."

"Will you tell them?"

"Will the PBSO?"

"In due course. There will have to be an investigation."

"I'll tell them."

"Do you want me to come over?"

"This isn't your job."

"It's not yours either, MJ."

"It's okay. I got it. I'll see you at home later."

"I'll be there. Call if you need me."

I hung up and stared into the darkness. In his last hours, Johnny had broken Stone's number one rule. He had fought outside the ring. I wondered if you were incarcerated, did the entire jail become the ring? Or perhaps Johnny had lost the muscle memory. His damaged brain just let it go. He had hit Ricky the Fudge outside the ring, and now he had done it in jail. He had probably been on the downswing. *Probably?* I shook my head at my own stupidity.

Then I heard Johnny's voice in my head. Something he said to me in our meeting at the detention center. Our final conversation. I had told him about the agreement for the five thousand dollars.

"So I was worth something after all."

I stood in the yard wondering if that was on Johnny's mind at the end. That he had signed the agreement to get Tina some money and that was the last useful thing he would ever do. His business on this planet was done. Was the document I had him sign his death warrant?

I clenched my fists at my arrogance. A man was dead and a family was grieving, and I was making it about me.

I opened the back door and found Tina still there, staring at the floor. I caught her attention and beckoned her outside. I stepped onto the grass and asked her to sit on the step.

"I got some news. It's not official, but I'm sure it's accurate."

She didn't move.

"I don't know how to say it, so I'll just say it: Johnny took his own life."

Tina's jaw set firm, but she made no sound and shed no more tears. She just sat there and breathed for a while. I couldn't begin to guess what she was thinking.

"Don't tell the girls," she said.

"Okay."

She stared into the darkness as I had. I watched her, wondering about truth and fact. The fact was that the mean reds had descended and Johnny was not in his right mind. Fighting in the jail showed that. The depression had gripped him so hard that he only saw one desperate way forward: to leave his wife and children and all the sadness behind.

The truth was something else. That he had done one last good thing for his family, gotten them some money—however little—the only way he could. That perhaps he had died a proud and content man.

I wasn't going to verbalize any of this tonight, but when Tina and the girls were ready to hear about him, I would. And I knew that the truth was always better than the facts.

Tina sat for a good long time until she jerked her head up like she had remembered she had left the oven on. She got up and went back inside and snuggled in between her daughters.

I stayed outside long enough to order a couple pizzas for delivery. The family would need to eat eventually and pizza could feed them now or wait for until they were ready.

The women didn't leave the sofa. I told Sofia's boyfriend that Tina had my number if she needed anything. Then Mick and I made our way out.

"You should go home," I told Mick as we approached his car.

"Longboard's."

"Muriel can handle Longboard's."

"Longboard's," he repeated.

I nodded as I realized what he meant. Longboard Kelly's didn't need him tonight. But he needed it.

I watched him pull away, then I got in my car and drove to Singer Island while I thought the whole time about Allan Samson.

I held Danielle for about half an hour. Then we sat, late into the night. I told her what I had learned about the death of Ricky the Fudge, and about what I had found out about Allan Samson.

"I don't think Johnny did it," I said.

"You might be right, but let me be devil's advocate for a moment. You've got evidence that he was in the area, but none placing him at the crime scene itself. You don't see him on the video at all."

"It's not the full picture."

"I get that, but you can't prove a negative. There's also no evidence that he was in the club. It's only theory that an assailant came through the door."

"You think I'm wrong?"

"I don't. I agree there are inconsistencies. This Samson being there at all is extremely suspicious, but I'm not thinking about whether he did it. I'm talking about what can be proven. The detectives and the prosecutors have a closed case. The alleged perpetrator is dead. No more case, move on. They won't go looking for more work. They're overworked as it is."

"So what are you saying?"

"I'm saying you need to present your case to Kelty, but you need to think it through first. Not now. Tomorrow or whenever. Look at the inconsistencies. Is there one link that looks better than the others, more likely to prove your point? If Kelty only has to pull one thread to make the whole thing come together, he's more likely to go with it."

"If he pulls a thread, won't it fall apart?"

"I'm not above a mixed metaphor either."

I nodded. "I see what you're saying. I'll think it through."

I leaned into her on the sofa and stopped talking and tried to stop thinking. One came easier than the other.

CHAPTER THIRTY-NINE

The next morning I didn't sit around thinking about my strategy for selling my theory to Kelty. That could wait. It wasn't going to bring Johnny back, and it wasn't going to help Tina and her daughters. Focusing on the job I had originally been tasked with was the best I could do for them.

With my wife, I stood outside the Palm Beach office building that was home to Fishook Financial. She winked, and I walked in alone. I made my way to the elevator and then to the office. I pulled on the door as I had before. It buzzed and I let myself in.

The receptionist with the eighties hair went through the same rigmarole of confirming my identity and escorting me inside. Fishook didn't offer to shake hands, and I was okay with that. I sat down as he straightened his tie at his desk.

"We don't usually do this," he said.

"I know, you told me on the phone. But as I explained to you, my client is going to lose her house today. The sheriff has the paperwork, and the landlord has said if there's no rent money by noon, they're out. So a company check is no good to her. It won't clear in time. And if it doesn't clear in time, then she's out on the streets, and we might as well drag this thing through the courts and see if we can't multiply that five thousand by ten or twenty."

"We don't need to get lawyers involved."

"I don't think so, but either you have a cashier's check or you don't. If you do, then it's as good as cash. If you don't, then we're done here. Which is it?"

Fishook opened a drawer in his desk and pulled out an envelope. He closed the drawer, placed the envelope on the desk, and straightened it so it was lined up with the desk's edge.

"Do you have an executed agreement?" he asked.

"I do." I handed him a manila folder. He removed the document and flipped to the last page, where the signatures were. He then opened a filing cabinet, put the agreement into a file, and closed the metal drawer gently.

"Now, I must make sure that you fully understand the terms. This is a one-time payment. There is no double dipping. And the nondisclosure means your client cannot mention this settlement to anyone."

"Don't worry, he won't tell a soul."

Fishook straightened his tie again and put his fingers on the envelope as if reconsidering the deal. Part of me wanted him to try. If he did, I was pretty sure he would try to keep the copy of the agreement document, and I was going to enjoy going through him and ripping his filing system apart to get it back.

But he didn't. He picked up the envelope and handed it to me. I took it but didn't put it away. I was sure the classy move was to slip it into my jacket pocket and shake hands like gentlemen, but I wasn't wearing a jacket and I didn't consider him a gentleman.

"You're opening it?"

"Yes." I took the check out to make sure it was kosher.

"You don't trust me?"

"Not one little bit."

But it looked good: a cashier's check issued by Bank of America in the amount of five thousand dollars made out to Johnny Cabrini. The money would go directly into the account he had shared with Tina. I stood, took my phone out, and slipped the check into my pocket in its place. Then I punched in a quick text message.

"It's been a pleasure," I said.

The look on Fishook's face suggested he didn't agree. He followed me out to reception. I didn't think it was courtesy, more the way you shoo a pest out the door. I got to the front door and opened it. A man was standing there, so I pulled the door wider to let him in.

Fishook stepped toward him. "Can I help you?"

"Nolan Fishook? I'm Agent Dorcas of the Florida Department of Law Enforcement." He showed Fishook his ID as he spoke and held up a folded document. "I have a warrant for your arrest and a warrant for the search of your office and home."

"What?"

"Agent Castle?" said Dorcas.

Danielle brushed up against my chest as she stepped in past me.

"Agent, can you please inform Mr. Fishook of his rights and take him into custody?"

"Yes, sir."

Danielle recited the Miranda warning as she cuffed him. The smile on my face grew and grew. I loved watching her in work mode.

Danielle directed Fishook out of the office, but he looked at me as he passed.

"You cannot say anything, Jones."

"Why?"

Fishook snarled. "I have an NDA."

I smiled. "Not with me."

Danielle pushed him the rest of the way out the door, and a couple other agents entered wearing latex gloves.

Agent Dorcas turned to the receptionist, whose eyes were like full moons. "Ma'am, what is your name?"

"Francine."

"Ma'am, you are not under arrest at this time."

"I don't know anything."

"We'll get to that later. But for now, I ask that you remain at your station here and witness our search." He turned to the other agents. "Let's do it. Documents, files, hard drives. The whole enchilada."

One agent walked into Fishook's office as the other began unplugging Francine's computer.

Dorcas came over to me. "Thanks for the tip."

"No sweat."

"And thank Lizzy again for me, will you? She did great work. We were able to verify thirty deceased persons on her list who received phantom payments."

"Marjorie Cartwright had plenty to do with that."

"She's been incredibly helpful."

"How do you think they were putting money into foreign accounts?"

"I'm willing to bet it was cashier's checks into a US dollar account in the BVI."

"He just gave me one, but he wasn't keen to do it."

"They don't want to use cashier's checks for actual, reportable disbursements. The paper trail looks more legit if the money comes from a trust."

"Can you trace where the money went?"

"We've briefed the FBI on it. We'll see where it goes. Financial treaties are stronger than they used to be. Speaking of which, you said you had spoken to Breyer Priestly, the president of GBC?"

"Yes."

"You don't have any idea where he might be? We'd like to chat with him."

"He's based in the Virgin Islands."

"We checked. He entered the country under a Canadian passport but hasn't left."

"He has an office at his brother's boxing-promotion company in Orlando. You might try there."

"Orlando?"

"Yeah. I can text you the address."

"Appreciate it. I wouldn't mind getting to him before he leaves town."

CHAPTER FORTY

Johnny Cabrini's funeral was held on a glorious Florida winter's day. The service was in a chapel at the funeral home. I was worried that Tina would not be able to afford a burial, let alone a service, but Mick and Samson split the bill. The congregation filled the space, and I noted a similar look among many of the men there. Former boxers thinking about their own mortality. Danielle and I sat near the back and let the family take care of its own.

The casket was closed because, as part of Dr. Abe's study, Johnny had donated his brain for research. The autopsy had been perfunctory since the cause was self-evident and the public purse had no appetite to delve into Johnny's substance-abuse issues.

There was a gathering after the funeral at the Pugilists' Club. I watched a quiet line of people shuffle past Tina and her daughters to offer their condolences, then move to the bar. One of her girls was in tears most of the day, but the other two kept her supplied with hugs and backrubs and more hugs. I saw Allan consoling Tina and getting her drinks. I wondered if that was his intention all along: to get rid of the competition and move in on her. He had certainly bided his time well if that was his plan.

Someone talking with a group of boxers called Allan to weigh in on their discussion, so Danielle and I walked over to Tina.

"Hey," I said.

"Hey."

"Have you seen this picture?" I directed her to the wall near the bar.

"I don't know."

I offered my hand and helped her up, then walked her to the photo of the three boys in the ring. She looked at it and smiled, then strolled a little farther down and stopped in front of the photo of Johnny the boxer, hands in the air in victory.

"That was him," she said. "That was his life. He loved everything about it. The training and the matches and just hanging out with the boys. Who knows where he would have ended up if Stone hadn't gotten hold of him. All of them. They were rascals, always looking for mischief. Stone sorted him out and set him right."

She looked at the photos for a while in silence. Then she looked at me. "I want to remember him like this. I loved the way he was then. I loved the way he would look at Sofia when she was first born. He'd hold her entire body in his forearm, tucked in tight against him. He'd have a frown on his face until he got her settled because he was petrified he'd break her. And he'd do the cooing and those things, but then he'd stop and just look at her. You never saw love in someone's eyes like that. Just—I don't know—so pure."

Tina made to wipe her eye, and Danielle handed her a tissue.

"The injuries, the CTE or whatever it was, it took that look away. It took that Johnny away." She looked at Danielle and me as she wiped her eyes. "I loved that Johnny."

"I know," I said. "And he loved you." I retrieved the envelope from my pocket and handed it to her. She slipped the edge of the check out to peek at the amount and let out half a profanity.

"I didn't think . . ."

"He took care of it," I said. "Johnny got it for you. And he was happy, Tina, at least in the moment, that he had done this for you."

She had no pockets, so she couldn't find a home for the check. I took it back and told her I'd drop it at her home. For a moment she smiled. Then she didn't.

"Do you think that's all his life amounted to? That this is his legacy? A check for a few months' rent?"

"No, not at all."

"You're just saying that, but thank you."

"No I'm not. His legacy is a whole lot greater than that." I pointed across the room, and Tina turned around to see her three daughters. Tina nodded and blinked back tears. Then she turned to me. "Thank you."

I just nodded. Tina walked across the room toward her girls. I glanced at Danielle, who was smiling, watching them play with one another's hair, a casual moment among the grief, perhaps the first day of lives that would go on to be lived well. I was about to say something when Danielle's face changed. Her smile disappeared as if a cloud had drifted across the sun.

"I'm going to use the bathroom," Danielle said, and she was gone.

I had no idea what had happened, but as I glanced across the room, I saw Allan Samson heading for the door. I sprinted and met him as he reached the stairs.

"Leaving already?" I said.

"Memory Lane really isn't my thing."

"Going home?"

"To the gym."

"I thought it was closed today. Mark of respect."

"It is. But I always got stuff to do there." He waved me off and headed down the stairs.

I stepped back into the club and found Danielle searching the room for me.

"You okay?" I asked.

"Yeah. Feel like going home."

"You don't seem so good."

"Funerals."

"Yeah. Listen, I need to go somewhere."

"Where?"

"To see Kelty."

"Okay. You want me to come with, help make your case?"

"No, I think I've got it. But I have to get you home first."

"Don't worry, I'll take a cab."

Danielle and I slipped out of the club without another word.

CHAPTER FORTY-ONE

I found Kelty in his office in West Palm, sitting opposite Detective Remington.

"The man of the hour," he said. "You got another drug tip?"

"No. But I think I know who killed Ricky the Fudge."

"Your man, Cabrini," said Remington.

"No. I don't think so."

"He's dead, Jones," said Kelty. "Let it go."

"And let a killer go free?"

"You can be a real pain in the backside sometimes, you know that?"

"Look, I want to be done with this business as much as you."

"Evidently not."

"But I have video of Allan Samson climbing the side fence into the lot behind the club shortly before the incident."

"Who the hell is Allan Samson?"

"He owns the gym they all go to."

"That's right. Stone's."

"Samson's now."

"We've already got video, Jones," said Remington. "Cabrini's on it, Fudge is on it, this Samson guy is not on it."

"That's because the video from the payday lender doesn't show the other side of the alcove. And I tested it. I can get from that side of the lot into the alcove without being seen by the camera."

"You're saying another guy went into the alcove with them?" said Kelty.

"No, I'm saying Samson went in before, but he didn't stay in the alcove. He went into the club."

"There was no damage to the door, Jones."

"He had a key."

"How did he get a key?"

"He bought the gym from Stone Mitchell's widow, Maxine. She gave him Stone's keys, a big ring of them. She didn't go through them, but she has the same big ring herself for the club she runs. She and Stone both had the same keys in case of emergency. She still has other keys to the gym she forgot to give Samson. And she never asked for any back from him."

Kelty sat up now. He didn't look happy.

"Then there was the call to Ricky's phone, just before he left the bar. It came from inside the club, and the video shows that Maxine had already gone home."

"How do you know that?" said Remington.

"Discovery from the prosecution."

"But how did you see it?"

"I've been working for the public defender. Pro bono investigation."

"So what, now you're cooking something up to justify your theory of your guy not being there?"

"No. Johnny was there. And I thought he was guilty too. I haven't been trying to clear him; I've been trying to mitigate the charges, to place him in a psych ward. Doesn't matter now, not for him. But I re-created the fight. It doesn't fit. Not the way it's laid out. I have no doubt Johnny punched Ricky in the face. But the deadly blow was from the back, and Johnny couldn't have done that."

"Why not?"

"Two reasons: one, Johnny was a good boxer, and a guy with his experience wouldn't go from the position of strength in the open side of the alcove to get penned in against the door. And two, that's the only place the blow could have come from. But I tried throwing one from in there and I couldn't do it. The only way it works is if the door is open."

Kelty and Remington exchanged a look.

"And there's the brass knuckles. The injury to Ricky doesn't match the knuckles you found in Johnny's garage."

"Jones, do you see what you're asking?" said Kelty. "We open this Pandora's box, we're opening the PBSO to a wrongful-arrest suit and, hell, a wrongful death. The family could sue. Even if we can't convict this other guy."

"Is that such a bad thing, Kelty? That this family that has nothing now gets a couple hundred grand thrown at them by the county?"

"It's not our job to make these people rich," said Remington.

"No, it's your job to put guilty people away, not the innocent ones. And do the math, Remington. Two hundred grand spread over what, twenty years of having no husband and father bringing in money? That's ten thousand a year. Is that rich in your eyes? You living on that?"

Remington sat back in her chair. I thought about Elissa Croix and the other side of the coin and being a bit more of a socialist. Although I didn't completely disagree with her, and I wasn't super eager on paying more in taxes, I could see a point in the Cabrinis' situation. The system had let him down, done nothing for his health, and then let him die.

"If that's how our tax dollars are spent," I said. "I, for one, am okay with that."

"I'd rather pay no taxes at all, thanks," said Kelty.

"Then you wouldn't have a job. Look, you do you. If you grow a conscience, Samson will be alone at his gym this afternoon."

I didn't stay for more chitchat. I walked out and headed for the bar.

CHAPTER FORTY-TWO

I HAD TO GET HOME. I WASN'T SURE WHAT THE FUNK WAS THAT HAD descended on Danielle, but I couldn't easily let it rest after seeing Johnny Cabrini's depression in action. But on my way, I wanted to stop in at Longboard's. I was sure Mick would pack in the Memory Lane thing like Samson had and head for his home base.

I walked into the courtyard and found Danielle sitting in my spot, sharing a drink with Ron. Muriel was behind the bar, and for a moment, everything seemed right with the world.

"I thought you were going home," I said.

Danielle shrugged. "I wanted to check in on Mick first."

"Is he here?" I looked at Muriel.

"He's here," she said. "Better to be busy, I think. How was the funeral?"

"How are they ever?" I said. "More people than I would expect at mine, that's all I can say."

"And the family?"

"Getting through it one moment at a time, the only way you can."

"Did you get Tina the check?" Ron asked.

"I showed it to her. It's not much, but it will help. I think there might be more in the wind anyway."

"How's that?"

Mick wandered out from the depths with a tray of napkin holders. "All right?" he said as if I had come in from a day's fishing.

"You know."

"What do you mean they might get more money?" asked Ron.

"Did you talk to Kelty?" Danielle asked.

"I did. He didn't seem that eager to open it up again."

"I told you."

"Open what?" said Ron.

"I don't think Johnny killed Ricky the Fudge."

I noticed that everyone had frozen in place, even Mick. He was watching me through a fierce frown.

"Go on," said Ron.

"I went through the fight in the alcove—reenacted it—and it didn't work. Johnny hit Ricky, but I figured someone had to have come from inside the club after Johnny had left, and killed him. So I did, you know, investigator stuff. I found a video of Allan Samson climbing over the wall to the lot just before the fight."

Mick slammed the tray of napkins onto the bar.

"And I think he has keys to the club from when he bought the gym."

"Stone's," said Mick.

"Yeah."

"Why would he do that?" asked Ron.

"Not completely sure, but it turns out he dated Tina before she left him for Johnny."

"Oh," said Ron.

"Oops," said Muriel.

I looked at Mick. He was not keeping everything on the inside anymore. I could see the emotion on his face as his nostrils flared and his jaw clenched. He turned and disappeared behind the bar.

"Where's he going?" said Ron.

Mick appeared on our side of the bar and stormed off. I ran after him and caught up at the exit.

"Mick, what are you doing?"

He didn't respond.

"Mick, be cool. The sheriff's office will handle it. I hope."

That didn't help. He strode to his Eldorado, got in, and started it. I didn't have any time to think, so I just jumped over the passenger door and into the seat as he skidded out of the lot.

I pleaded with him all the way to the gym. By the time we got there, I hadn't convinced him of anything, but he had cooled down a touch. He parked and walked across the lot to the black-painted glass door. He pulled on the metal handle, but the door was locked. He yanked on it again, and the whole thing shook.

"Mick, let's just think about this."

When he jerked the door harder, the frame groaned. Then he put two hands on the handle and pulled with his entire body. He ripped the aluminum frame from the hinges, but the lock held. Mick gave it another tug and pulled it open in reverse, then let the door fall onto the ground and stepped over it into the gym.

I followed and saw Allan Samson coming out of the locker room.

"What the hell are you doing?" he yelled.

"You!" screamed Mick.

"What is wrong with you?"

Mick charged at Samson. "You killed him!"

The two bodies collided with a sickening thud.

"What has gotten into you, man?" spat Samson.

"You killed him."

"What? Who?"

"Johnny."

"Are you crazy? Johnny died in jail."

Mick pushed him but didn't take a swing. Maybe he knew his limits after all. Samson boxed for a shot at a title. Mick didn't.

I stayed near the door. "He means you killed Ricky the Fudge and let Johnny take the fall."

"What? Are you crazy?"

"You parked in the lot next door," I said. "I've got video."

Samson froze and looked at me.

"And I know you have a key to the club. You called Ricky from inside, and you were there when he arrived, and after Johnny left you snuck down the stairs and attacked him from behind."

"You two are out of your minds. Now get out of my gym." He looked at Mick, but Mick didn't budge. Instead, he pointed at the boxing ring.

"In the ring," Mick said.

"What? You want to fight me? You're out of your mind, Mick. I'll kill you."

"Good." Mick strode over to the ring and pulled a pair of gloves from a hook on the wall.

"We're not doing this, Mick," said Samson.

"Stone's rule." Mick pulled the Velcro tight on one glove and used his teeth to close the other. Then he banged the gloves together.

"Mick," I said. "Maybe this is not the right way to go."

He kept his eyes on Samson. "Coward."

Apparently, that was a trigger word, because Samson snatched his own gloves and put them on.

The two men climbed through the ropes without the grace of youth and moved to the center of the ring.

"You want a mouthguard?" asked Samson.

Mick shook his head.

"How many rounds?"

"To the end."

They touched gloves, and suddenly they were squaring off. I wanted to tell them to stop, but I didn't think they'd listen, and I couldn't take my eyes off them. They were similar in build, but Samson was taller and had Mick for reach. As they eased around each other, I thought of the fights I had seen with Harv, how the young athletes danced around the mat. This was not that. This brought forth thoughts of the player who went one season too many.

They continued moving around in circles as if summing each

other up. They were two middle-aged guys who had known each other since childhood. They weren't going to learn anything new here, and for a moment I felt relief thinking they were going to prance around until they were spent or got bored and then trash-talked it out.

Then Mick stepped in and punched Samson in the face. It wasn't a massive hit—a jab—but it rocked Samson back and established the parameters of the engagement. Samson shook his head and snarled.

"You killed him," said Mick again, dodging and weaving.

"You're insane." Samson feigned a jab.

"You were his brother," said Mick.

Samson stepped in and hit Mick with a double jab. Mick didn't take a backward step.

"He was just someone I knew," said Samson. "He could have been any guy on the street."

"Jealous," said Mick, hitting Samson in the gloves with a jab and then connecting with a hook.

Samson shook his head from the blow. "Jealous of him? He lost his mind."

"He got the shot."

"That was my shot," Samson spat as he stepped in with a flurry of punches. He wasn't controlled anymore. The sparring session was done. Samson started throwing wild punches like the fighter I had seen with Harv. Looking for the big hit, strategy and skill be damned.

Mick held his hands up in front of his face and took most of the blows on the gloves, but plenty landed in one way or another. Mick ended up against the ropes, and Samson kept hammering away. Mick didn't try to move. He just took the punishment. I wondered if that was the point of the exercise—that he felt like he deserved the hits for not doing more for Johnny.

But then Samson stopped. He was puffing like a steam train. The moniker seemed apt now, for the wrong reasons. Like the boxer at the casino, he had given his hardest shots in the hopes of landing the knockout punch, but Mick had taken his best and was still standing. Samson stepped back to the middle of the ring, his hands by his side and his chest heaving.

Mick dropped his guard and stared at his old friend. He wasn't breathing hard at all. He looked just like he did standing behind his bar, barely awake and completely unflustered.

"Jealous," Mick said again.

Samson stood hunched, sweat dripping from his face. "My shot."

"Not the shot!" said Mick. "Tina!"

Mick was a stout guy with legs like concrete bollards. He didn't move with the speed of Sugar Ray or the grace of Ali. He was more like a charging rhino. Mick came upon Samson before he knew what was happening, and as Mick cocked his arm back, I thought about Dr. Abe and what kind of punch would hit the head in the worst possible way. I held my breath.

And then Mick skidded to a halt, stopping right against Samson's chest, nose to chin. The two of them stood there, breathing heavily as if they had just missed the bus.

Then Mick lifted his gloves and pushed Samson in the chest. It didn't seem all that hard, and Samson took a half step back, but he looked defeated, as if he wasn't even worthy of punching. Mick used his teeth to rip the Velcro open, then he stuffed the glove under his armpit to wrench it off.

"Think she'll have ya now?" he said, throwing the glove at Samson's chest.

Samson dropped his head. "She was never going to have me. Not then, not now. She only ever had eyes for that damn cuckoo."

"Then why?"

"I didn't do it to get her back. I did it to save her. She wasn't going to leave him, and one day he was going to completely snap and kill her. You know it's true."

For a moment, I wondered if there was some kind of warped honor in what he was saying. But Mick pulled off his other glove and threw it at Samson's head. Samson dodged it, and in doing so, he lost his balance and fell to the canvas.

"Did you slip?" Mick gave one last sorry look at Samson, then climbed out through the ropes.

"Shall we go?" I asked.

Mick nodded.

Detectives Kelty and Remington noisily climbed over the broken door and into the gym with two more detectives and two uniformed deputies.

"Where's Samson?" asked Kelty.

I pointed at the man lying in the ring. Kelty directed the deputies to collect him and told the detectives to look around. They removed the gloves and replaced them with cuffs. As the deputies led Samson away, I looked at Kelty.

"You changed your mind?"

"Nope," said Kelty. "You can thank Remington."

I raised an eyebrow at her.

"I remembered that there's a new licensing recommendation for establishments that serve or sell alcoholic beverages to have security cameras on premises."

"Okay."

"And you said Samson was inside the club. Well, the club serves alcohol."

"I didn't see any video cameras."

"We just came from the club. There's just one. Above the register, looking at the door."

"And you didn't check that before?"

"The club wasn't a crime scene," said Kelty. "We had no reason to look for anything up there."

"But isn't Florida a two-party consent state for recordings?"

"That's only audio," said Remington. "And it doesn't matter because consent was given."

"When?"

"It's not a public bar, it's a members club. Ms. Mitchell said there's wording in the membership agreement about possible recording."

"But nobody reads that stuff."

"Maybe they should. Samson should have because she just showed us video of him creeping around in the dark during the time of the incident. He goes downstairs just as Mr. Cabrini arrives."

"We looked at the brass knuckles we have in evidence," said Kelty. "They don't match the autopsy report."

I was about to say, "Didn't think so," when one of the other detectives came out of the locker room carrying a plastic evidence bag. He held up a pair of brass knuckles. They weren't like the ones Barry had described. These had the same sort of rings around the fingers, but they had short rectangular nubs sticking up, clearly designed to scrape and cut open an opponent.

"Found in a locker," said the detective.

"Make sure you note which one," said Remington. "No mistakes with chain of evidence."

"Done. It had two names on it."

"Let me guess," I said. "Stone and Samson."

"Got it in one."

"Why would he keep those things if he'd committed murder with them?" I asked the ether.

"These guys get pretty attached to their knuckles. It's a thing," said Remington. "Plus, he probably thought he had done the perfect crime. Hubris. Pride cometh before the fall."

"Not sure you'll ever be able to prove it, but Samson planted the ones you found at Johnny's. He knew Johnny was drunk and where he went to sleep it off—his garage."

"We'll look into it," said Kelty.

I had nothing further to say on it, so I turned to Mick. "I think our work here is done."

Mick didn't speak or nod. He was looking around the empty gym. Perhaps he was wondering if it was the end of an era or if it would have to close. I really couldn't say.

"We might need a statement," said Kelty.

"Call my office after I've had a decent night's sleep. And, Remington, thanks for not ignoring me."

"Don't get used to it."

I wasn't sure if she was kidding, but her delivery was deadpan. "I won't."

Mick and I stepped across the fallen door and walked back to his car.

CHAPTER FORTY-THREE

I got some sleep, but it wasn't good. My mind didn't want to shut down. But rather than curse it, I was thankful it still worked well enough to keep me up with coherent thoughts. I was yawning as I worked with Lizzy, finalizing packets of information for both the FDLE regarding the fraud and the PBSO regarding the murder.

Five thousand dollars would keep Tina and the girls off the eviction list for a few months at most. But there were other options to look at, and I wanted to close out the case by making sure she knew what those were.

I went into my office and sat down, then I picked up my phone and pulled up the contact record Tina had created for me. On a whim, I hit the little information icon in the corner.

"Huh, would you look at that?"

I decided that a visit was more in order than a call, so I drove down to Lake Worth. Tina opened the door when I knocked. She looked tired but not so bleary-eyed. She asked me in as the two girls ran by to meet up with two other girls who were standing on the street outside.

The room was as it had been before, but all the drapes were opened and the windows cracked so a breeze wafted through. The place was brighter for it. It wasn't like things had turned over a new leaf the day after they had buried their husband and father, nothing so trite. Maybe it was just the first step on the endless road to healing.

"Would you like iced tea?"

"Sweetened?"

"I can put some sugar in."

"No, unsweetened is better, thanks."

She poured two glasses of iced tea as I watched the girls talking outside. When she came in, we sat.

"A guy called me about fixing the hole in the wall," she said.

"Good."

"I asked for a quote, but he said there was no charge. It's on Mr. Mondavi, he said."

"Yeah."

"Who's Mr. Mondavi?"

"My guardian angel."

"Well, thank you for that."

"No problem."

"Thanks for all of it."

"You bet."

"The landlord's off my back. For now."

"Glad to hear it."

"So what can I do for you, Miami?"

"Couple of things. First, I know it was you that called Johnny in the bar the night of the incident."

She dropped her tea onto the floor. Without saying anything more, she went to the kitchen and returned with a dish towel. She got on her knees and blotted the carpet.

"I know that Samson called the other guy, Ricky. But Johnny wouldn't have listened to Samson if he had called him, so Allan told you to call."

"I didn't know this would happen." I could see the fear in her eyes, perhaps envisioning a future where she was in prison and her daughters were goodness knows where.

"I know. He told you that the guy was a dealer and was selling drugs at the school. That the girls were in danger."

The color had left her face, but I saw the stoic Tina in there again. No tears, just determination to take on what she had been dealt.

"No. He told me to tell that to Johnny. He said that would get Johnny there. He said they would probably fight, and worst case was Johnny would be arrested for assault. He said nothing would stick because the other guy was a drug dealer and he wouldn't testify."

"Why though?"

"He said because we had no money, Johnny would never get treatment, but if Johnny assaulted someone, we could go to court and have him involuntarily committed into a psychiatric hospital because if the court said he was sick then they had to take him for free. He said we had to do it before Johnny hurt me or one of the girls."

She finished soaking up the tea and sat up on her haunches. "He wasn't supposed to go to jail, Miami. He wasn't. That was not the plan. I didn't think for a second that Johnny would kill that man."

For a moment I thought about not telling her, but Samson had been arrested and would hopefully stand trial, and she would learn about it sooner or later.

"He didn't kill anyone," I said quietly.

Tina frowned. "The drug dealer."

"No. Johnny hit him, just as you planned, but he didn't kill him."

"But how? What are you saying?"

"I'm sorry, Tina. Samson killed Ricky. He was inside the club when Johnny hit him and left. Then he came out and killed Ricky and made it look like Johnny did it."

Tina's eyes were darting all over as if her brain was playing catch-up.

"No, he wouldn't. He couldn't." She said it, but she didn't sell it. She looked up at me. "Why?"

I knew she knew, but I told her anyway. "Because of you. He was in love with you."

"No, that was a long time ago."

"It was for you, Tina. Not for him. A long time ago, he lost his title shot and then the love of his life in quick succession, and he never forgot it."

"I left him before the title shot. I was with Johnny before the two of them ever fought."

"Not sure Samson saw it that way."

"What are you saying? That he set up Johnny to get him out of the way after thirty years so he could have me for himself? That's ludicrous. I loved Johnny. I always loved Johnny."

"Actually, I think Samson knew that and wasn't trying to get you back. I think he was genuinely concerned that Johnny was going downhill. There was a fight at the gym and he banned Johnny just like Stone had banned him after he got drunk and went after Johnny all those years ago. But Samson saw Johnny at his worst, and his only thought was you. He likely figured it was just a matter of time before Johnny turned his anger on you."

"He did all that to prevent Johnny from hitting me?"

"Well, I suspect he also blamed Johnny for everything that had gone wrong in his life. In a warped way, he thought it was reasonable to put Johnny in jail when he was so sick anyway. Same for killing a drug dealer. Many would agree. Do you?"

Tina stood. "No. I do not."

"Me either. Take a seat, Tina."

She sat in the chair.

"Him taking his life might have happened anyway. His brain was damaged. It was all downhill from here."

"That doesn't matter. I know he wasn't getting better. I spoke with Dr. Abe. But I wanted him to get help, not to die alone in a prison cell."

She looked to the floor where the tea had spilled. The mess was gone, but a wet stain remained.

"What happens now?"

"Samson may be tried for murder."

"But I called Johnny. Am I an accessory?"

"Tina, wives call their husbands at bars telling them to come home all the time. Nobody but you and Johnny know what was said. Maybe Johnny went to the club despite your plea."

"Allan knows."

"I don't think he's telling anyone anything."

"What have I done?"

"You've protected your family from a situation that had no fairy-tale ending regardless of how it played out. But if I were you, I'd hire an attorney. I can recommend a guy."

"You think they'll come for me? What about the girls?"

"No, I don't think they'll come for you."

"So why do I need a lawyer?"

"To sue the county."

"What?"

"They arrested, jailed, and ultimately let a man die under their watch."

"You don't think they were wrong to have arrested him?"

"No, I don't. The evidence as it stood was obvious and damning. The arrest was the right move under the circumstances. But after that, the system should have done better by him. Honestly, I think it's the sport of boxing that should pay. A lot of people are making a lot of money off those guys and washing their hands of them after, and we the people are paying for it. They provide laughable insurance and nothing once a boxer retires—for a sport that is almost guaranteed to result in brain injury. But on they go. I think five grand is the most you'll see from them. But a settlement with the county for wrongful death might get you somewhere permanent to live and maybe put the girls through college, if that's what they want to do. It's no kind of quid pro quo, but it's something."

I stood and told her I had places to be. She walked me to the door, and we watched the girls hanging out on the street.

"I don't know what to say," said Tina.

"Then ask yourself, what would Mick do?"

"He'd say nothing."

I smiled. "Go with that."

CHAPTER FORTY-FOUR

Beer is beer, but some days it just tastes better. This was one of those days. The sun was falling across the courtyard at Longboard Kelly's, there was a good crowd enjoying the mild evening, and the mood was easy.

It wasn't the conclusion of a successful case that elevated my mood. I didn't see too many positive outcomes. I had gotten the Cabrinis a nice chunk of change, just at a hell of a cost. But now I was sitting on my favorite stool at my favorite bar, and the world was starting to feel like it wasn't going to spin out into the endless universe.

Danielle sat next to me with a vodka tonic, and beside her, Ron was sipping a beer. Muriel was pouring, and Mick was grilling grouper sandwiches in the back.

"How's Fishook?" I asked Danielle.

"He's more bird than fish because he's singing like a canary," she said. "Dorcas had Breyer Priestly picked up in Orlando, and Fishook's blaming him for all of it. Apparently, someone told Dorcas that Priestly was a foreign national, so when they went to his office and saw him working, that meant he was here illegally—he didn't hold a work permit. And because he doesn't have a US residence, the judge denied bail on account of him being a flight risk."

"Is he at Gun Club Road?" I asked. "I'd like to visit."

"You leave him to Dorcas."

"No fun."

"And it looks like Samson will have to sell the gym to pay his defense lawyers. But he's had an offer from LA Fitness."

"That feels wrong," I said. "Where will all those kids go?"

"Sadly, I don't know."

"We should form a syndicate," said Ron.

"Like a joint venture?" said Danielle.

"Yeah. Cassandra has a capital investment firm on call. They could advise."

"You want to invest in a stinking gym with a busted door?" I asked.

"Yep," said Mick from behind the bar.

"Oh. Hey, Mick. You doing okay?"

"Yep," he said to me, then to Ron: "Sign me up."

"Let me look into it," said Ron.

Mick held up the plates in his hands. Grouper sandwiches. The fish was grilled with nothing more than seasoning and then placed inside a hoagie roll with mayo, but I couldn't re-create the same taste from my grill at home if my life depended on it. But I need not worry. That's why I had Mick.

I bit into my sandwich and did a little happy dance on my stool. "You're a genius, Mick. What's your secret?"

"Fish," he said, walking back into the kitchen.

"Fish," I repeated. "I should have known."

The sound of laughter was welcome. Muriel poured me another beer. "You guys should taxi tonight." She looked from me to Danielle.

"Why?"

"Because you wouldn't accept payment for the case."

"So?"

"So he told me to comp your bill."

"Forever?"

"In your dreams. This is Mick we're talking about. For tonight. Like Sinatra. One night only."

I looked at Danielle and she smiled. "You earned it on this one."

"I'll take another one of these fish sandwiches."

"Done."

"We're still going for a run tomorrow morning," said Danielle.

I stared at her with wide eyes. "But this is like Halley's comet. Once in a lifetime."

"You should see your face right now." Danielle winked and turned to Muriel. "Another vodka tonic. Thank you, Muriel."

"Coming up."

"Am I in on this deal?" asked Ron.

"What will the Lady Cassandra say?" I asked.

"She'll say enjoy this once-in-a-lifetime event and sleep on Miami's couch tonight. So?"

"The tab was for Lenny Cox Investigations. You work there, don't you?" said Muriel. If Ron had been a Labrador, his tail would have wagged him right off his stool.

* * *

I don't know what time I got home. When I woke, the sun was up, I was lying on a lounger on our back patio, and my tongue was stuck to the roof of my mouth. I looked to my right and saw an empty lounger. The sliding door whooshed open and closed, and Danielle sat down. She handed me a glass of water.

"Good night," she said.

"Yeah. Did I sleep out here?"

"We both did."

"Well, that's okay then."

"Nice to know we still have it in us."

"I am not drinking for the rest of this century."

"How about a run?"

"Don't. Just don't."

"Ron's on the sofa."

"Good. That might have saved his marriage."

We drank our water, and Danielle went and got refills. Then she lay down beside me.

"You doing okay?" I asked.

"Didn't we do that already?"

"I don't mean that."

"What, then?"

"At the funeral. I don't know, you seemed funny."

"Funny ha-ha?"

"You know what I mean." I sipped my water.

"It was a funeral. It just got me thinking."

"About dying?"

"Yes."

"Oh. That's no good."

"Actually, it is good. I don't mean lying around depressed about it. I mean acknowledging that it will happen and you shouldn't take life for granted. You should do things, say things. Live with less fear."

"You live with fear?"

"We all do. I'm just saying it made me think, that's all. Nothing bad. I just want to be more aware. Thoughtful. Grateful. Considerate."

"There's a lack of that in our world, I'll give you that."

"And it starts with the man in the mirror."

"You saying I need to be more grateful?"

"I don't think you need to do anything. I love you as you are. And I know what you just did for the Cabrinis, and that makes me proud, MJ. I was once married to a man who was destined for greatness but never goodness. You, on the other hand, are a good man. You just need to believe it a little more."

"And greatness?"

"Comes in many forms."

I took a deep breath—in through the nose and out through the mouth—and then a long drink of water. I watched the birds play across the sky, ducking and weaving, diving into the water, maybe for food or maybe just for the sheer joy of it.

"Oh, and, MJ, do you remember signing a napkin last night?"

"No. Did someone want an autograph?"

"Not so much. But I think you might have bought a share in a gymnasium."

IF YOU ENJOYED THIS BOOK

One of the most powerful things a reader can do is recommend a writer's work to a friend. So if you have friends you think will enjoy the capers of Miami Jones and his buddies, please tell them.

Your honest reviews help other readers discover Miami and his friends, so if you enjoyed this book and would like to spread the word, just take one minute to leave a short review. I'd be eternally grateful, and I hope new readers will be too.

ALSO BY A.J. STEWART

Miami Jones series

Stiff Arm Steal

Offside Trap

High Lie

Dead Fast

Crash Tack

Deep Rough

King Tide

No Right Turn

Cruise Control

Red Shirt

Half Court Press

Past The Post

The Ninth Inning

Big Thaw

Devil's Backbone

Below The Belt

Three Strikes

John Flynn series

The Compound (novella)

The Final Tour

Burned Bridges

One for One

The Rotten State

Lost Luggage

Lenny & Lucas series

Temple of Gold

Danielle Castle novella

Little Packages

Baskin Island Mysteries

Clearer Waters

ACKNOWLEDGMENTS

Thanks to Lisa, for creating diamonds out of coal, and Stacey for rubbing off the remaining sharp edges.

As always, all errors, omissions, and fictionalizations are on me, except for that one last bout. Sometimes you need to know your limit, and sometimes you need to stand up and fight.

ABOUT THE AUTHOR

A.J. Stewart is the USA Today bestselling author of the Miami Jones mystery series and the John Flynn thriller series.

He has lived and worked in Australia, Japan, UK, Norway, and South Africa, as well as San Francisco, Connecticut and of course Florida. He currently resides in Los Angeles with his two favorite people, his wife and son.

AJ is working on a screenplay that he never plans to produce, but it gives him something to talk about at parties in LA.

You can find AJ online at www.ajstewartbooks.com.